COACH IZZY:
Full Circle

*Book Three
in the
Cheetah Basketball Series*

Roger Johnson

ISBN 978-1-7364368-6-8 (paperback)
ISBN 978-1-7364368-5-1 (ebook)

website: Roger_Johnson.com
email: rogerj47@gmail.com

The following people made this three-book series possible, and
I am forever grateful.

Mike Vagher
Skye Sisson

Beatriz   Neyva
Ceci   Julie
Cyndii   Katie
Danii   Maritza
Michelle   Fatima

ACKNOWLEDGMENTS

Self-publishing is such a misnomer! A number of people provided support and expertise, mostly friends who want only to see me succeed. Continued appreciation to my small group of readers over the years, mostly from Colorado, but also around the country and in Australia, who have encouraged my "hobby."

Special thanks to

- Wally Towne and Wendy Constantine
- Jay Johnson and Julie Christensen,
- Cheryl Johnson
- Joe DesGeorges

Books in the Cheetah Series

On Point

Gifts: The Return

Coach Izzy: Full Circle

Coach Izzy: Full Circle

Roger Johnson

IngramSpark

2021

Coach Izzy

"That's what I want you to remember . . .
the becoming a family."

Coach Isabella Soto

CHAPTER 1

Studying the tear-stained faces of her charges, Coach Isabella Soto understood what her high school basketball coach had felt when that team lost in the State semifinals ten years earlier. It was not sadness or regret over losing, it was pride and love. The score wouldn't change and no longer mattered. Coach Izzy and her three assistants hugged each player and offered quiet words of comfort. Then, she walked back to the front of the locker room and gently said, "Hey, hey, eyes up." One by one, twelve girls lifted their heads, some wiping tears away with their warmup jerseys or palms of their hands. Coach Izzy smiled warmly and wiped her tears with her knuckle so as not to further smear her trademark stylish eye make-up.

"I could not be more proud of you." She allowed that sentence to settle over her team like a down quilt. She bit her quivering lower lip and sniffled, trying to compose herself. In a voice just slightly above a whisper, she continued. "It hurts, I know, because we came so close, and you gave it your all. One possession short." That was enough to say about a missed call with nine seconds remaining that would have given them the last possession, the last shot. "All of you have been in this program, in this family, for at least two years, some as long as three, so we all understand what we put in to get here. That's what I want you to remember: the sweat, the sprints, the drills, the scrimmages, the daily competitions . . . the becoming a family." Izzy Soto paused, allowing herself time to remember those practice moments. "That's what I'll embrace, twelve girls working harder than you thought possible to achieve something intangible.

That something is this." Coach Izzy stretched her arms to encompass the entire room and held her girls. Her lip quivered again, and the tears flowed. As they did, her girls rose as one and walked into her arms.

§

The noise level in the Prospect View High School cafeteria prevented conversational communication: a single lunch period for 250 or so students. Many of the seniors and juniors left the campus in their cars for the fast-food chains close to the interstate, leaving school much like their parents had left their homes five hours earlier to commute to the high-paying jobs in Denver, Boulder, and Ft. Collins. Prospect was where mostly college-educated adults slept, but the happenings seemed to occur elsewhere. Prospect was a town of houses and new apartments, and Prospect View represented the trend, nice and comfortable but not a place of permanence. Many of the town's citizens, especially those without children yet, didn't even know the name of the high school.

"Coach Soto, if you have a few minutes after school, I want to run something past you."

Dr. Kerrigan always called Izzy "Coach" at school instead of Ms. Soto. At social events off campus, the principal called her Izzy. Setting is always important, a lesson Coach Izzy slash Ms. Soto stressed to her basketball players and English students. Every stage has different requirements and expectations. Now in her fifth year at Prospect View, Izzy had established both her classroom teaching and her more visible coaching assignment as standards of excellence for the school. For each venue, it had taken time, step-by-step, year-by-year. Izzy nodded to Dr. Kerrigan and hurried off to her lunchtime duty, an assignment for which she had volunteered. "Lunch monitor," she often joked, but at least it wasn't hall duty or study hall. Lunchtime was interactive in the same vein as her classroom or the gym, and Prospect View was exactly what Izzy, now at age 28, dreamed of when she started down the path to become a teacher nearly a decade earlier. She felt a part of something larger than herself.

"Coach, when do open gyms start? We gotta get better! I bet those private Denver schools have already started." Bailey Rockwell reminded Izzy of her high school point guard, not physically, but full of fire and drive. Bailey would be the lone full-time starter returning from this year's team, a team that made it to the State 3A semifinals just three weeks earlier. Next year's squad would challenge Izzy's coaching skills, but if she could choose just one player to build around, it would be Bailey. Coach Izzy, quickly transforming into Ms. Soto, pulled Bailey into a shoulder hug and asked her if she had finished her English essay.

§

At four o'clock, an hour after her last class ended, Izzy finally made it to Dr. Kerrigan's office. Izzy respected her principal, who had arrived a year after Izzy. Avery Kerrigan had been hired from a nationwide pool of candidates, a search that stressed the need for a leader not afraid of the challenge of a district in transition, from rural to suburban. Prospect, Colorado; north of Denver, east of Boulder, south of Fort Collins, close to I-25, had been discovered as an affordable alternative to those cities, and it would no longer be known as the cinnamon roll capital of Colorado. But even as its population swelled, the name Prospect seemed apropos.

"Nice assembly this morning, don't you think," said Dr. Kerrigan as she handed Izzy a diet soda and motioned for her to sit. At 5'6" with long, straight black hair, orangy-red lipstick, and a clear complexion, Izzy could easily pass for a college student. But Teacher Soto also had a confident look about herself, a person not seeking approval. Her jaw protruded very slightly, and her dark eyes, always impeccably made up, could alter from welcoming to challenging to shielding . . . depending on her intention, on the setting. "I think you embarrassed Coach Sabka by having him walk your trophy over to the students."

"He's easily embarrassed, such a gentle soul. More of a background guy, but so important to my program. The girls just love him, and he knows his Xs and Os."

"We're going to miss him if he follows through with his threat to retire." Dr. Kerrigan sat down at the small table with a clear glass of liquid. "You have a nice staff."

"I do," smiled Izzy. "I wish I could pay them all. I wish I could keep them all too, but Tanya wants her own team, her own varsity team, and she's ready. She already has her antennae up for openings."

Dr. Kerrigan nodded. "She sure brought your JVs along. Did they even lose a game after Christmas?"

"Just the one to Roosevelt, but that was when I had to use two of her starters, because the flu hit my girls so hard. I'll be counting on those girls next year, and I think we'll be just fine," said Izzy.

Dr. Kerrigan leaned into the small table. "Our boys team continues to struggle, and it's not as if the cupboard is bare. Coach Miller turned in his letter of resignation yesterday . . . keep that under wraps for right now . . . and I was wondering about whether you might have any suggestions or recommendations on filling his position."

"Wow," said Izzy softly. "Brad's such a good guy, maybe too nice sometimes. I've heard there's been some talk among the parents, but I didn't know it had gone that far."

"There were some disgruntled parents for sure, there always are, but I would have given him another year. He just wanted to step away. I think the fight at the end of the year was the last straw, sort of convinced him that he didn't have control. He has plenty on his plate with his AP class and AVID starting up." Dr. Kerrigan paused. "Anyway, I'd like to know your thoughts."

Izzy shook her head. "I don't really know the boys' side of the equation. I watched them practice some, but not enough to really say. They were an undisciplined bunch and pretty mouthy. Maybe a little more talented than their win-loss record indicated. Whoever you hire will need to correct those traits immediately to have any success. You'll need to have his back."

Dr. Kerrigan nodded again. "That's sort of what I saw, sort of what I was thinking." She paused and continued nodding. "Well, here's my proposal. How about I hire you as the boys coach and promote Tanya to the head girls position?"

§

Later that evening, after the noises in her head quieted and her heart resumed its normal beat, Izzy called Morgan Summitt, her high school coach, the gentle old man who in the summer of 1995 told her she had a nice stroke and convinced her that she could be a quality player if she practiced diligently. It had been a magical summer, and over the next two seasons, her team became the best small school team in the state, winning the championship in 1997. *Her team.* No, it had been Molly Rascon's team, but that team had been the epitome of *team*, and its success taught Izzy how important basketball could become in her future. It had given her lifelong friends and a mentor who attached no conditions to love. And a portal.

"Coach, it's Izzy. How are you and Mrs. Summitt doing?"

"Izzy, so good to hear your voice. Just a minute, let me turn down the TV."

After a few minutes of catching up, Izzy turned to the gist of her call. "Coach, I have a dilemma. My principal has asked me to become the boys varsity coach, in effect, to give up the girls program, which I've been building for the last five years, and take on a dysfunctional group of boys." Izzy stopped there to allow Morgan to respond.

"You had a wonderful season this year, and I'm very proud of you. Always have been." He allowed a moment for that to sink in. "Your principal must think very highly of you to ask you to do this. It's not just a dysfunctional team, but boys. I know you're aware that women don't often coach boys. I can only recall one instance in Colorado where a woman coached a boys basketball team, and she had played some pro ball."

"I know. When I started coaching, I knew exactly the kind of program I wanted for my team, one that mimicked your program for us. Two of my college years with *The Screamer* showed me what I didn't want to be. We weren't very talented, but he never took that into account. After he left, the next two years were pretty fun, and we always played to our abilities. I was confident when I came here. This, though, I'm just not sure."

On his end of the phone, Coach Summitt nodded. "I suspect

you want to keep working toward that championship trophy too. You're so close, but that big gold ball is not the end-all."

Izzy smiled. "You taught me that, but it's a symbol sometimes. I love my girls."

"Izzy, when I couldn't coach your team for your senior year, I didn't stop loving all of you."

"You're not going to tell me what I should do, are you?" She laughed and then continued to smile on her end.

"No, Izzy. Each team gives different rewards, and whatever you decide, I trust you'll do well."

It was Izzy's turn to nod her head. "Thanks, Coach. Love you. Tell Mrs. Summitt that I love her too. I'll be up to see you both this summer." Izzy flipped her phone shut and grabbed a legal pad to continue this discussion with herself. Dr. Kerrigan had asked her to consider it over the next few days and give her an answer on Monday, so they could all move forward. Izzy realized that if she took the boys coaching job, she would not get her girls back, that Tanya would grow into that job and be successful. Izzy needed to talk with an old friend before making her decision . . . and a young point guard.

§

Izzy arrived at school at 6:45 on Friday, the first teacher in the building. After dropping off her coat and books in her room, she walked to the main office to wait for Dr. Kerrigan. The office door was still locked. Izzy had questions. First on her list was whether she would be free to select her own assistants or whether she would be required to accept Coach Miller's crew. Could she pay Coach Sabka for one season if he would remain as an assistant for Tanya? Could she be guaranteed three years to get the boys program rolling? And finally, at least for now, if she accepted the job, could she be allowed to announce her decision to both the boys and girls on her own timeline? If Dr. Kerrigan agreed to all these questions, then Izzy would take the weekend to make her decision. A part of Izzy considered this new challenge, the competitive side, but her heart had yet to be persuaded.

"You're here early," said Virginia Polis, the school's head custodian, as she unlocked the office door. "I mean here earlier than normal. You're one of the early birds anyway."

"Just like you; things have to get done." Izzy waved as Mrs. Polis stepped back out of the main office. "Thank you," said Izzy as she watched the bleached blonde, athletic looking janitor walk down the hall pushing a mop bucket. *A good one*, she thought. Taking a seat, she read over her notes wondering if she really wanted to pursue Dr. Kerrigan's request. At seven o'clock, the office secretary arrived followed closely by Carl Porter, the activities director. His greeting to her indicated he did not know about the possible coaching changes.

"Are you waiting to see Dr. Kerrigan, Ms. Soto?" asked Doris Finkle as she arranged the office for students. When Izzy nodded, Ms. Finkle said that Dr. Kerrigan wouldn't be in this morning, that she had a downtown district meeting. "She'll be in around noon, and I'll tell her you were here."

Returning to her classroom, Izzy wondered if she had just received a premonition, a warning about taking the boys coaching position. The more she thought about it, it seemed as if it was the idea of a single person, and maybe Dr. Kerrigan's reasoning wasn't for the good of the students per se, but to make a political statement. Taking out her phone, she called Ms. Finkle to tell her that seeing the principal today wasn't important, and that it could wait until Monday. The part of Izzy that thought this coaching position could be a new challenge shrank back behind her heart. She folded her notes and tucked them inside her purse. It was time for sophomore language arts, not to be confused with full-court run-and-jump presses.

§

Never much of a beer drinker, Izzy still agreed to join a few of her colleagues at the local pizzeria for a Friday Afternoon Unwind, but after drinking her usual half-glass of beer and eating a slice of pizza, she excused herself. In her car, she called her good friend Bianca Acero in Fort Collins. "Hey, Big Stallion, do you want to have dinner with me? I can drive up and get you?"

"Mexican? Are you buying?"

"See you in thirty."

§

Since high school Izzy had been amazed at the amount of food Bianca consumed at a single setting. Tonight, she ordered a smothered burrito and two tacos, while Izzy got two enchiladas. Good friends from poor families who had achieved success, Izzy as a teacher and Bianca as a veterinarian. It had been a basketball season ago since they last sat down together to catch up.

"Rosa's pregnant again. Due in September," said Bianca.

"When are you and Adam going to start having kids?" asked Izzy.

Bianca laughed. "You always ask that, but at least we've been talking about it finally. We've been able to save up a little money now that we both have real jobs, and I'm not getting any younger." She finished her burrito and took a breath. "You and me and Molly are about the last holdouts in that arena. Stevie, Cindy, Elena and Sophia all have at least one, and Alondra's up to four. Gloria has two, I think, and she waited until her thirties, so we have time." Bianca looked up seriously to Izzy. "What do you hear from your ex?"

Izzy shook her head at Bianca's use of the term *ex*. Izzy hadn't married, just moved in with her steady. "Nothing for over six months; maybe he's finally got the message that I want nothing to do with him ever again. That was the stupidest thing I ever did."

"I'm sorry; I shouldn't have brought it up." Bianca lowered her head for a second and then started giggling. When she looked up, Izzy too started to laugh. "I tried to talk you out of it," said Bianca.

"I know, but he was just so beautiful . . . and he could hoop."

"And ignorant and lazy. Good riddance."

"By the way," said Izzy, "I met a new guy. Not as cute, but nice. Don't know if it will go anywhere though."

"Well, tell me!"

"At a Hispanic Educators conference in Denver last week. You can guess why I was my school's rep. His name is Jorge. He teaches in Ft. Meade, some music, some English. At the evening social, he came up and asked me to dance." She raised her eyebrows. "He can really dance! We were in a salsa line, but he began to bachata. So fun!"

"Not like your ex, I hope."

"No! Nice looking but no Adonis. His youngest sister played basketball for Ft. Meade, and he said he remembered me from last season when we were beating them so badly and she got so frustrated. He walked me back to my room and thanked me for dancing with him. That's it."

Bianca tilted her head. "A kiss?"

Izzy blushed slightly. "A polite one. The next day between sessions, he asked if he could call me sometime. We've talked on the phone a few times. He's two years younger than me, than us. He plays soccer, never liked basketball except to watch his sister, grew up in Denver, still lives with his family. They moved to Ft. Meade after he graduated from high school."

"*El nino de mama?*"

"I have no idea," said Izzy, "but he's interesting to talk with on the phone. He loves his teaching."

"What's he want to teach you?" kidded Bianca. "Well, keep it light and don't go all in so fast."

After the two friends stopped laughing, Izzy asked Bianca, "Do you ever miss it?" Bianca cocked her head as if she wasn't sure what Izzy meant. "Basketball. Do you ever miss being a part of a team or the competitive aspect; just the whole everything?"

After a moment of thought, Bianca leaned forward. "Iz, I played for a different reason than you . . . or Molly. From the very beginning, I played because it was safe and because I was accepted for who I was. You guys and Coach protected me and Rosa. It could have been volleyball or chess. I played not to let you down. Yeah, over time, I came to love basketball too, but you guys made it possible for me to move on, and then I discovered horses, and that led me to this next life. Adam says I need a hobby now, and he may be right."

"Bea, I need your opinion on something. You've known me for eleven years now and seen what I'm kind of made of. You and Adam took care of me after I broke up with lazybutt and allowed me to continue teaching and coaching while I worked through the trauma. My principal asked me this week to give up coaching my girls and become the boys coach." Izzy bit the inside of her cheek and paused. "Do you think I could do that?"

"Why would anyone want to coach boys?" asked Bianca. "All they do is trash-talk and posture. It seems like all they want to do is show each other up. They play for an entirely different reason than we always did, and I still haven't figured out what that is." Bianca shook her head and stopped.

"That's certainly the case with my school's boys team. So cocky with no reason to be. They won four games last season and still strut." Izzy went quiet and Bianca waited. "I owe this school so much," said Izzy almost as if she were talking to herself.

Bianca continued to devour her tacos, giving Izzy time to continue. When she didn't, Bianca said, "Seems like you're solving your own dilemma. It's not like there aren't lots of men eager to be high school coaches. Heck, call your old JV coach and see if he's available."

Bianca's reference to Izzy's first high school coach made her laugh. "Yeah, everybody's best friend in his own mind." She waved her hand in front of her face. "We don't need to go there. Regardless, I'm going to lose my JV assistant, Tanya . . . I think you've met her . . . anyway, she'll get a varsity job soon. So, do you want to be my new JV coach?"

§

Coach Izzy met Bailey after church on Sunday at Starbucks. Bailey bounced in wearing a Phoenix Suns jersey with Jason Kidd's last name on the back. Izzy thought back to Bailey's sophomore year and how she had rapidly changed over two years. As a tenth grader, Bailey was a chubby, five-foot-seven-inch bundle of enthusiasm. The coaching staff slotted her as a center on the C-team. Izzy certainly hadn't seen any inkling of a varsity point guard, but

Bailey was a three-sport athlete with decent footwork, and Izzy understood that girls who show up that first year often develop into something quite different, and often extraordinary, over the course of their high school careers. Bailey had moved to Colorado from San Francisco, the Oakland area, where her father played high school ball with Jason Kidd. Bailey took to the ball-handling drills with a determined enthusiasm. Over the course of her sophomore year, her body lost much of its baby fat, and she was another inch taller. She began lifting weights, and Coach Tanya brought Bailey up to her JVs. They began to see in Bailey what she could become. Izzy instructed Tanya to move Bailey to guard, "because a program can't have too many point guards." As a junior, Bailey became the team's best guard, all-conference, and honorable mention all-state. Izzy predicted continued improvement.

"Hey, Coach, what's up?" said Bailey as she gave Izzy a brief hug before sitting down.

"Oh, I just wanted to run some spring and summer plans by you, since you're going to be running the show next year. Thought I'd turn over all my responsibilities to you now rather than waiting until December."

Bailey understood the sarcasm. Will I get your paycheck too?"

"I think they still have rules against paying players. Anyway, open gym starts Monday. Make sure you spread the word. So many of you are out for spring sports, so I think I'll hold it late, start at eight. The boys can come in earlier and play grab ass for an hour."

Bailey laughed as she shook her head in agreement. "Do you think we can be as good as we were this past year?"

"As long as my point guard stays healthy and we develop our younger girls over the summer, I think we can be." Izzy paused, took a sip of her latte, and looked at Bailey over the rim of the cup, raising her eyebrows. "Maybe even a tad better."

Bailey bounced in her chair. "It's basketball season again."

Izzy raised her coffee cup as a toast to what Bailey said. "I'm going to have Coach Tanya do more this spring and summer. Maybe if I give the two of you more responsibility, I can take some time off."

"Yeah, like that's going to happen, you taking time off or delegating responsibility."

"Well, I need to give Coach Tanya more responsibility, so we don't lose her. She's varsity ready, you know."

Bailey looked concerned. "We can't lose her, not for my senior year. Not only for basketball, but she's such a great math teacher too. She has me actually understanding calculus. Has she said she's leaving? Can I talk to her?"

"Bailey, she's always had the goal of being a varsity coach. She's worked hard and deserves her chance, but I'll see what I can do to keep her around for a little while longer."

§

Sunday, March 26, 2006. For the NCAA Basketball Tournament, Bailey had set up a Sweet Sixteen party for a half-dozen of her teammates and invited the coaches. Izzy begged off, saying she had grading and lessons plans to complete, a claim that was mostly correct. However, Izzy feared that eating pizza with her girls as they watched the games would be difficult if she decided to leave them. Coach Tanya would be there; that was enough. From her second story apartment, Izzy looked across a field to the rooftop of Prospect View High School, the newly remodeled Prospect View that was being redesigned to take on the Twenty-first Century. Another classroom wing still needed to be completed. Her home over the last five years. Her eyes saw the building, but her thoughts remained focused on Dr. Kerrigan's proposal.

Why are you even considering this, Iz? Kerrigan said she was okay with it if you refused, that she would certainly understand. You have nothing to prove to anyone about your coaching abilities. She just said she thought you were the right person for the job, that you would be a good fit for the school too. Izzy turned back into the living room of her apartment but didn't sit down. She went to the fridge for a bottle of water, swallowing half of it before setting it on the counter. *You won five games that first year, but your girls bought in. If the boys only win five this next season, do you think they'd be gung-ho for summer ball? What if you can't get them to play this spring and summer? Might not even win five. You worked your butt off those first two summers, Iz. It was the foundation.* Izzy took a deep breath and exhaled slowly. *But you had players, Iz, even if they didn't realize it. The boys all think they're Division I players, even though they wouldn't make the teams in Broomfield or Longmont or Loveland.* Izzy bent over at the waist and placed her forehead on the counter. *Every boys team you've ever been around has underachieved and was no fun to be near. High school, college, and now here. It's always been the girls who worked hard and listened.* She lifted her head and thought about calling Dr. Kerrigan. *You'd have to be a miracle worker, Iz. Who do you think you are? Pat Summitt? Tara VanDerveer?* Izzy started pacing, shaking her head as she walked, as if she was in front of her bench during a game, arguing with a referee, gesturing with her hands. *You're comfortable and safe, Iz, and you have another special team coming back. You don't have to yell at them much. That would change with boys. The first year wouldn't be as much about basketball as it would be about behavior. You've earned this chance for next season, and it might not come again soon.* That word *chance* reminded her of what Coach Summitt always used to tell her and her teammates back in high school. "All I want for you is a chance, and when you get it, seize it!" *Dammit, Coach, which path is the chance?* Izzy realized she was rolling her tongue rapidly behind her lower lip, a habit she did when she was angry or stressed. *You're such a prissy, Iz, always the timid girl. You always have been. Everything of value for you has come easily, too easily.* Izzy's chest heaved with those last thoughts. She swallowed hard in an effort to ease up on herself. *Remember when Coach Summitt referred to you as the most delicate flower on his team as a junior. When games got physical, he substituted for you. But you used that to toughen up; you showed them. Coach Noones at Western praised you as the heart and soul of his squad over your last two years, that your teammates followed you into battle.* Izzy lowered her head and rubbed her temples with her fingers. She turned and walked slowly back to the sliding glass door that looked toward her high school, still under construction. Standing there, alone in her thoughts, Izzy Soto folded her arms around her chest, as if she were hugging herself.

CHAPTER 2

Team first!

On Monday, just as she had on Friday, Izzy arrived at school before the office doors were unlocked, and just as before, Virginia Polis showed up to unlock them, minus the mop bucket. "You got a raw deal in that State game, you know. Refs took away your team's chance."

Izzy nodded in agreement. "You were there?"

"Yeah. I see most of the home games for both the girls and boys. Kind of stand in the background, then clean up after. Your teams are easy to watch; it's all about basketball and no bullshit. I made a point of going to your two games at State. I wish you'd have had one more." Virginia gave Izzy a peculiar look. "My nephew played on the JV team."

"I don't recall a Polis boy."

"Different last name. Sampson. He could be pretty good." Virginia smiled that. "Well, you understand." She turned and walked back down the hall.

Moments later, Dr. Kerrigan arrived with AD Porter. "Sorry to keep you waiting."

§

Sitting at the conference table in her office, Kerrigan spoke. "I'm assuming you've given this a good deal of thought."

Izzy unfolded her list and straightened it out with the palm of her left hand. "I have. No decision yet. I have several questions, if I may." The principal nodded for Izzy to proceed. "First, if you can, tell me what you're looking for in the boys program; what are your goals?"

Porter looked to his boss and then answered. "We talked at length after Coach Miller resigned. Yeah, we want a competitive program, but then we stopped ourselves and decided that was setting a pretty low bar. We want to challenge for championships when the talent is on the table, the old adage, 'take ours and beat yours; take yours and beat ours.' That takes a special coach."

Izzy looked at Dr. Kerrigan. "I was under the impression that you had made this decision by yourself. I'm kind of relieved that Carl is in on this."

The principal nodded and let the AD continue. "Obviously, we're going to hire a coach who represents our values, and one who has a vision. Prospect is growing by leaps and bounds; we're going to be bumped up in class within the next few years, and our new coach is going to need to grow with us. We want our school to be a nurturing place, as you know, not simply a modern Front Range building. Kind of that small-town feel."

Kerrigan leaned in, a technique she often used to gain the floor. "Izzy, you can coach, no doubt in our minds. You've proven that in spades. Your players model our school's values. The faculty likes you and you're engaged in programs beyond the gym. Still, when Carl and I first started thinking about who to hire, I need to admit, we were thinking of a man. Your name never came up. I still have my own gender biases to overcome, I guess. I also want to say that this is a horizontal move for you, not a move up. You would be filling a need for our school. We've been trying to keep this secret; we asked Coach Miller to delay his announcement for a little while, but rumors get out. A lady whose nephew plays in the boys program heard the rumor and came to Carl and suggested we talk with you. The more we discussed this idea, the more we liked it."

Izzy smiled to herself.

"What questions do you have for us, Coach?" asked Dr. Kerrigan.

"My first one is not so much a question as a demand. If I take the boys job, can you guarantee me that Tanya will be hired as the girls coach? I'm not going to leave if she goes too."

"Let's do this," said Kerrigan. "We haven't spoken with Tanya yet, so if we can settle on your other demands this morning, we'll meet again tomorrow morning, the four of us, and find out if she would be interested." Kerrigan had smiled when she said the word *demands*. She indicated to Izzy to proceed.

"First, I want to pick my own staff, and I don't want any of Coach Miller's assistants."

§

Izzy sat on the bleachers watching the boys' open gym antics. No drills, just five-on-five games, winners keeping the court, loosely supervised by the sophomore coach, a young man who didn't teach in the building but had a connection with Coach Miller's past. Lots of wild shots and bad passes and trash talk. Of the eighteen boys participating, Izzy recognized only a handful as varsity or JV players from the previous season. She grimaced frequently. As eight o'clock drew closer, her girls joined her in the bleachers to watch, as did Tanya Hatton.

"Any idea what Kerrigan wants to talk with us about tomorrow morning?" asked Tanya.

Yes, I do, thought Izzy, but she replied differently. "Next year's scheduling, I think. That and she wants to tell us again how wonderful we are." An errant pass from the boys sailed into the bleachers and was caught by one of the girls sitting near Izzy who tossed it back. Bailey laughed and yelled "Turnover," to which several of her friends chuckled. Izzy had imagined this moment in her head and heart all day, the short time at open gym when she would be sitting with many of her players and her assistant coach watching the final minutes of the boys open gym. Her last open gym as the girls coach if discussions played out as they could. Kerrigan approved every one of Izzy's requests, answered every question to her satisfaction. The deal would be sealed if Tanya accepted tomorrow's offer to be the girls head coach, which Izzy was certain she would.

Izzy bent forward to put her head near Bailey, who was sitting in front of her coach. "What do you think, Bailey? Do you think you could beat them five-on-five?" asked Coach Izzy.

"Maybe not their full varsity, but these guys? Yeah!"

The skins won the final boys game just before eight, and their coach told them to gather up their stuff and head out. He took the only boys ball, looked to Izzy and Tanya, and said the floor was all theirs. Twenty-plus girls leaped out of the bleachers, took balls from the rack, paired up, and began scripted ball-handling drills without direction from either Izzy or Tanya. The two coaches sat and watched.

"I love open gym," said Tanya. "Nice to see a couple of our seniors here tonight. Do you think any of them will play in college?"

"Sarah and Olivia said they're going to try. Metro may offer Olivia some money, but their coach definitely wants her. She came a long way with her studies to qualify. Sarah had such a great State Tournament that a few of the small colleges got on board. She's been accepted at CSU, so she'd have to change her mind about that if she decides to play on. She's not D-1 caliber." Izzy motioned with her head about the girl who had just entering the gym. Both coaches rose to greet her.

"Rosie, it's so good to see you," said Izzy. Both coaches hugged the girl on crutches as her teammates stopped their drill work to gather around their teammate who had been injured in a car accident two weeks earlier. "How are you feeling?"

"Well, duh, my leg is still broken, but the doctor said I'll be fine by the end of the summer." Behind her, Rosie's parents walked in smiling. While Rosie's teammates stayed with her, the two coaches moved to speak with the parents, who assured them that their daughter was indeed going to heal and be ready for next season.

"You're welcome to stay and watch tonight," said Izzy to the parents. Rosie was a promising player, a tall and athletic girl who was being counted on to be in next season's starting lineup. Unlike Bailey, Rosie's potential had been obvious from the moment she entered Prospect View.

It was Bailey who yelled out, "All right, girls, enough sympathy for Rosie. We have work to do," and she led her team back onto the court. Rosie and her parents sat on the first bleacher row, and Izzy and Tanya began walking among the girls offering words of instruction and encouragement. After a half-hour of drills, Izzy blew her whistle, and her team ran to the rack to put the balls away. Then they lined up, roughly tallest to shortest.

"Count off by fours," yelled Tanya. Five teams were created, and two half-court games began. "Call your own fouls! Be shot aggressive but don't force anything!"

"You take Bailey's group," said Izzy to Tanya. "I'll watch Lauren's. Don't let Bailey get away with that cheap spin move against the younger kids." As a player, Izzy never had a spin move, her high school coach disapproved, and now she thought of his coaching techniques and slogans. *Amazing,* she thought, *how engrained those words and ideas became . . . and how important they are to a player's growth.* For the next 45 minutes, Izzy forgot about Dr. Kerrigan's plan and simply coached her girls.

§

Tanya Hatton's response surprised the others. She sat silently and stared straight ahead, not looking directly at Kerrigan, Porter, or her friend and mentor Izzy Soto.

Izzy and Tanya were confident women, both in their late-twenties, and fit. Since being paired together three years earlier, they had become good friends apart from the gymnasium. Because they attended basketball clinics together, coached summer leagues and camps together, spent hours and hours together discussing coaching techniques and philosophy, they had grown close. They socialized, worked out, double-dated occasionally, and ate dinners together. And, they were both basketball geeks.

In a few moments, Tanya refocused on the people in the room. "This is a surprise. I'm not sure what to say." She stopped there and turned to Izzy, who was sitting next to her. Tanya didn't speak, aloud, but her face registered concern. She turned back to Kerrigan. "Would it be possible for you to get someone to cover both Izzy's and my first period classes?"

Carl Porter said he would take care of that, and then Tanya and Izzy left to find an empty space at Prospect View. Kerrigan turned to her activities director. "What just happened there?" she asked.

"I sense that Tanya felt she was taking something from her

friend. I'm not sure though."

§

"Hear me out, Iz," said Tanya as they sat in the women's coaching office in the PE area. "I was offered a head coaching job this past week at a 2A school near Pueblo. I turned it down because I wanted to stay here and work with you for a few more years. It was a good offer and I considered it, but I am so happy where I am, especially working with you. I'll get my opportunity, I'm sure of that. I don't need to take your job. Kerrigan wrapped this all up in a bow like we would both be staying here as coaches and teachers, and that would be best for our students, but . . ." Tanya hesitated.

"Tell me," said Izzy.

Tanya waited. Finally, "That boys team is rotten . . . toxic. Everyone connected with the varsity and some on the junior varsity would have to be cut to even give you a chance, and I know you. You'll keep them all if you can. You're the best coach I've ever been associated with, but I think those boys will eat you up just like they did with Brad. He's not as good as you, and he left the program in terrible shape. I don't want that for you." Tanya reached over and took Izzy's hand, and they went quiet.

"You're a good friend, Hat. Thank you." Izzy smiled. "When were you going to tell me about the job offer?" It was a rhetorical question. "You're wrong about one thing. The boys program is rotten, but the boys aren't. I know I won't save them all, but if I accept Kerrigan's offer, I'm going to try and put the program on the right footing, so that the boys will have a chance. I don't expect I'll have much fun this year, so I'm going to rely on you to pump me up, not allow me to stew alone in my apartment." She stopped to give Tanya an opportunity to affirm that she would, which Tanya did. Then, Izzy continued. "I talked with Coach Sabka, talked him into staying on for another year, told him we'd pay him, so you'll have him. Georgia's staying too. And after this year, if I hate it and you don't go to State, I'll come back and take my job back."

Tanya understood the last sentence to be a joke and nodded.

"How do you want to tell your girls? They're going to be so disappointed."

"We'll do it together."

§

Dr. Kerrigan set the meetings for Friday immediately after school. Izzy and Tanya would meet with the girls in Ms. Hatton's room, while Coach Miller would announce his resignation to the boys and whatever parents chose to attend in Ms. Soto's room. Between Tuesday and Friday, Izzy wanted to get her staff hired and tentative summer plans in place. She decided not to attend Wednesday's open gym, letting Tanya supervise alone. The boys open gym was cancelled. During lunch hour, having Tanya cover her duty, Izzy went to the gym. Finding who she was looking for in the PE office eating a giant, homemade, sub sandwich, Izzy put her sack lunch on his desk, closed the door behind her, and pulled up a metal chair.

"Hey, Coach, got a minute?" Izzy asked Donnie Romero.

Romero made a pretense of straightening a place on his cluttered desk for Izzy to eat while wiping the corners of his mouth. "Of course. What's up?"

"I need to ask you something in confidence, at least for now." Romero nodded. "I trust you're aware of the rumors about Brad resigning." Romero nodded again and took a bite of his sandwich. "Well, the boys are in need of a head coach now."

Romero put up both hands like a stop signal. "Whoa, Coach. I've got way too much on my plate to take that job. If Kerrigan sent you down here to get a reading on my feelings, you can finish your lunch and go tell her I'm not interested."

Izzy laughed. *If you want something done, ask a busy person,* she thought to herself. "No, she didn't. I'm pretty sure she and Porter already have someone in mind." She stopped there and unwrapped a basic ham and cheese sandwich, took a bite, and looked back up at Romero.

"No. You?"

Izzy smiled a tight smile and nodded. "Yeah. Crazy, huh?"

"Well, I'll be go to hell."

After a moment of staring at one another, Izzy spoke. "The boys program needs so much, and I can't do it alone. I need a first-rate staff, and I want you as my JV coach." Romero started to speak, but Izzy cut him off. "Hear me out, Coach," she said raising her right hand. "You're the strength and conditioning teacher and the assistant football coach. The boys respect you a ton. I also know you played high school basketball and were pretty good. You scored a few baskets last year in that fundraiser game. I can get Kerrigan to arrange your schedule so that seventh period would be a sports weight-lifting class, which, as you probably know, would help all of our teams."

Romero leaned back from his sandwich. "How long do I have to consider this?"

"Hey, we have 30 minutes or so to finish our lunch."

"I tend to yell a lot."

"Oh, I know that. We'll complement each other."

Romero moved back to his sandwich, but before he took another bite, he looked up at Izzy. "Head boys basketball coach, huh. Izzy, you got some guts." He shook his head. "Not sure about the brains, but some guts."

§

For her C-team coach, Izzy plucked Miles Minturn from the Middle School. Only in his third year, Miles coached both eighth grade boys and girls teams and had college playing experience from Izzy's alma mater, Western State. He had coached several of the players who now played on the high school teams. Kerrigan agreed to hire him as a teacher in the building to fill a projected science vacancy at Prospect View, but only after she did her homework on Minturn's teaching credentials. "Classroom teachers first, Izzy." Now, Izzy wanted a volunteer assistant or two, one to help the C-team and one to work with her and Romero. Coach Sabka was her choice, but she had promised him to Tanya and gotten him a paycheck. Izzy had time to find the right people to fill these spots, a whole summer, in fact.

With her staff in place, Izzy began to steel herself for informing her girls that she would not be their coach any longer and for introducing herself to her new team. She understood which would be the more difficult task. Moreover, a part of her felt she was abandoning her girls just as they were at the cusp of something special; a sinking feeling that only eased because Tanya would be replacing her. But still. Before the scheduled meetings, however, Izzy needed to meet with one player. Bailey Rockwell deserved to be told in private and not be blindsided. And Izzy needed to do this for herself also, so she could then face all her girls with a semblance of composure. A proper break and sendoff.

§

Ms. Soto's planning period was seventh hour, the last period of the day, like most of the head coaches in the building. On Friday, a half-hour before she was to meet with her team, Ms. Hatton ushered Bailey into Coach Izzy's room, tapped her fingers on the Mary Oliver poem that Izzy had posted near the door, and then excused herself. Perceptive as always, Bailey's eyes registered concern. She looked at her coach, turned back to reread the closing lines of the poem—*Tell me, what is it you plan to do with your one wild and precious life?*—and then looked back to Izzy.

"It's not as bad as that, Bailey," said Izzy, who stood just an arm's length from her point guard. "Come on, let's move back away from the door." The two ladies sat in student desks just in front of Ms. Soto's desk. "Coaches and teachers are not supposed to have pets, and for most of my tenure here, I've managed to follow that guideline. This past year, however, out of respect for who you are and how you've conducted yourself with the team . . . and so much more . . . I've," Izzy caught herself and swallowed hard. She reached across the two desks and took both of Bailey's hands. "Last week, Dr. Kerrigan asked me if I would fill a need here at Prospect View, one that would not be of my choosing, but one where she thought I could be of even more help to our school. At first, I said no, but she's persistent, and there's Coach Tanya." Izzy paused again to wipe her eyes.

"You left out a part, Coach," said Bailey softly.

"Yeah. I have a difficult time saying it aloud. She asked me to give up my team, you gals, and take over the boys program. After lots of thinking and talking with people close to me, especially Coach Tanya, I accepted. It's been the most difficult week of my life, and this is the hardest decision I've ever made, to give you gals up."

Bailey scrunched up her face as the tears formed, and she squeezed Coach Izzy's hands tightly. Both ladies remained quiet as they sniffled through the tears. The older young lady had immediate second thoughts but dismissed them. She had made her decision and now had to push forward.

"The only way I could do this is because Coach Tanya will become your coach now. She's ready. Remember last week when you pleaded with me to keep her, not let her get away? This isn't quite what I envisioned, and she tried hard to talk me out of my decision, but she'll be staying for the foreseeable future, and we're hired first and foremost by the District as classroom teachers, and she's an excellent one." Izzy realized that she was rambling a bit. Bailey rescued her. Bailey had been Izzy's rock on the court, both in games and at practices, and now the younger lady tried to compose herself.

Bailey pulled her hands from her coach's and wiped the tears from her cheeks. "Remember when the ref blew that last call?"

"Yeah," said Izzy, "of course."

"I immediately looked to you and you handled it, almost like you were all right with it, it seemed."

"Actually, I wanted to scream, to contest the call, but we didn't have time to argue. I didn't want to give their head coach extra time to draw up a play. They were out of timeouts, and the ball was at our end. They had to go the whole length of the court."

Bailey wiped her nose with her wrist. "But they scored anyway." Her words were more of a question than a statement of fact.

"A lucky shot by a player who didn't want the ball. You kept it out of their best player's hands. That other girl hit a hook shot." Izzy wanted to say more, but she realized Bailey already understood. "Now, my precious point guard, it's time for you to take care of

Coach Hatton and your teammates with the same fervor as you have taken care of me."

They stood and hugged tightly for a few minutes. "I want you to be at the meeting. I'll say a few words and then turn it over to Coach Tanya. Then, I'll go meet with the boys and some of their parents. I don't know what to expect there."

Speaking into Izzy's neck, Bailey said, "I'll miss you so much, Coach."

"We can still review your games on the weekends, and I'll still be in this room, so I won't be gone."

"Coach, I said I'll miss you."

"And I will miss you, Bailey, more than you'll ever know."

§

Having met with Bailey prior to the telling her girls goodbye, and having coach Tanya at her side, made the first meeting bearable for Izzy. There were tears, but most of the returning girls had been on the junior varsity or C-team, Hatton's and Sabka's and Georgia Winters' squads. Izzy told the team she loved them, would follow their every game, and that she expected a deep run in March toward the championship. Then, she hugged Tanya and turned the meeting over to her.

Izzy was met in the hall by Dr. Kerrigan who surveyed Izzy's composure and, finding her ready to move ahead, asked her how she would like to be introduced to the boys. "There's several parents in the room," said Kerrigan as she escorted Izzy to her next appointment. "Coach Miller's goodbye certainly didn't elicit any tears." Outside her own room where the boys were gathered stood Donnie Romero and Carl Porter.

Romero handed Izzy a whistle attached to a pink lanyard. Izzy smiled and slipped it around her neck. "Kinda clashes with the orange blouse, don't you think?" She turned to Dr. Kerrigan. "Just be matter of fact about this, and Coach Romero and I will take over from there. Omit any mention about gender; I think they'll recognize that immediately." She winked.

Coach Miller had been informed about Izzy's hiring that

morning, and he shook her hand when she entered as well as Romero's, then waved to the crowd and left. Dr. Kerrigan stepped in front of the boys and their parents and the one local sportswriter in attendance.

"It's nice to see you all here on such short notice. Thank you for coming. I'd like to introduce our new head coach and her assistant, Coach Izzy Soto and Coach Don Romero." With that, Kerrigan stepped to the side with a nod to the two coaches. There was no applause, but there was an audible murmuring.

Twenty minutes earlier, Izzy's emotions were on display. Now, she surveyed the room as if she was objectively evaluating players for her varsity squad. Off to her left stood Virginia Polis, to whom Izzy nodded. Izzy's voice was steady as she began. "Coach Romero and I are anxious to get started. When we finish our short talk, we'll stay around to meet any of you who have specific questions, and there is a handout that provides as much information as we have today about our spring and summer programs, which will be quite extensive, including costs for camps and tournaments." She paused briefly. "As a brief introduction, I'm Isabella Soto, Izzy to my friends, Ms. Soto to my students, Coach Soto to those of you in this room. Transferring over from the girls program is exciting. I was a three-year starter in college, and this is my fifth-year coaching here at Prospect View. Coach Romero is in his thirteenth year with the football team and is the strength and conditioning coach." She looked to Romero and nodded. "To you parents, our job is to make your sons become better basketball players, to mold them together into a championship team, to—with your help—guide them along their path to responsible adulthood, and to create a culture that leads each one to be a reliable teammate and representative of Prospect View." Izzy paused again. "Those are words that nearly every new coach says, but you'll find that I'm serious about these things. I want to let Coach Romero say a few words, and then I'll touch on a few specific things to close and take any questions." Izzy stepped back as Romero stepped forward.

"Most of you know me, and I'm a no-nonsense guy. When Coach approached me about being her assistant basketball coach,

I was hesitant because I've been out of basketball for a while, but after hearing her out, I agreed. What she just said goes for me too. This school has watched her teams perform at the highest level, and she will expect the same kind of effort from you." Romero paused to correct a word in his last statement. "We won't *expect* that kind of effort, we will *insist* upon it." He looked to Izzy and stepped back.

Izzy stepped forward again. She bent down to pick up a box containing game tapes and notes. "Now, to you boys, as we begin, and the new era begins now, let me address a couple of negative issues. Over the past few nights, I have been studying film and taking notes. First, fighting. Over the past two seasons, both in practices and open gyms, and at one of your games, skirmishes seemed to be a part of your personality. Mostly posturing. That behavior stops now. It's phony toughness. Toughness is getting in the weight room, diving on loose balls, fighting over screens." Izzy caught the eye of one of the boys who had initiated the fight with Elgin High. She held his eyes for a moment before continuing. "You've had your warning on this. What happened up to now is over, but I will not allow it to go forward. Second, being here at Prospect View has allowed me to watch you up close, especially at practices where your true nature is exposed. Your reputation around the league is that you are a soft team, and I've seen that at your practices. You simply get outworked by everyone, and you're loose with your habits. Coach Romero and I will not allow that to define you any longer."

In the days leading up to this meeting, Izzy had wondered about her audience. She decided she would present her words for two individuals and let that project to the entire room. She would speak to one player as if he represented all the players and to one adult whom she knew would be on board from the get-go. Boyd Smith was a 6'3" sophomore who had been a JV starter. He was in Izzy's language arts class, so she knew him and sensed his frustrations with his teammates. Virginia Polis was a no-brainer.

Coach Soto continued. "With the unpleasant issues out of the way, let's begin. Open gym resumes on Monday at 7:00. We won't be scrimmaging at all this spring. We'll be working on offensive skills, particularly ball-handling and shooting, lots of shooting.

Don't dress out in t-shirts with drug or beer logos on them. Come in with the positive attitude that you want to get better. Next, get with Coach Romero on a weight training schedule. Parents, if your son has any aspirations about playing college ball at any level, he needs to lift weights. For summer, we have two tournaments and a team camp lined up, and we'll hopefully get into a league. Coach Romero and I will also be running an underclass league on Saturday mornings, so we have a lot on our plates. With all that said, I want to encourage all of you to play other sports too. I know that several of you play baseball, so do that and we'll work around it. Same with football." Izzy moved one step forward. "There was a story in the paper a few weeks ago about Floyd Larson, the Dallas football running back who led the league in rushing last year. He's a Denver native, Denver South, I think. Anyway, he said he never had an off season, that when he wasn't out for football, he played baseball or basketball or ran track. That way, there was no burnout and he was always with his friends. Think about that this summer."

Izzy cleared her throat, turned to Romero to ask him if he had anything to add. He shook his head no, so she continued. "I want to close with a few words to the seniors, I mean you juniors who will be next season's seniors. Often, when a program changes coaches, the new coach will want a fresh start and will be tempted to cut seniors. I have no intention of doing that. If you are one of our best players, if you are a good teammate, if you work hard over the summer, expect to be included on next year's squad. I will be talking with each one of you next week at open gyms, as will Coach Romero. Know that there will be no secrets between Coach and me; our common goal is to put the best team we can on the court, and we will work together to do that."

With that, the formal meeting ended. A few of the boys introduced themselves, as did most of the parents on their way out. The young newspaper writer asked a few questions about Izzy's background but didn't ask about gender bending. More of the boys spoke with Coach Romero at the door as he handed out schedules. When the room emptied, Izzy thanked Romero and Porter, who had stayed to get a read on Coach Soto's first day.

"Too macho?" asked Izzy.

"I don't think so. Just the right tone," said Porter. "We expected no less from you."

"Just like we discussed," said Romero. "You did good." Izzy smiled. Romero shook Porter's hand as the AD left, and then sat with Izzy. "My wife wants you to come over for dinner tonight. She wants to meet the woman who's going to be stealing her husband for hours and hours over the next year. Don't worry, she's a great cook."

Izzy accepted and then did a funny thing. She crossed her arms over her chest and felt under her armpits. "Yew. I'll need to go home and shower first."

Izzy started to stand, but Coach Romero put his hand on her forearm, much like she had done to Bailey an hour earlier, and she sat back down. "Before you go, . . . Isabella," he paused and smiled. "No second thoughts. You signed up for this . . . the problems. I admire your start just now, now don't back off. For better or worse, they're your boys now. I understand how difficult it must have been to surrender your girls for the good of Prospect View." Romero leaned in and lowered his head slightly.

A casual observer might have interpreted the scene as a father speaking with his daughter, but Izzy saw it a different way. This gruff bear of a man was telling her that he had her back for the coming year, no questions asked. Three years earlier, she had waded into a fight in the school's hallway near the cafeteria and found herself unable to stop it and about to become part of the collateral damage. Out of nowhere, Romero appeared and separated the two boys, one of his big paws clutching the collar of each boy. At that moment, he thanked her for breaking the scuffle up and marched the boys down to the office.

CHAPTER 3

The seniors-to-be didn't quite understand what they were protesting, but they stayed away from open gym that first night. The boys who did attend, a handful of juniors and fifteen sophomores, received the full attention of three coaches, each one demonstrating technique or correcting bad habits. Coach Romero, with his linebacker's build and gruff demeanor on the football field, found himself enjoying the pure instructional nature of Izzy's coaching method, the hands-on approach of his new head coach and classroom voice Izzy used to teach basketball skills. "It'll come back to me," he told her, but she jokingly warned him not to allow that to change his demeanor, that it was going to make them a unique coaching combination for the boys.

"Start your shot from the knees. Basketball is played with bent knees. Don't allow your guide hand to fully extend. That's it; that looks really good." Coach Izzy would pat the boy on his shoulder and have him repeat the move. Romero began recalling instructions given to him two decades earlier by his high school coach, began to understand that those old instructions were not much different from what Izzy was saying, just presented with different words, different phrases. *Bent knees,* he thought. *About the same meaning as, Get your ass down!*

"At the end of the game, the team that puts the ball in the hole the most will be the winner. It's that simple. My job is to get you in positions to take good shots, but it will be your responsibility to practice making good shots." Izzy walked over to Romero and Miles Minturn, allowing the paired shooting to proceed on its own for a few minutes. "Oh, if it was only that simple. Eric over there has a nice shot, but at 5'5" and 120 pounds, he has to get it up over players a half-foot taller and quicker." She smiled at her coaches. "No problem, huh."

Minturn responded. "Well, at least we're seeing a bunch of promising JVers and C-teamers."

Romero laughed. "Building from the ground up, Coach. I'm assuming all but one or two of these kids will make up my JV squad."

Around 7:45, girls began arriving and stretching. Bailey Rockwell walked directly to where Izzy was standing under one main court basket and gave her a quick hug before joining her teammates off to the side. Coach Tanya had come early, but after she wheeled out the rack of balls, she too had stepped onto the court to work with two boys on their free throw shooting. For the last ten minutes, Izzy put the boys in a pass-and-cut drill that would eventually work its way into her motion offense. At precisely 8:00, she pulled her boys off the court and had them sit on the floor away from the girls.

"Good work out there, guys. I see some real promise. We have a long way to go, but it's March. Don't let open gym be the only time you're practicing." Izzy turned to her assistant coaches.

Coach Romero cleared his horsey throat. "As some of you noticed, I'm a bit rusty with this roundball thing, but I'll be up to speed in another week or so. I enjoyed working with you tonight. Make sure you get your homework done before you go to bed." Romero nodded and stepped back.

It was Miles Minturn's moment. "It was nice to see most of you again," he said referring to the fact that several of the boys had played for him at the middle school level. "Also, good to see that you're all taller. Now, get in the weight room and get stronger!"

"I'll know all of your names by the end of the week," promised Izzy. "Take advantage of these days when others aren't here. See you all on Wednesday."

Several of the boys lingered to talk with the coaches, most with Coach Minturn, seemingly happy that he was a part of the high school coaching staff. Most of the boys thanked Coach Soto as they were leaving. When they had dispersed, the three coaches held their first post-practice meeting.

"The Sampson kid is a comer," said Romero. "He'd make a dynamite split end."

Izzy laughed. "You'll probably always see football players out here. See, this is just a recruitment gig for you. Hard to tell about his toughness, but he does have good hands and is smooth. Very coachable." She took out a notepad. "Any others who grabbed your attention who might be varsity caliber?" She stopped herself. "I mean for the upcoming season."

"They're all gems, Coach," said Romero, "we just gotta polish them." He checked to see if Izzy understood his humor . . . or sarcasm. "Winning is still about talent. We need a baseline amount."

Izzy agreed. "I think we can teach shooting. I've always believed that skill could be taught at this level. Passing can be too, but we need to demand its execution since it's not a flashy skill. The one skill that I've always thought was learned early, even as an elementary kid, was dribbling. We'll do all kinds of drills but having that one kid who can really handle the ball is a gift." She shook her head and smiled. "Until Bailey showed up, I couldn't get the girls to that last step. Good but with limits."

"So, a point guard is sort of like a middle linebacker," grunted Romero. "Wider vision."

Izzy nodded. "On paper at the beginning of the season, last year's girls didn't have a real chance to make the State playoffs, but then Bailey burst onto the scene. All capitals *BURST*. We were solid, of course, but not top sixteen. Amazing what one player can do."

§

Two more boys from the JV squad attended Wednesday's open gym as well as three more sophomores. The numbers were down on Friday, but they always were because of the weekend parties. Still, another sophomore from the JV team came, and all three of those boys had the makings of varsity players. "Up to four," teased Romero."

"Please find me some guards," said Izzy.

§

On Saturday, Izzy ate lunch with a realtor from Boulder who had gotten her name from one of Izzy's colleagues and was looking for a relationship. She politely thanked him for the meal but said no to future dates. *Way too old*, she thought. *Probably can't dance fast either*. Later that afternoon, she drove to Ft. Collins to spend time with Bianca and Adam, having dinner with them and laughing at her decision.

"How's this working out?" asked Adam.

"Ask me next year at this time. I should have a better feel for an answer."

"What about your JV coach?" asked Bianca, referencing Izzy's earlier request that Bianca be on the staff.

"Romero's been terrific. Funny. His first name is Don . . . Donnie . . . but I've gotten into the habit of calling him Romero. He's never been a head coach which surprises me, but he has a different perspective than I do. I've never been an assistant. He and I and my C-team coach, when he can get to the high school, are meeting at lunch to discuss our needs. They think the absence of upperclassmen may actually prove to be a positive early on, that we'll be able to set a pattern for our program before they show up. We'll see, but they may have a point."

"What do you see as the biggest difference so far?" asked Adam.

"For me or between the girls and boys?" asked Izzy.

"Between your players."

"Easy. Size and athleticism. Not that my girls weren't athletic, but in height and jumping ability and maybe a little quickness. The old adage is that the boys game has a faster pace, but that certainly hasn't been the case at my school since I've been here. We've always played faster." Izzy laughed aloud. "The ones I've worked with, however, sure lack for basketball sense and competitiveness. One of my better decisions was to not hire the old staff. Romero's football genes have already kicked in, and Miles wants to coach a real team, not like the middle school intramural teams."

§

The weekly local newspaper, *The Prospect Times*, came out on Monday with a short story about Prospect View's coaching changes. The focus was clearly on a woman becoming the coach of a boys team. In addition to providing a quick bio of Izzy, the story alluded to the fact that, as far as the *Times* could ascertain, Colorado had only had one female head coach of a boys major sport at this classification or higher over a decade ago. When Dr. Kerrigan discussed the article with Coach Soto, they both commented that there would be several tennis, soccer, swimming, and track coaches who might object about the reference to "major" sports.

"I hope some of those coaches write letters to the editor making that point. There have always been women coaching boys in high school athletics," said Kerrigan. "How did your first week go?"

"Surprisingly well aside from the fact that some of the kids who played on the varsity last season are staying away from open gym. They didn't like coach Miller, wanted him gone, but they don't approve of me for the obvious reason, I guess. I don't know who's leading the protest, but in actuality, it's probably only a half-dozen or so boys who are boycotting. Rumor has it they're playing at the rec center in the evenings. At least they're playing."

"If they think I'm going to change my mind, they're sadly mistaken," said Kerrigan.

Izzy smiled. "Oh, darn. I'm stuck then." Both women laughed. "Have you had any calls about your decision?"

"Three. All from mothers, which surprises me. The gist of each one is that if their son is to get a basketball scholarship, he would need a man to be coaching him, that it wasn't fair."

"I hope you told them that Colorado has open enrollment, that they have several high schools nearby where they might go."

Kerrigan nodded. "As a matter of fact, that's exactly what I told them. Just so you're clear, without me joking, you're my coach, Prospect View's coach. I'll take these calls and handle them, and unless you ask specifically, I'm not even going to mention them to you."

"Thank you, Dr. Kerrigan. Has Carl taken any calls?"

"Yes, but I asked if he wanted me to speak to the caller, and he said no. We're on the same page. I think his might have been from a father."

Izzy shook her head. "So, the women call you, a woman, and the men call Carl. Interesting."

Their conversation was interrupted by a call from a counsellor wanting Coach Soto to come in to introduce herself to a move-in student who was interested in coming out for the team. "Let's hope he's 6'10"," said Dr. Kerrigan.

§

He wasn't. Sitting in the counselling office was a below average-sized boy and his mother. The counselor introduced everyone and then sat behind her desk.

"You're the coach?" asked Nick Patterson, standing to shake Izzy's hand.

"Yes, I am," answered Izzy. "Were you expecting someone . . . older?"

Without missing a beat, Nick said, "No, taller." Everyone in the room laughed.

Taking a seat, Izzy spoke, "I understand you're interested in playing basketball. What year are you?"

"I'll be a sophomore next year. I have to go back to Illinois to finish this year, but I'll be here next year."

"When will you be moving out?" asked Coach Soto.

Nick looked to his mother, who answered for him. "We should be out around Memorial Day. If you have any summer programs, he'd like to be included, if that's possible, and I'd like to get a list of expenses, if possible."

"I imagine you played back home?" asked Izzy.

"I was on the freshman team there. I'm pretty average, but I really like basketball."

"He loves basketball," interjected Mrs. Patterson. "He started on his team. He's always dribbling the ball around the house. I think he'd sleep with it if I let him."

"Well, I'll make a note that you'll be arriving in late-May and include you in our plans. I want you to call me when you get in.

We're in a tournament that last weekend in May, so I might not be here at school. You would be welcome to come watch us and see how good we are. We're pretty raw at the moment. Have you had a tour of the school yet?"

"All I want to see is the gym."

"I have a few moments before my next class. Let's go down, and I'll introduce you to Coach Romero, my JV coach. He's also an assistant football coach. Do you play football?"

§

A month of open gyms taught Izzy that the actual coaching of boys varied little from coaching girls. The court still measured 84 feet by 50 feet; the basket remined at ten feet, and the three-point line was nineteen feet nine inches from the hoop. The most notable difference was the size of the basketball itself, which took a bit of getting used to for Izzy. Throughout high school and college and continuing for the five coaching years, she could shoot better than almost anyone around her. Switching to the larger ball threw her out of her comfort zone, but after several weeks, she was returning to her level of expertise. She certainly could outshoot any of her boys. But the coaching part remained constant; basketball was basketball. Roll the balls out and get after it. Where Izzy felt a difference was in why boys played compared to her girls' reasons. It didn't seem like boys were concerned as much with friendships. They wanted to be with their friends, of course, but the boys open gyms had a different feel. *Tentativeness?*

While Romero and Miles obsessed over the missing boys, Izzy mostly put it out of her thoughts. She would coach the boys who showed up, not the ones who didn't. She assumed that after their bluff had been called, they would return. They would have missed some valuable time to get better, but they would walk out on the court, their tails between their legs, and compete for varsity time. Of the protesters, only Atticus was in her classes, although she had taught three of the others in sophomore language arts. They avoided her. The two people they could not avoid were Coach Romero and the head football coach. Both men sought them out to challenge their obstinance, but to no avail. The father of one of the boys called the head football coach warning him to lay off his kid.

"He needs to quit being babied by his dad," said Romero. "Notice how none of the parents actually called you or me. Always someone *around* us."

April open gyms separated the participants into two groups, potential varsity players and for-sure non-varsity players. The first group had five boys, but the second group's numbers were growing weekly. None of the boys at open gym seemed to have any problems about being coached by a woman. Coach Romero's prodding each night at the end of open gym about getting in the weight room was having its desired effects, as at least a dozen boys who had never lifted weights began showing up to his zero hour weight room class. One of those was Charlie Sampson, and his growth was an example to the rest of the boys. One month into her tenure, Izzy figured she had one varsity starter and four reserves.

On Monday, May 1, Coach Izzy began to incorporate scrimmages into her practices. She knew that while half-court offense and defense would look ragged during the summer, if her boys could not break presses, they would be embarrassed consistently in tournaments and at team camp. For five years, she had utilized the same plan for breaking both full and half-court presses, but the plan relied heavily on a quality point guard, which she did not have. *Maybe*, she thought to herself, *I could borrow Bailey for games.* After trying various methods at open gym and endless discussions with her two assistant coaches, Izzy said, "Screw it!" I'm going to use what I know and work like heck to develop point guards who can fill our need." With Romero's and Miles' input over beers at Romero's house, they compiled a list of six boys who showed the most promise, including one who was 5'5"and 120 pounds.

Looking at the list, Miles shook his head and said, "We have our work cut out for us, but at least we now have a goal."

Romero took his copy, arose from the table, and walked around his kitchen rubbing his head. It was more like pacing. He would stop six inches from each wall, hesitate, then turn and head back, much like a prisoner in a small jail cell. While Izzy and Miles sketched out variations of lineups to compliment the mystery point guard of the future, Romero began to hmmm. After a few minutes, he returned to the table, took Izzy's list and added a name. Charlie Sampson.

"What's wrong with having a 6'3" point guard?" he asked. "Who knows, in time he may become a 6'6" point guard."

With her arms under the table, Izzy leaned way forward, her nose almost touching her list. Without rising up, she turned her head to Miles. "What do you think?"

Romero popped his third beer and answered before Miles spoke. "You'll need a backup and the JVs will need two, but at least we can cut this list by three, add Charlie, and move forward with a more manageable number. Miles can assume he has all the rest and develop them normally."

Miles agreed. "He might not be the smoothest ball-handler, but with his height, he can throw over the top, and that's a big part of this press break method. I like the idea."

Izzy lifted her head and took a drink of her soda. "If nothing else, it'll add to Charlie's skills. He'll be better for it even though he'll struggle during the summer." She put Charlie's name at the top of her point guard list. We're going to be putting a lot on his plate. Help me monitor that."

§

On Wednesday night, Coach Soto gathered the four boys on her point guard list, sat them down on the bleachers, handed them a list of drills to be executed on their own, and began Point Guard 101. On Thursday, Bailey asked Coach Soto if she could have the handout. "Always something more to learn."

"As point guards, you're in charge out there. A coach delegates his responsibility to you while the clock is moving, but it's an awesome responsibility. It takes a special player to take charge of a team. I will be looking to each of you to step up." Coach Soto paused. "It isn't easy."

§

With two weeks left in the school year and two weeks left before Prospect View would play its first summer game, the coaching staff reviewed its team's status at Coach Minturn's apartment while waiting for pizza to be delivered. His wife was the guest of honor at some party at a friend's house. No seniors-to-be had attended open gym, so the Pronghorns would go to battle starting four juniors-to-be, all of whom had played on last season's JV squad, and a sophomore from the C-team. That group would be backed up by a junior and three sophomores with almost no JV experience. The one sophomore who had varsity experience, Atticus Felton, was still a no-show. On the bright side, as Coach Soto said to her assistants, "With our numbers, we'll be able to field two JV teams in our Saturday league. Each of you will have a team."

"We'll have fun," said Coach Minturn.

G Charlie Sampson, jr, 6' 3" (best player)

G Morgan Rexford, jr, 5'10 (baseball player, but comes to open gyms when he can)

G Jimmy Yang, soph, 5' 9" (JV at best)

F Rob Broyles, jr, 6' 0" (still on the fence)

F Boyd Smith, jr, 6' 3" (a hopeful maybe)

"Bunch of skinny kids," said Romero. "Not enough meat and potatoes. Too much junk food." They all laughed. "We're going to get hammered on the boards!"

"Charlie can help on the defensive side, since he'll be guarding a forward or center. Only on offense will he be considered a guard. Morgan will be the defensive stopper. Thank goodness he's been coming in after baseball practice. I wish a couple others from the varsity would show up." Izzy giggled. "Gawd, we have no other defensive stoppers."

"Go zone, Coach," teased Romero.

"Never happen during the summer. Never happen."

The pizza arrived and the planning continued. Minturn suggested Izzy take two extra kids down to the tournament, and he gave her two names. "Those two have been to every open gym and would love to carry the ball bags. Have them keep stats."

Romero started laughing again. "Just have one of them chart all the turnovers. That may be a fulltime job."

"Hey, where's your optimism?" asked Izzy sarcastically.

"Coach, that's realism," answered Romero. "We're going to lose all three games. Be prepared for that. This tournament doesn't have any other patsies. We're it. Charlie and his friends have done all we've asked, but they're not in the class with those Denver area teams. We're 3A and every other team is 4A or 5A. Make sure your kids know that winning isn't the goal in this tournament. It's getting their first varsity game experience."

Minturn nodded in agreement. "Coach, it's doubtful we'll even be competitive in any game. This will all be about showing up, getting their feet wet, and not getting hurt. At least we won't be getting in any fights. Goal one accomplished."

Romero looked very seriously at his head coach before speaking again. "Are you gonna eat that last piece of pizza?"

§

Four of the five seniors-to-be, along with Atticus Felton, showed up at open gym on Wednesday, May 17, albeit ten minutes late. Two dozen underclassmen working at six baskets were already into their second drill of the evening, this one a shooting drill with mild defensive pressure. The four seniors stood near the locker room door for a few minutes waiting for a coach to acknowledge their presence. Shortly, Coach Soto walked to them, told them to tie their sneakers, split up, and join a group. "Watch and see what we're doing and try to get it right."

As she turned away, she heard one of the boys say to another, "I wonder how long until we scrimmage."

Coach Soto turned back. "The team will be working on some half-court, four-on-four stuff in about twenty minutes. You're free to watch when they do." Then, she pivoted and rejoined Jimmy Yang's group at a side basket.

Rather than join any group, the seniors stayed together and sat on the bleachers. Coach Romero strode to the group. "You've got a choice. Get on the floor or get out. This isn't a spectator event." The four seniors stood and left. The one junior-to-be removed his cap and asked Coach Romero which group he should join. *An act of bravery*, thought Romero.

After open gym, when the girls took the floor, Soto, Romero, and Minturn sat in the bleachers reviewing the practice. "Did you tell them they couldn't participate?" asked Miles.

"No. I told them to split up and join a group. They just came to scrimmage. Didn't want to work hard, just to show up the young kids." Izzy smiled. "Or more likely to show up me. Little do they know. It was encouraging that Atticus stayed." She left it there.

"Did you notice which kid wasn't with them?" It was a rhetorical question by Romero. "Brooks Danson, the best player. Coach, there's a rumor he's transferring to one of the nearby schools."

"I've heard that rumor. His parents have already met with Kerrigan about me. Don't worry though, she's got our backs." Izzy cracked her neck. "In numbers, we're fine. Plenty of kids for three teams. Miles, you'll have more than a dozen. It's those six or seven kids from last year's varsity and JV squads who are missing. It's puzzling that they would skip out for so long. It can't be just that I'm a female coach, especially without even coming in to talk."

Romero rubbed his chin. "With Danson, it might just be you're a woman, but I can't believe all the others would feel the same way. No, since we aren't missing any of the younger kids, it's a varsity thing. For some reason, they think they were targeted, I think, and now they have to make a stand. This first year might challenge you; with only these kids, you might not win as many as they did last season." Romero smiled. "Did I say *you*? I meant *we*."

"Any ideas, Miles?" asked Izzy.

"You read about cases where a team loves its old coach and resents the new one. That's not the case here. Other times, it's the parents who inject their insecurities onto the situation. I guess there may be a little of that, but I doubt it. You were pretty definitive at the first meeting about fighting and their team being soft, so maybe they took offense and got together as a group to make a statement and it got out of hand." Miles tilted his head and raised his hands as if to say, "Who knows?"

"Your point at that first meeting was right on target. Don't over-analyze that," said Romero. "There's a fine line in sports between toughness and fighting. 'Stand your ground,' 'don't be a pussy' . . . pardon my lingo, Coach. The boys basketball team has been pushed around on the court for several years, and not being able to win on the scoreboard, they compensated by fighting. At least, that's what I think. Embarrassed." He paused. "You called them out on it, and that hurt their feelings. The newspaper article emphasized that."

Izzy tried to recall what the paper had written about that meeting. "I'll have to go home and reread it." The coaches went quiet for a moment.

"By the way," said Romero. "Rexford's getting better fast. You know he's going to be our starting running back next fall, and now he seems to be taking ownership of this team. That kind of stuff is contagious."

"I haven't asked you this before, Coach, but are there any big football kids that might help us on the boards?"

§

. . . and the new coach quickly addressed the issues of the team's image of playing soft and fighting, without directly mentioning last season's melee near the end of the year that led to three suspensions, saying that would not be tolerated in her program.

Izzy cringed at the wording in the sentence but had to admit that it might have caused a rift between her and Coach Miller's boys. She skipped down to read the words that the sportswriter had written about the girls' team.

Tanya Hatton will be inheriting a gritty program known for winning, with three consecutive trips to State, the last one to the Final Four. Coach Hatton will also have the team leader returning in all-conference guard Bailey Rockwell.

Izzy thought back to when she was hired as the girls coach five years ago. *Soto said she is excited and anxious to begin, to get to know the girls, and build a program the school and community can be proud of.*

Izzy took a deep breath and exhaled slowly. She did it again, shook her head from side to side, and then folded the clipping about her recent beginning on this new journey. She clasped her hands on top of her head and leaned back on her sofa. She wondered if she still had that t-shirt Molly had given her as a gift when she was first hired five years earlier. She rose from the sofa and went to her bedroom dresser. Finding what she was looking for in the bottom drawer along with her college shooting shirt, she unfolded the long-sleeve t-shirt and spread it out on her bed. With baby blue lettering on the gold shirt, it read, "A coach is someone who can give correction without causing resentment." John Wooden. Molly purchased two of them, the first one for herself, saying she needed to heed Coach Wooden's advice more than Izzy would.

§

After an evening of stewing and a night of restless sleep, Izzy went to school early again to spend a few minutes with Virginia Polis. Izzy found the custodian in one of her offices having a cup of coffee while she perused a request to build shelves in a back closet off the band room.

"Morning, Coach. Do you need me to unlock the office again?"

"No, I came to ask you something."

Polis assumed Izzy needed something repaired in either her room or the gymnasium. "Let me write Mr. Lennon a note, and then we can go take a look at your problem."

"No, everything is okay; I just want your perspective on a couple of students."

Still not sure of what Izzy wanted, Polis put the note down to give her colleague her full attention. "Okay, Coach."

Izzy began. "I think, in my push to not be seen as weak in this new position, which I hadn't thought I was going to worry about but evidently did, I think I may have made a mistake. You were there at that first meeting, and I wanted to make a strong point about behavior, about how I expected my team to . . . represent our school. I don't know if you've had any conversations with your nephew about open gyms or his perceptions, but I've liked how the boys have taken to instruction. We're making some good strides."

Polis sensed Izzy's uncomfortableness. "But some kids aren't there."

"Yeah. I knew who the kids were who were the leaders of that misbehavior, and I wanted them to know that I knew, but it was never my intention to drive them away. It's like I cut them from the team at that first meeting." Izzy's face registered a bit of pain. "And when they didn't show up at open gym that first week, I didn't reach out to them to get them back, I just sort of let the problem fester." She looked at Virginia Polis to check for comprehension.

"Sit down, Coach. Do you drink coffee?" Izzy waived off the offer but did sit. "Charlie and I talk a lot here at school. He always comes around needing lunch money. He's loving open gym and feels very comfortable around his teammates and coaches. He says his friends feel the same way."

"I'm glad to hear that, and I feel that vibe, but my job is to coach all the boys, and I want to give them all a chance."

Polis reached back to rub her neck. "So, what's your question, Coach?'

"You watched a lot of the boys games last year, for the last couple of years, and I'd like your opinion about what those boys are like off the court." Izzy scrunched her mouth into her nose, an act of discomfort. "Do you think any of those kids would deliberately undermine what I'm trying to get done?"

Polis breathed out hard and scratched her chin. "That varsity team was out of control, and they ran the show. I have no idea who started it, but it wasn't just last year. It started with the kids who have already graduated, and it seems like each new senior class is supposed to carry on the tradition of being jerks. Sort of like hazing; it's a tradition. I don't know if it's because of what they see on TV or just macho teenage bullshit, but it's been going on for a couple of years.'

"Did Coach Miller try to stop it?"

"Not that I'm aware of, but most coaches give lip service to behavior. I'm pretty sure it's why he quit, not because of his win-loss record. He was worn out," said Polis. "He'd get frustrated at practice and make them run sprints, but it didn't carry over to games."

Izzy agreed. "Only sitting on the bench or suspensions have long-term effects." She stood. "I've taken up too much of your time, and I know you have work to do, but thanks. I appreciate your insight."

From this meeting, Izzy went to see Carl Porter to see if he would facilitate a meeting with seven boys who had seen some varsity time last season but had not attended any open gyms.

§

Immediately after lunch on Friday, Coach Soto and Coach Romero entered the office conference room where Porter was casually conversing with seven former basketball players. Instructing them to sit, Porter told them that the two coaches wanted to have this meeting to clear the air about their non-participation.

"Seems more like an inquisition," quipped Brooks Danson, and the other boys laughed.

Sensing Romero's anger, Izzy nudged his leg under the table with the back of her hand, an unseen gesture meant to have him hold his tongue. "Wow," she said calmly, "your cleverness is noted . . . as is your lack of respect." She looked at the other boys, three of whom she had taught as sophomores, who now averted their eyes.

"I asked for this meeting, a meeting I should have held six weeks ago, to apologize for my part in maybe shining an unwanted spotlight on last year's team. At that first meeting, I should have said how excited I was to get the chance to work with you all." She paused. "I am excited. I love to coach." Izzy spoke deliberately maintaining eye contact. "Instead, I began with two negatives. Those issues got the spotlight in the newspaper article, and for that, I'm sorry. They needed to be addressed, as I'm sure you would agree, but probably not at that time. The first open gym would have been a better time." She took her pen and checked off an item from a list and then continued. "Coach and I have wondered if all seven of you were offended at that time and each one of you, on your own, decided not to play basketball any longer. It's a question that Coach and I can't answer, but quitting a sport tends to be one of those decisions that adults later in life cite as being a regret." She looked to Romero for his silent assent, and he nodded.

Brooks Danson again popped off. "Can we get to the heart of this meeting? I've got a class to go to."

"Shut up, Brooks, and let Coach finish," said one of the students who had been in Soto's sophomore language arts class.

Izzy smiled to herself, and she was sure Romero did too, and then she asked the boys, "What would it take for any of you, either individually or collectively, after you consider this attempt by Coach Romero and me to reach out and make amends, to sit with us and discuss your decision about quitting basketball?" She allowed her offer to linger in the air. Then, "Brooks, I've heard a rumor that you have been accepted at Broomfield High School for next year, that you will be transferring. I hope that's just a rumor and that you'll be open to giving us an opportunity." It was obvious that Brooks' friends did not know this.

Brooks shot back. "Where'd you hear that?"

Calmly, Izzy answered. "I received a call from the Broomfield coach wanting to know if I knew why you were leaving."

Brooks abruptly stood. "Shit! I'm out of here!"

Carl Porter started to speak, but suddenly stopped and allowed Danson to leave. After Brooks slammed the door behind him, Porter asked if either coach had anything to add or ask. Romero leaned in.

"Guys, I've worked with all of you either in football or the weight room. Coach Soto has made a fair offer: come in and talk. She's got the program up and running. Ask your other teammates; they'll tell you. She knows what she's doing. Don't allow this boycott to smear your reputation."

Porter looked to Izzy. She nodded. "Last thing. I really would like to work with you, but know that we're moving ahead regardless. Summer play is critical to any team's development, so if you'd like to play, don't wait. We have a practice tomorrow at four. I hope to see you there. Thanks for listening to us."

The meeting ended and the boys left without speaking to either of the coaches or each other.

Romero put his left hand on Izzy's forearm as he had done after the first meeting. "That's all we can do; the ball's in their court now."

"I wonder how the town will react," said Izzy.

"I'm not sure Prospect cares a whole lot about what goes on here, Isabella. What I mean is that it's growing so fast, and the new population has no ties to the school. Parents graduated from somewhere else, so they don't react to events on our campus. This isn't a poor community. It's upwardly mobile, tech savvy, and isn't looking for nostalgia. It's looking for championships and resume building. No allegiance yet. Think of the low numbers of fans in the stands or bleachers. It's hard to get people to come for any sport."

"It's even harder for the girls. We're big winners, but we still don't fill up the stands for any of our games. The boys get as many people as we do, and you know how they've done the last few years. How do we change that?" Izzy looked at Romero, waiting.

Romero punched her in the arm gently. "Win bigger, Coach. Win bigger."

§

Win bigger. Izzy paced her small apartment entering each room almost unconsciously. Intuitively, she knew how to coach girls, to work with them as a high-performance unit. *High goals to supplement my vision, a vision you learned from your high school coach. Even though he was calm, he expected us to win. Stretch them; they want to be challenged. Toughness; physically of course, but more importantly, mentally. Every drill. And let them know they are loved, that they are yours, Iz.* The Prospect View girls had climbed to the highest level, and now that culture was in place. Those first two years for Izzy created a testing ground for her as she put in place the stepping-stones for a first-class program. Each girl received personal and detailed feedback about what to improve upon. Advice was direct but delivered in a positive manner. Even when a player fell short of her goals, even if it was because of lack of effort, Izzy stayed positive and supportive. But still demanding. "I will not demand of you anything you are not capable of doing, but you must do your part."

Each time Izzy's pacing brought her to the kitchen counter, she jotted a note on her pad. If she had nothing to write, she avoided passing by the counter. *These boys are cliquish, confused, and unaware of possibilities open to them. They will be resistant to break out of their comfort zone, out of their fears of pushing past that comfort.* On her last pass, she stopped and nodded, picked up her pen, and wrote one last note to herself. *Trust yourself and Romero. These boys don't look like much of a team today, but that's what you have been hired for. Be tougher than the environment! Win bigger? Hell, yes! Win more than they did this season!*

CHAPTER 4

Find great teammates! Be one yourself.

While Izzy wanted last year's players, all of them, to be members of next year's team, she had to admit that open gyms were running conflict free, that a culture she envisioned along the lines of her girls program was developing. When four more boys showed up on Friday, including Atticus Felton for the second time, she split them up and incorporated them into existing groups who understood the drills. The three boys who didn't show up had the most varsity experience but having the additional four boys enhanced the talent level of the practice exponentially. As of May 19, all four of them were good enough to be considered for starting positions come next December. However, none would play in the upcoming Memorial Day tournament, but each expressed an interest in attending the games. All signed up and paid their fee for the league and team camp.

"We'll get a look at the younger kids next weekend," said Izzy to Coach Romero as Friday's practice was winding down, "and then restructure the teams a bit."

Romero laughed. "There are at least two kids who will be happy they won't have to play varsity this summer. They know they're not good enough and really don't want to be thrown into that pit. Besides, their friends are all on the summer JV team. I also think Charlie is a little relieved he won't be our forever point guard. We need him at that forward spot anyway."

"Mason slotted into the drills easily. He just might be the answer to our guard dilemma. Mason and Morgan. That has a nice ring. Morgan is coming, just like you said. Don't let him get hurt in football. He brings toughness to our team." Izzy walked back to her group of six, moving them one basket over to work on feeding the post. "Show target hands. Go get the pass; don't wait for the ball to come to you. Passer, relocate to the corner and get your feet ready!"

When practice ended around 5:30, Izzy called her boys to mid-court and sat them down. "Next week's practices will all be at 7:00, one hour only. Since Thursday's the last day of school, some of you will need to hit the books to pass final exams. If you need the extra time to study, stay home. For those of you who will be playing in the Memorial Day tournament, pick up a schedule after I finish. Our first game is Friday at 6:00 against Aurora. They'll be good again. I'm not expecting miracles, but I will expect you to compete. I've heard a rumor that if you don't, Morgan will be speaking with you privately." She looked at Morgan Rexford and smiled. "For the rest of you, Coach Romero and Coach Minturn will have you scrimmaging a lot next Saturday beginning at 9:00. Your league begins the following Saturday, June 3. If you're going to be out of town for the holiday, let your coaches know." She looked at her boys for questions. "Now, Charlie and Wes have challenged me to a three-point contest." The boys made various sounds to indicate doom or support. "Do you guys want me to go first or last?"

Charlie went first and drained five threes in the one-minute session. Wes shot next, also making five. Izzy removed her sweatshirt, picked a ball from the rack, and went to the right wing. "Start the clock," she said. She missed her first shot and the kids hooted. Then, she reeled off four in a row before missing again. Three more makes, a miss, and then finishing with two more makes. The buzzer sounded. She raised both arms in victory and did a little dance, receiving high fives from Minturn and Romero, while Wes and Charlie received the razz from their teammates.

"The gym will be open tomorrow morning at 10:00 for extra work. It's not mandatory. Have a safe weekend!"

§

The 6'8" Aurora High School center controlled the opening tip, then received a back screen at the top of the key to free him for a lob dunk over Prospect View's Boyd Smith. Coach Soto silently laughed at the thought that never had an opposing team dunked over one of her girls. Boyd seemed dazed when he turned and ran to the other end of the court. However, it was his responsibility to inbound the ball after a made basket. Charlie Sampson grabbed the ball, but had no teammate to throw it to, which resulted in a five-second violation. Aurora's subsequent possession led to another dunk by their center. This time, Boyd filled his role, but Charlie was immediately trapped, causing another turnover.

In the informal introductions before the tip-off, as the Aurora coach shook Izzy's hand, he asked if she was a mother filling in for the day. Was Prospect View's coach going to be at the tournament for the weekend? He seemed genuinely surprised when Izzy told him she was the head coach, that she had been hired two months earlier. "Oh, I'm sorry," said the Aurora coach. "What should I call you?"

"How about 'Coach'?"

This first game of the summer proved difficult in many aspects; certainly Prospect View was over-matched in talent and size, and the kids felt, at least in the short run, embarrassed by the final score, but Coach Soto thought she saw some things to build upon. Morgan Rexford relished the opportunity to defend both of Aurora's quick, mouthy guards and had the physical tools to do so. Boyd Smith returned to the low post each possession to battle Aurora's seasoned center, never asking for a breather. Charlie Sampson, playing out of position and clearly frustrated by Aurora's press, still managed to score eight points, almost half of Prospect View's total. And, the four players who did not play but sat behind their teammates gave vocal support throughout the game. After the game, Izzy deconstructed the game to her team, emphasizing positive points and recognizing the areas where improvement could be achieved.

"First, guys, remember what you were up against. That team is 5A and returns several players from a deep run in State last year. We won't play anybody that good next season." Izzy checked for comprehension. "That first play was a set up. Boyd, you got double screened so they could get that dunk. I like how you competed for the rest of the game."

As Rob Broyles put a light headlock on his teammate, Boyd said, "Yeah, he only dunked on me four more times." The team laughed.

"He's going to dunk on a lot of good players, so you'll be in good company." She stepped forward one stride to give Boyd a high-five and then spoke to the entire squad. "What were your expectations coming into the game?" After a moment for reflection, she received several answers.

"To win."

"To have fun."

"Sort of like last year."

"Not a blow-out, that's for sure."

Izzy looked to the boys who hadn't played. "Do you think you could have made a difference?" she asked without resentment or as an accusation.

They looked to each other and gave a general nod. Sal Palagi answered for the group, "We still wouldn't have won, but maybe it would have been a little closer." Then, he looked away from Izzy toward the boys who had played. "You guys did pretty good though. You played hard." Sal returned his eyes to Izzy.

"I think so too," said the new coach. "This team is, in so many ways, starting over this season. That's not a bad thing. At any beginning, it's healthy to know where you stand . . . where we stand. We know now that we won't be good enough to win the 5A State Championship next season." Izzy paused and smiled, waiting for the boys to see more than just the humor in her statement. "If this last hour is any indication, I like our beginning. I can go home tonight and begin making lists of where each of you fit, all sixteen of you who, and this is the important part, hung together and kept battling. I'm including those of you who didn't suit up." Izzy had lots more to say but cut herself off. There would be time after games tomorrow and Sunday to continue this theme. For now, get back into the vans and make the drive home fun. She gave them tomorrow's schedule, told them to get a bite to eat at the concession stand, and said she wanted to make a few notes before they headed home.

"Coach Soto."

Izzy turned to the woman standing a few paces to her right. "Oh, hi, Mrs. Patterson."

"If you have a minute . . ."

"Yes, of course. Let's sit, so we can get out of the way of this next game." They climbed a few rows into the bleachers. "I noticed you and Nick during the game. I'm not sure we gave an encouraging account of ourselves tonight."

Mrs. Patterson waved that off. "Nick went over to the aux gym to check on another game. He's always looking for a game. He was adamant about coming here tonight."

"I hope he's still excited about the move. Watching us might cause a bit of consternation."

Mrs. Patterson shook her head. "Actually, quite the opposite. Back home, he hoped he might have a chance to make the JV team next year. His high school has about 2500 kids. He said he thought he had a chance to make your varsity."

Izzy tightened her lips. "Lord knows we can use a point guard."

As if on cue, Nick returned to the main gym and joined his mother. Izzy stood and offered her hand.

Nick shook it and said, "I liked your plan for breaking that green team's press."

§

Izzy met Jorge for a casual dinner a few hours after her last tournament game on Sunday. He had played in a soccer match in Brighton and was interested in telling her about his goal, his first of the summer. He liked that she understood the game a little but confessed again that basketball confused him with all its scoring. She laughed, telling him that soccer teams might score more if they didn't celebrate for a half-hour after each goal. Jorge continued to act amazed that she was coaching a team of boys. After dinner, he asked if he could see her again, maybe have a real date where he picked her up at her apartment, maybe go dancing. Izzy said she would like that if he would first read up on basketball a little. She drove home with a smile.

Coach Minturn called Izzy on Sunday night to get an update on the weekend tournament. He detailed his and Romero's time with just the lower-level kids on Saturday morning, and thanked Izzy again for "bringing me on board with the boys program." He was also excited about moving to the high school as a teacher in the fall.

"As we expected," said Izzy, "we didn't win a game, but I don't think they were discouraged, and some of the holdouts came down all three days. That was so positive. I think they were trying to get into the good graces of at least their teammates. Not sure about me yet."

"Any word on the other three?" asked Minturn.

"Brooks did transfer, but I have nothing new on Jed and Kelly, and the other boys haven't heard anything or at least aren't saying. That code of silence, I guess."

Minturn told Izzy of his and Romero's ideas for running the Saturday league and summer practices, ideas that the three coaches had discussed at length over the past month. Izzy understood from Miles' tone how excited he was to be coaching at this level, remembering her own anxiety over that first season five years ago. It occurred to her that she hadn't had those same feelings this past weekend in her new position. She had simply coached. Her anxiety came from a desire not to let Dr. Kerrigan down . . . and from walking away from her girls.

"By the way, Miles, you'll be getting three or four boys back. I talked with them this weekend and they understand they're not varsity quality yet. Actually, all of them will be Romero's. We have a move-in who may also be joining you, a sophomore, but I told him he could come to my practice on Monday. I'll let you know."

"Hey, Izzy, I haven't told anyone yet, but my wife is pregnant. Well, Romero knows, but no one else around school. Franny is due around the first of December, just as the season begins."

"Congratulations, Miles. Tell Franny too."

The conversation ended and Izzy went to the kitchen to look for something to eat. She fixed herself a salad and thought about starting a family. *You might want to get married first, Iz, or at least have a stable boyfriend. A family would be nice though.* She pulled her notepad alongside her salad and began jotting lineups. Her guards now could include Mason Nichols paired with Morgan Rexford. Neither handled the ball as well as she needed, but she had six months to work on skills and leadership. Jimmy Yang as backup for both, but he really was more suited for the JV team. Charlie Sampson back to forward along with Sal Palagi, a couple of 6'3" athletic kids who could compete in the league. Atticus Felton might push out Sal, but at least those three could be solid in the conference, and all would be juniors next season. *The strength of my team right now.* Boyd Smith at center. *What a pleasant surprise, Iz. Way too skinny, but he battled this weekend. Funny kid, too. Who are you kidding, Iz? Your whole front line is skinny.* Izzy continued to juggle lineups, writing notes next to each name about skills each boy needed to improve upon. She worked late into the night. There was no school tomorrow; she could sleep in.

§

Twelve boys began ball-handling drills at 4:00 o'clock on Monday. Four guards, one center, four forwards, and three "tweeners." From this group, Izzy needed eight players. The others would eventually split time between the varsity and JV teams next winter. She figured that she had six as of the start of the summer.

"You need a different sweatshirt, Coach," said Morgan as he jogged past her to retrieve a loose ball. "One that doesn't say 'Girls Coach' on the front." He smiled as he said it. Izzy didn't have to look down to understand. She reached up with her right hand and touched the embroidered logo, a basketball swishing through a net with the words, Prospect View Pronghorns Girls Basketball Coach. *I'll just get some tape and cover it,* she thought.

Unlike the other boys, Nick Patterson used two balls for the dribbling drills. Head up, eyes alert. He crouched in the back row trying not to attract attention, learning the drills by observation. Izzy strolled past each boy. "Bend over more, Morgan." "Harder bounce on that crossover, Mason." Words of encouragement, words of instruction. She got to Nick and watched. He looked up at her briefly but returned to his forward stare. She nodded her head. "Looks good, Nick."

Next up was the power series. Power layups from both sides of the hoop. Bounce powers, baby hooks, footwork at the basket. Extremely important for the forwards and Boyd. The squad moved to dribble layups, and Izzy noticed that Nick was lefthanded even though he made every shot from the right side too. *What a different level this practice is, Iz. Your boys might even win a few games this summer.* She realized her practice plan would need to be altered in a good way, to account for a more advanced skill level. After a half hour, she blew the whistle on the pink lanyard and called the team together after a quick water break.

"Nice work, guys!" she said with enthusiasm. It was the first time this group of twelve had worked out without two dozen other boys taking part of her time. "I saw some really positive things just now. Let's keep that focus for next hour. We're going to do a lot of shell drill . . . four-on-four half-court work now. On defense, the emphasis is not on stealing the ball, but on footwork, positioning, and talking. On offense, I really want your passes crisp. Remember, pass away from the defense. Make your cuts hard and get to the basket. Guards up top and the rest of you at the wing spots. Boyd, you'll be the only center. We aren't going to pass to you much, but I want you to get a feel for where you should be as the ball moves along the perimeter. I'll be helping you with screening too. Curt, I want you working with the guards." Coach Soto clapped her hands and the boys moved into the drill.

Izzy found herself ignoring Boyd's movements as she coached the perimeter play. She needed an assistant, a knowledgeable post coach, otherwise Boyd's development would be delayed. When the drill ended, she called Boyd over and told him she would work with him individually when the others shot free throws. Izzy also decided she would teach Benny to be Boyd's backup. She ended practice at 5:30, a half an hour before Tanya's girls would arrive for their open gym. *Oh, to have Tanya or Sabka working with her and this team. Or both."*

Gathering the boys at center court like her high school coach had always done, like she had always done with her girls, she sat them down and debriefed the practice. "I liked what I saw out there. In that fast break drill, I want you to understand that we go on make or miss. Those of you who are assigned the outside lanes, our two-guards and our small forwards, you must sprint your lanes all the time. The right-side lane runs deeper, the left-side goes past half-court and looks to help back if needed. Our guards are going to work so hard this summer on their ball skills that we won't need much help, but for the moment, two-guards, be alert to help back." She asked for questions and answered a few, noticing that Nick Patterson's attention never wavered. "Okay, we'll meet here at 4:30 to travel to Brighton for our first summer league game. I'm pretty sure we aren't playing Aurora." Izzy smiled and the boys laughed. "We play at 6:00 and 8:00 so bring a sports drink. I want to see Boyd and Nick before you go."

"Boyd, I'm going to find an assistant to help me help you. I get focused with the other eleven boys and you get neglected, but I'll find one who understands post play and bring him in." Boyd said he understood, thanked Izzy, and left.

"Did you have fun out there today, Nick?" asked his new coach.

Nick nodded. "You do a lot of the things my old school did, so most of it I got. I tried not to mess things up."

Izzy just looked at him for a moment and nodded her head. "You're going to be a sophomore, correct?" Nick nodded. "Are you all registered?" Nick nodded. "Did your parents find a house?" Nick nodded. "You thought you'd make your JVs back in Illinois?" Nick nodded again. "I'm pretty sure you'll make varsity here. I'm going to count on you. Think you can fit in tomorrow night?" Nick nodded and smiled. "I'll get you a jersey for the summer. Don't be late tomorrow afternoon. I don't tolerate tardiness." The young player smiled and started to turn away. "Oh, one more thing, Nick. Get in the weight room."

§

Morgan Rexford wrestled the ball away from the taller Adams City forward, pivoted, and passed back to Mason Nichols. Mason quickly dribbled towards their basket as the clock moved toward 0:10. His dribble was tipped away at the mid-court line, but it bounced ahead to Sal Palagi. Sal understood the situation, took one hard dribble to free himself from the defender, and fired up an awkward fifteen-footer. The shot skimmed off the rim into the hands of Boyd Smith, who powered the rebound back up and in. Prospect View had its first win under its new coach.

With her girls after a win, Coach Izzy would exchange hugs. With the boys, Coach Soto exchanged high-fives. *A subtle difference,* she thought, *but proper.* The game confirmed many of her previous evaluations. The forwards were solid, Boyd competed, and her guards were inadequate offensively. Izzy's top six out-played Adams City's starters, but PV's second unit dropped the ball. Except Nick. While he hadn't seen much time in this first outing and hadn't taken a single shot, he consistently penetrated the Adams City defenses and had no trouble breaking their press.

"Well done!" said Izzy with enthusiasm, and the boys clapped and hooted. "Adams City is a tough team to play; they kind of force you to play helter-skelter, but you managed to settle in enough to do what we've been practicing. Way too many turnovers, but again, this type of game will cause that. However, . . . this is the last game I'll let you use that as an excuse. I hate live-ball turnovers, as you'll find out." Jimmy Yang interrupted his coach to ask how a live-ball turnover differed from a regular turnover. "Good question! A dead-ball turnover results in the official blowing his whistle and the ball is taken out of bounds. We get to set our five-player defense." Izzy stopped herself and laughed. "As a long-time girls coach and player, we called our man-to-man defense player-to-player. I'll get back to using the term man-to-man shortly. Anyway, a live-ball turnover is a bad pass that can lead to a fast break against us. There is no whistle stop. Bad passes are a stain on my genetic code, so you'll find that I go ballistic about bad passes." The boys laughed, and Izzy remembered Coach Wooden's saying.

She made a few more comments, all positive in nature, and then released them to hydrate and get a few bites of food to prepare for their next game. She watched them, noticing that there didn't seem to be one leader. The three seniors acted more like juniors, and Izzy wondered if last year's team leaders had all decided to transfer or not participate. She would need to find her leaders, but for now, having a team in search of a personality was okay.

Izzy juggled her lineups in the second game. Playing against a small school varsity with missing starters allowed for her to give the bottom five extra minutes. Two wins on the first night of summer league; misleading of course, but it created a positive vibe. There would be many double-digit losses in the coming months, but she saw a foundation on which to build.

§

Mr. Robles, Jorge's professional name at Ft. Meade, taught summer school four days a week. On Tuesday, Izzy sat with him in his classroom after his second class of the day sharing lunch. She had driven over to surprise him, checked in at the main office, and was escorted to his room where he was just finishing a lesson on sentence diagraming with freshmen.

"I do this to make a few extra dollars," he smiled. "Keeps me from spending all my time at home bugging my parents."

"I teach writing, but we don't do diagraming," said Izzy. "How many are in each class?"

"They keep them small, fewer than ten in each class." He took the burger and fries from the sack that Izzy had brought and smiled. "Thanks. The district pays less per class for summer school, but it helps my family a little, and I enjoy the different atmosphere of the summer."

Izzy bought herself a chicken sandwich and a diet soda. "I always considered myself rich in Oro Hills . . . in a poor way. I had it way better than my friends." She laughed. "I got a few new things from the thrift store every fall before school started."

"It's all relative, isn't it," said Jorge.

"Yeah. My first paycheck that first year seemed like I'd won the lottery. More than my dad made, I think."

"How did you end up in Prospect?"

"I thought I was going to teach in northern New Mexico. I had interviewed but hadn't signed a contract. I was going to also get a thousand dollars or so to be the assistant basketball coach too."

"For girls?"

"Of course. Anyway, I was excited about it, but the Prospect View job showed up on the website, and I applied with no expectations at all, mostly because of the salary difference. About $12,000 difference per year, and the coaching was for the varsity job. I got an interview and the old principal offered me the position that day, mostly because of my basketball credentials he said. I drove back down to Prospect the next day and signed a contract. Right place, right time. I later found out my college coach knew the principal and vouched for me."

"Cool."

"And why are you here?" asked Izzy.

"Family. My sibs were all going here while I finished my degree at Metro. Night school. During the summer, I worked with a teacher here and he put in a good word with the principal. Like you, knowing someone in the system helps." Jorge stood, went to his desk, and pulled a book from the top drawer. He sat back down and handed it to Izzy. "I know you don't have a lot of extra time these days, but my regular classes are reading this, and I thought you might like it. No basketball though."

§

Eight games into the summer league, Prospect View's record stood at four wins, four loses. On Monday, June 12, simultaneous baseball games and a football clinic diminished Izzy's usual roster to six. To compensate, she added two of the JV kids who had played in the Memorial Day tournament, a guard and a forward. Coach Soto was excited about having two games where she would be forced to use Nick and Jimmy, both sophomores, as the starting guards. She was particularly interested in turning the ball-handling duties and generalship over to Nick. She also wanted to see how her two senior forwards, Curt and Bryson, would perform. Those two had slipped behind the three juniors, Charlie, Atticus, and Sal, on the depth chart. Having alternative lineups during the summer always brought surprises, often, pleasant surprises.

Prospect View's 5:00 o'clock game pitted them against a

quality team from a Denver suburb that had made it to the State Tournament the previous season. The Tigers extended a one-three-one zone with long-armed wings, making it difficult for Prospect View to operate its offense. Nick and Jimmy were especially frustrated. Izzy's adjustments helped, but the Tigers were a more talented and experienced squad. In the second half, most of Prospect View's offense came off quick shots after just one pass, shots that were not a part of Coach Soto's scheme. She continually instructed her team to swing the ball in order to create more favorable driving lanes and rebounding conditions. Her directives were particularly aimed at Curt and Bryson, both of whom shot quickly. What little success Prospect View had came with Nick and Charlie effectively using Boyd at the high post to reverse the ball and get open shots with backside rebounders. Late in the game, Coach Soto substituted the JV player for Curt after a particularly bad shot in order to talk with him.

"Curt, those first side, fifteen-foot jumpers are not what I'm looking for," said Coach with a bit of frustration.

"It went in, didn't it? Isn't that the point of a shot?"

Izzy shook her head. "No, that's not the point. We're trying to work on things that will help us get better, that will make us a better team during the season."

"We're not going to win this game anyway. Our guards can't do anything." Curt turned his head toward the bench disengaging from his coach.

Izzy moved to get in his view again. "How did doing things your own way work out for the team last season? Take a seat!" As Curt sat down on the bleacher bench, he slapped his hand hard on the wood, a resounding sound that echoed through the nearly empty gym.

Each team congratulated the other after the game, walking in a line to shake hands. Immediately afterwards, Coach Soto moved her team to a corner of the gym to critique their play. "Remember when we started, about me telling you we had an inexperienced team overall? That certainly was the case tonight." She looked at Jimmy and Nick. "That was a tough zone, especially because we haven't had time to practice against any zones. You'll get it; you'll get better." She looked up to the forwards. "Wide zones really restrict our ability to shoot wing threes, but again, when we have more time to practice, we'll be more successful. I also understand that sometimes what I'm instructing you to do seems counterproductive to winning the game, which is, as it should be, high on your list." Izzy looked at Boyd. "How many offensive rebounds do you think you got off first side shots tonight?"

Her center shook his head. "None, I think. Maybe one. I was usually ball side and trying to post up. Maybe I should have started high or weakside, huh?"

Izzy moved her head to show approval and understanding. "So, Curt and Charlie and Bryson, even though it's hard to get the ball moved to the other side of the court, we need to work on it. We get better rebounding opportunities when we do, not just for Boyd, but for the three of you too. And against a high and wide zone like we saw tonight, that backside rebounding position gets more available . . . but only if we reverse the ball." She paused. "Questions?"

It was Bryson who spoke. "Last year, Coach Miller just put someone at the backside post and told us to shoot quick. He had us overload the zone and we got shots."

Izzy rubbed her chin. "That's one way to attack a zone, and for you and Curt, because you played under that scheme, you tend to revert to his plan. That's understandable. But this summer, I need you to do it my way." She paused, pursed her lips, and nodded ever so slightly. "Lots of what I tell you to do won't work right away. Until we get repetitions in practice, it won't be perfect. But I am telling you this, it will in time. So, do what I ask. Give it a chance!" She emphasized her last word and then excused the team for its short break before the second game of the night. She watched as the boys moved to get their sports drinks and snacks from their bags and move to the bleachers. Six boys sat in the stands together, the underclassmen, but the two seniors climbed to the far end of the bleachers to sit with a spectator, Brooks Danson. Izzy wrote down a few notes and then moved to the bleachers to get her own bite to eat.

§

As the team began to stretch in preparation for the second game, Nick sat with Coach Soto. "Do you think this next team will play zone, Coach?"

"From what I remember, I think they play man, but we'll see," replied Coach Soto.

"Jimmy and me and Eddie will do better," promised Nick. Then, "Coach, I'm just a sophomore, but during the game, could you tell me what you want the guys to do and then let me tell them? I can huddle them up on dead balls."

"That's a great idea, Nick! Whenever there's a dead ball, I want you to run to me, not just look at me, but sprint over, and I'll give you instructions."

Nick smiled and joined his teammates.

During her college years, Izzy did not play with extremely talented point guards as she had in high school. Her last college coach utilized high screens by the center to help the guards get past pesky defenders, so Izzy told Boyd to do the same thing, to set a "Mountaineer" screen for Nick and then roll to the basket or pop back to reverse the ball. A simple maneuver, but it made all the difference in the second game. Nick's confidence soared as the game progressed, finding his forwards on their cuts and feeding Boyd on the post. Charlie went off for his best game of the summer, as did Bryson, and Prospect View got a solid win, albeit against a weaker team. Nevertheless, after being thumped earlier, getting a win buoyed her team's spirits.

"We're finding our way," Izzy said to her team. "The shots we took were about the same as the ones in the first game, but they came after an extra pass or two, so there was less pressure and we hit the boards better . . . more effectively. You really dominated the glass." She had other specific comments for each player before releasing them to drive home. "I want to stick around to write down some thoughts. Be careful on the way home." Not old enough to drive, the three sophomores had ridden over with Coach Soto, so they took seats together in the bleachers to wait. Two players hesitated while the others moved away.

"Coach," said Curt, "I wanna apologize for popping off in the first game."

"I appreciate that. No harm done," said Izzy.

"I don't know what you've heard, but Bryson and me aren't leaving."

Izzy tilted her head slightly, an indication that she hadn't heard anything, and a pause that allowed Curt to continue.

"Brooks wants us to transfer too, but we're not."

"Good," said Izzy. "The team will be much better with you guys on it."

Then the two boys did something touching in Izzy's mind. They each reached out to shake her hand before walking away to join Brooks at the far exit door.

Izzy climbed the bleachers to join tonight's backcourt. "Did you guys have fun in that second game?" They said they had. "You do know, don't you, that it's okay for guards to shoot occasionally?" The three boys laughed.

"We didn't really need to. The other guys were doing so good," said Nick. "It was fun just to make the assists."

"Well, you certainly had a ton of those," said Izzy. She took out her pad and began writing. *Pair Nick with Morgan more. Those two have leadership qualities and can defend the perimeter. All the guards need to improve their 3-pt shooting!*

§

"Bianca, it's Iz. I need you!" Izzy practically screamed into her phone.

Bianca laughed on her end. "What? Coaching boys not what you imagined?"

"No. I've discovered I need a post coach, an assistant who works full-time with my center. He's got some real potential, but he gets lost when I'm working on the perimeter, and I don't understand the little intricacies that boys need with the extra size and athleticism. Come on, my earlier offer still stands."

"That's your own fault, Iz. All you ever concerned yourself with was standing at the three-point line waiting for Molly to throw it to you so you could shoot." Izzy knew Bianca was teasing. "My answer is still the same. But I may know someone. Can it be a woman?"

Izzy laughed at the irony. Her mind's image had been a tall man. "I just need an assistant who can teach post moves and screening on the offensive end, and who demands toughness on the defensive end.

"Well," said Bianca coyly, "think back to *The Evil Empire.*"

Izzy had no idea what Bianca was talking about. "Which episode?"

"No, *sweetheart*, Academy Prep."

§

Izzy met Bianca and *The Younger Sister* at Starbucks in south Ft. Collins on Friday afternoon. Allie Monroe. They all ordered flavored lattes.

"We never called you by your name. You were always The Younger Sister," said Izzy.

"I know. Bianca explained all that to me. I'll tell you what I told her when we first met. I still don't like any of you." Allie Monroe smiled broadly and they all laughed. "Can you believe that was ten years ago?" Allie recounted some details about their six games against each other in high school, confusing some of the events and being corrected by Izzy and Bianca, all to loud laughter. It was clear they liked and respected one another. "Izzy, you kept messing up our game plans. We had to pay such attention to Molly and Bianca, double-teaming them much of the time, but it seemed like whenever we did, you'd stick another three, and we'd just shake our heads. If you and Molly hadn't cracked your heads open in that one game, you'd have beaten us the last four in a row."

"Lots of blood," said Izzy, pulling her hair back to show a two-inch scar. "I haven't thought of that in years, but when I would talk to my girls about achievement, about competition, about all the good things in athletic contests, I would always bring up our games. Oro Hills versus Academy Prep." Izzy paused and smiled. "I still won't buy any clothes that are powder blue, your school's colors." She shook her head. "We always held your team in awe, and you and your sister were like goddesses."

Allie waved the compliment away. "Maybe some of you did, but not that little turd, Molly. She probably had my picture taped to her wall and threw darts at it. Bianca tells me you're looking for an unpaid assistant."

"Yeah, for boys. Or more specifically, for two or three boys who play center. You always had the best moves down there."

Allie started giggling and placed her hand on Bianca's forearm. "You don't know how many hours I worked on those moves, just to gain an advantage over you, and then you'd just use that big body to nullify all my moves. I thought it was simply that you were stronger, and then I'd watch film and see that you were putting in just as many hours at developing your skills. Your footwork was amazing. That's when I gained so much respect for your team. We kind of assumed it was all Molly, but it never was just her."

Bianca placed her off hand on Allie's. "In the beginning it was. Having an All-State guard on our team did give us a bit of an advantage."

"Not just All-State. She was about the best player in any classification," said Allie.

While Izzy explained to Allie what her team needed, the time involved, and other details of the job, incidents from their past competition would be recalled interrupting the interview. The three former foes would laugh, sometimes so hard that they would need to wipe tears from their eyes.

"Allie, it's a volunteer position, but I'll always buy the pizza. I'd want you to start next week, but you said you could do that. My JV coach is monitoring weight training in the mornings, so it would only be afternoons and evenings." Izzy leaned toward her former adversary. "It would be great to finally have you as a teammate."

CHAPTER 5

Surround yourself with good people.

Coach Soto introduced Allie Monroe to Coach Romero and Coach Minturn at the Saturday morning JV league on June 17. The league consisted of twelve JV and C-team squads from eight different area schools playing two games each weekend at Prospect View High School. The sounds of basketballs and shoes squeaking were heard at all times as games were conducted simultaneously in the two gyms, while boys from other teams waited for their time. The refereeing was amateurish: boys from varsity teams, parents, and occasionally idle coaches. Somehow, it all came together to give underclassmen the opportunity to grow their games.

Izzy had told her two assistants she was on the lookout for a varsity assistant, something both had earlier encouraged. As with Izzy, their image had been of a male with some college experience. "Well," commented Allie, "at least you get the college experience part. Three years at Northern Colorado before my knee finally said enough." Now, three of the four coaches on staff played college basketball, while Romero played college football. Romero warned Allie about his tendency to use colorful language, and said he was looking forward to the in-season practices when the three of them could "get after it in a closed setting." He also mumbled something about not understanding women. Romero and Miles left to run the JV league, leaving Izzy and Allie sitting in the bleachers to discuss how to get the best from her boys and watch future Pronghorns in their infant stage.

"On defense, all man-to-man during the summer. When it's over, we'll talk about adjustments, whether we want to use some zones, how much to press, so on. Ball pressure and three-quarter front on the post, no switching, but I'll defer to you on post defense. I know that you know summer is about player development and not wins," said Izzy.

"It's good for the kids to win some though," added Allie, to which Izzy agreed.

"Where your role becomes crucial is on offense. I want Boyd and whoever backs him up to look to you for guidance, not to me. You've got lots to teach me about post-play too. My impression so far is that he's open to as much as you can pour into his muscles and brain. Romero has him lifting weights, and I've told his parents to speed up the genetic process of gaining height. His dad's about 6'5"."

Izzy told Allie about one of the early calls Dr. Kerrigan had received from a concerned parent. It was from Boyd's mother. Her comments centered on low expectations if the school was hiring a woman. Prospect View's history was lower half of the league, and Boyd's mother was hoping for a splashy hire, one who might motivate the kids from the get-go. She offered the caveat that, "Of course Coach Soto has had success with the girls, but it's just not the same."

Allie shook her head while she made a noise resembling a sneer. "Will I be expected to smile at those who oppose you without giving you an opportunity?"

Izzy chuckled. "Yeah, you will." She laughed again. "I can deal with those people. You just teach my bigs how to score." She paused and then returned to the teaching part of their partnership. "We've been running motion, four around one, but Boyd and Benny have been lost much of the time. What did Northern Colorado run when you played?" asked Izzy.

"All motion, but at times, it was five out. I think it helped my understanding when I did those perimeter drills. We ran a plethora of high post stuff. I don't think I ever shot a three during a game, but I did shoot a thousand jumpers."

Izzy hmphed. "My first high school coach wouldn't allow us to shoot the three. Imagine how my life would have turned out if he'd have stayed as my coach. Much differently, that's for sure. The game is constantly evolving." Izzy knew that without basketball as taught by Coach Summitt, she would indeed have led a different life, and not one remotely similar to the life she now lived.

Allie nodded. "Sort of like life." She paused in thought. "Still, if you wouldn't have shot threes, I might have won a state championship." She smiled. "Anyway, I can teach the post game."

"Sounds perfect for Boyd and Benny. Any time in practice you feel the need to interrupt, do so. Any time in drills when you need to tell my perimeter players how and when to throw the ball to your post players, do it. Get angry if you need to." Izzy stopped herself. "I can't recall you ever showing anger back then, just this stoic intensity."

"My college coach yelled. She wanted me to be more vocal with my teammates, so she would bait me, get right up into my face. I didn't like it, but I did respond. For some players it works, and for others, it doesn't. My guess is boys accept yelling more than girls. I don't know if boys will accept a woman yelling at them. Are you a screamer?" asked Allie.

"I wasn't with my girls . . . mostly. I had my moments though."

"I'll let you be the screamer. I'm going to try to be a calm teacher. Demanding, but calm." Allie jotted a note in her pad. "I'd like to meet Boyd and Benny on Monday, if I could. Will the gym be free in the morning, maybe after they lift? Maybe work with them for a half-hour or so to get a feel for where their skills are at this moment. Also, could you have a couple of your guards there to pass to them?"

"I'll arrange that. I'm taking three teams to team camp the first weekend in July, then we're in one last tournament the week after. Any chance you could go? Romero and Miles are going to team camp, so it will be a great opportunity to evaluate what we have."

JV games ended on the hour. At 10:00 o'clock, Bailey Rockwell entered the main gym from the aux gym and saw Coach Soto. Bounding up the bleachers two at a time, she hugged her former coach.

"How come you're here?" asked Izzy.

"I run the clock in there," pointing to the aux gym. "How are you doing?"

"Allie, I want you to meet my point guard, Bailey Rockwell. I guess she's my old point guard now. Bailey, this is Allie Monroe. She's going to assist me this summer and next season." The player and coach shook hands, and Bailey sat on the bleacher in front of them.

"So, you're the Prospect View version of Molly Rascon," said Allie, as much of a question as a statement. Bailey looked confused. "Molly was Coach Soto's point guard in high school. She was the best player I ever played against at any level. Went on the be a great college player and now she coaches in college out in California. Molly made Coach Soto what she is today." Allie smiled at Izzy.

"I think what Allie is trying to say," said Izzy, "is that point guards rule the hardwood." Izzy turned to Allie. "Bailey made honorable mention all-state last season. I thought she should have been second team, but I may be a bit biased."

"Maybe Bailey could be your point guard then," said Allie.

Bailey blushed. "Coach, how's Morgan doing? He said he's really enjoying summer ball."

Izzy straightened up and cocked her head. "Do I sense some kind of vibe in the air?"

§

Don Romero loved the weight room, always had as both a player and coach. He called it his classroom and many of his students did not play sports but simply enjoyed the discipline and health benefits. Romero yelled encouragement, a genuine enthusiasm for the efforts of his lifters. He received no additional pay for opening the weight room during the summer, but he never complained. "All teachers work for no pay in the summer doing something for kids out of sight from the public," he would say. "This is what I do." Nearly every football player hit the weights at Prospect View, but basketball participation had always been spotty. Izzy added him to her staff to change that. Opening the weight room at 6:00 in the mornings, he said there was no excuse for anyone to miss. On Monday morning, 35-40 boys and a handful of girls worked at various stations in a serious but welcoming environment. Ten of those boys made up the bulk of Izzy's summer lineup, ten of the twelve who were being considered as next year's varsity squad.

Izzy showed Allie the weight room when they arrived at 7:30. They stood just inside the double-doors, two women wearing sweat suits, one who every boy recognized and one newcomer. After introducing Allie to Romero, Coach Soto walked to the bench press machine to speak with Benny and Boyd. The boys noticed and talked about this six-foot blonde standing with the much shorter weight coach.

"Let's go get the balls out," said Izzy when she rejoined her new assistant. "They're wrapping up now."

Ten minutes later, standing under a main court basket, Coach Soto introduced Coach Monroe to seven boys, soon to be joined by three others. Izzy had each boy introduce himself. As each did, Coach Monroe shook his hand and repeated his name. Then, she spoke. "Rather than tell you about my qualifications, let's get right to work. If you have any questions when we finish here, I'll be happy to tell you. Boyd, set up on this block. Benny, you go to the other. If you're a guard, grab a ball and go to the wings, about fifteen feet out." Turning back to Boyd and Benny, "I need to see how you receive the pass and then drop step and score."

Coach Monroe watched each boy catch three passes before she stopped the drill. "Okay, I've seen enough. Hold the balls, guards." She surveyed the group. "None of this is acceptable," she said firmly, "from the setup to the catch to the shot. I know I just asked for a demonstration, but from this moment forward, every drill is full-on game speed. Am I clear?" Allie turned to Izzy. "Coach, have the guards deliver a bounce pass to the forwards. We'll just work the right side, one at a time."

Shortly, with Boyd standing in front of her, Allie gave instructions. "Set up a half-stride above the block. Get your butt down and extend your arms." Speaking directly to Boyd but to every boy at the baseline, "This is your area, OWN IT! Above the block pushes the defender another step away from the hoop, YOUR HOOP! A wide base gives you greater balance. Then, it becomes an arm battle. You want to have higher hands. Use a strong armbar!"

The tone was set, and for the next 45 minutes, which had previously been scheduled as just a half-hour, Coach Monroe took ownership of the post players and gained their respect. Teaching and encouraging at the same time, with strict adherence to minor details, she walked Boyd and Benny through the basics of post play. Charlie, Sal, and Atticus had repetitions too, but the focus was on the centers. "Good, now check your location. Target hands this time. You've got to go get the ball! High on the glass, never up, never in."

On the perimeter, Coach Soto was just as demanding, but louder. "Ball fakes; move the defender's hands first! Every pass, every time! If you make a bad pass, run a suicide, and go to the back of the line. Excellent, now do it again." When they finished, Coach Soto told the boys to run five sprints and meet her and Coach Monroe at the end of the court. As the boys ran, Izzy put her arm around Allie's shoulder. "I think you got their attention. You're a natural."

When the boys completed their running, they rejoined their coaches. Coach Soto deferred to Coach Monroe who told them of her college experience but downplayed that. "I want to tell you when I first became a basketball player. My sophomore year, we beat Coach Soto's team by 50 points. 50! The next season, her team beat my team two out of three, including the District Championship. I played on a really good team all three years in high school, but we got beat because her team flat out outworked us . . . and every other team in the state. She won the State Championship her senior year, and her school had never been any good at basketball. From what I saw this morning, you guys can be really good, but you have to put in the time." She stepped back and looked to Izzy.

Izzy scrunched her nose. "Yew, you guys smell." The boys laughed. "Our games tonight are back-to-back, 7:00 and 8:00. Let me know if you have a baseball conflict. If you need a ride, be here at 6:00. Coach Monroe will be going. Boyd, I want to see you before you leave." She excused the boys, several of whom thanked Coach Monroe for helping them.

"Boyd," smiled Coach Soto, "I know your parents have some reservations about me as a woman coach. This might add a little more to their concerns."

"It's my mom mostly, she's . . ." He stopped himself. "I can handle it, and Atticus will talk to her too. He'll support you. I'll sit her down and show her on paper what Coach Monroe worked on today, and then take her out on our driveway to have her watch me."

Izzy smiled broadly. "The driveway is certainly the place to get better. Call one of your friends and work on these things together." As Boyd walked away, Izzy recalled a driveway in Oro Hills where she spent hours improving her game . . . and making lifetime friends.

§

Monday's games demonstrated how rapidly Boyd had taken to Coach Monroe's instruction. His parents were in the stands, and Izzy had no doubt they were pleased. The other player to show improvement was Nick Patterson. Since both Morgan and Mason were baseball players, Nick, Curt, and Jimmy were receiving extra time in the league. After his spring rebellion, Curt was settling into his new role as a guard after Coach Soto moved him from a short forward who would find little playing time behind her trio of 6'3" forwards. Still, it was Nick who possessed the most ballhandling skills and best understood where the ball needed to go on offense. Defensively, Nick was a pest and an excellent, if slightly undersized, on-ball defender. With three potential starters missing, Izzy started Nick and Curt at the guards, Charlie and Sal at forwards, and Boyd at center. She had ample big subs, but only Jimmy Yang to back up the guards, and only Nick possessed point guard skills. Curt was tutoring Nick during the game, leaning in on dead balls to offer advice.

"Your team is designed to play fast," noted Allie. "Charlie will benefit from this pace."

"We're still weak at the post and small in our conference, but you'll correct that, or I'll cut your pay." Izzy smiled, "By that I mean you'll have to buy your own pizza. My chief concern is my guards. I think we'll be able to defend, but we haven't handled the experienced guards well this summer."

"How many of your guards play football?" asked Allie.

"Morgan's the stud, but Mason and Curt both play. Not sure about Jimmy."

Allie smiled like the next question's answer was obvious. "Guess who that leaves to guide your summer games?"

§

Dr. Kerrigan gave Izzy a gift certificate to a new deli in Prospect, and on Tuesday, Izzy treated Tanya and Allie to lunch. "Since at least one of us is busy every night, I guess this is the best *Girls Night Out* we can do." Allie had not met Tanya but had heard good things about her.

"So, you roomed with Izzy for a while?" asked Allie to Tanya.

"Yeah, but she's so hard to live with," teased Tanya. "She gets up at 5:30 every morning, two hours before school starts. I needed more sleep."

"It only lasted about three months. Tanya has a boyfriend in Boulder, so she lives there a lot," said Izzy. "She saves on rent money, and I don't have to listen to her phone calls."

Allie's face registered a question. "A lot? What does that mean?" she asked Tanya.

"During the school year when I need to be here to teach and coach, I'll just go home with my parents. Too far to commute to Boulder, but I stay with my beau on the weekends. I'm living there this summer, but on Tuesdays and Thursdays, if I have a late game, I'll just go home. My parents just live a few miles from here. They would prefer we'd get married; they like Jeremy, but they don't like me *shackin' up*, as my dad calls it. Unbecoming of a schoolteacher."

For most of the meal, they talked basketball and team makeup. When Allie asked Izzy if she'd had any direct feedback from any of the boys about being coached by a woman, Izzy shook her head. "No, not directly, but I do get secondhand reports from my girls." She looked at Tanya. "From YOUR girls. Bailey told me that Morgan had been concerned, but she told him to shut up and just listen, that I knew more than all the boys put together. That made my day that day."

Tanya asked Allie, "What do you do? I know that you were Izzy's nemesis in high school and that you went on the play in Greeley, but what do you do now?"

"I paint. Not houses. I'm an artist. It's why my time is so flexible."

"Do you sell much?"

"Not so much yet, but my husband works in the tech world and has patience . . . and confidence in me. I have a studio at home south of Ft. Collins."

"That's where she met Bianca," said Izzy. "Taking riding lessons. They recognized each other immediately. Small world."

"So, how're your girls doing this summer?" asked Allie to Tanya. Allie noticed a slight pause from Tanya, as if she was measuring her words. Allie also realized that Izzy hadn't been forthcoming about the path of the girls team in the few days since Allie had joined the staff. Allie quickly surmised that Tanya might be shielding Izzy from the pain of missing her girls. Or maybe Tanya hadn't quite accepted the role as a co-equal to Izzy, a head coach in her own right.

"Good, as was expected. They have a way to go to be anywhere near as successful as last season, but we have a nice core. They're such a fun group to be around." Tanya reached up to scratch her head, almost, it seemed to Allie, as if she wanted to reach out and reclaim that last sentence and make it disappear. "Anyway," added Tanya, "Izzy created such a wonderful culture, all I have to do is roll out the balls and sit back."

Izzy squinted her eyes and stretched her mouth in rejection of Tanya's caveat. Izzy looked to Allie. "If anything, Hat will work them harder than I ever did."

"Well, like the boys team, we have some roles to fill before next season," said Tanya.

§

June ended and, with it, the end of the league part of the summer season for both the varsity and sub-varsity teams. The boys finished seven and nine, which seemed about right to Izzy given how many boys missed because of participation in other sports. The dust had settled, as Romero said, over the absence of four seniors who chose not to be a part of the team. The drama queens had moved on and had been replaced by Charlie, Sal, Boyd, and Nick. Coach Soto would not see the boys over the Fourth of July holiday. She would hold a mass practice on Wednesday, the fifth, with the 28 players who were attending team camp at the University of Wyoming in Laramie on Thursday through Sunday morning. Four coaches, three teams, eight games for each team. An extended time for Izzy to take stock of her talent after three months of "exploration," as Romero described it. Team camp would be the first time that Izzy's top ten would play together with no one being gone for baseball or tennis or football or vacations. "A real look!"

In the five days from the last league game to the mass practice on the fifth, Izzy's hours were spent making lists, all basketball related, but not from her apartment in Prospect. She drove to Oro Hills to spend the holiday with her parents and extended family, . . . and visit Coach Summitt and Mrs. Summitt. Their home was her cocoon, as it was for a half-dozen other girls. Even as the Summitts approached eighty, and despite his stroke from a decade earlier, his health and attitude remained positive, and their home welcoming.

On Monday, the third of July, Izzy and her cousin Elena, and two other championship teammates shot baskets on Coach's driveway while he sat in a personalized director's chair, a gift from his girls five years earlier when four of them received their college degrees that May. Molly from La Tech, Bianca from Colorado State, Izzy from Western State, and Stevie from Adams State. Surprisingly, it had been Stevie, the most transformed of all Coach Summitt's girls, who organized the event.

"You know, Coach," said Izzy, "coaching is coaching. The drama of this whole switch has been off the court. Once practice starts or games begin, it's just basketball." She tossed the ball to Elena, walked over to Coach Summitt, and placed a hand on his shoulder. "Are you going to just sit here and not rebound?" They both smiled. "We head to team camp this week; looking forward to that. Like you had to at Adams State, I'll be staying in a separate dorm. My two assistants will be monitoring the boys at night, so I'll be able to go out with the other coaches. My volunteer assistant, Allie

Monroe, will be with me."

Morgan Summitt smiled. "I remember her. I don't know if I ever told you, but her grandfather and I played on the same high school team. He grew up here too. I reconnected with him when you guys were sophomores, and he would gloat about his granddaughters who kept kicking your butts. It was nice to turn that around."

"I didn't know that," exclaimed Izzy. "I'll have to ask Allie about it."

"Is Allie the older sister or the younger one?" asked Morgan. "Both of them could really hoop."

§

Prospect View's first game at team camp was played on one of the narrow courts in the fieldhouse. Three courts, side-by-side, with a hundred high school boys milling around waiting for their games. As of July 6, the Pronghorns' starting lineup included just one senior, Mason Nichols at the point, with Morgan Rexford as his running mate out front, and three slender bigs: Charlie Sampson, Sal Palagi, and Boyd Smith. Atticus Felton kept challenging for a starting spot and might edge out Sal when December rolled around. Regardless, Izzy now had ten kids who could play, so she could design a fast-paced game and not worry about fatigue. Her primary concern when she accepted the position had been fighting instead of playing, but that issue never reappeared. Now, her chief concern focused on guard play. Her starters could defend, but neither Mason nor Morgan was above average offensively, and they were below average with their ball skills.

The narrow court accentuated that deficiency. Prospect's first opponent pressured Izzy's M and M guards from the opening tip, and they struggled. Standing together in front of the five reserves, Izzy and Allie analyzed the flow of the game. Allie suggested subbing Nick for Mason, but Izzy said she wanted to wait on that move. "Maybe in time, but not yet." She substituted five for five after six minutes and trailing by seven to a solid Wyoming squad. She squatted in front of her starters.

"I like your energy." She paused for a moment and looked

each boy in the eye. "Once we got into our offense, you showed good confidence." She smiled and quipped, "Did I forget to tell you the ball is designed to go into that orange thing?" The boys smiled back. "Keep firing; those are good shots. Now, against their pressure, Boyd, you need make yourself available to Mason in the middle. When you get doubled, Mason, remember you have Sal behind you as a release. Don't force it up the side. Look ahead, but don't force it."

As Izzy reviewed her starters six minutes, Allie coached the reserves.

§

None of Prospect View's teams won on the first day, but the coaches were pleased with their boys' efforts. Coach Soto held a brief team meeting before dinner, giving them Friday's game schedule and warning them about their dorm behavior. *A leaderless group,* she thought to herself. "Coach Romero and Coach Minturn will be monitoring you."

At the cafeteria dinner, the four Prospect View coaches sat together to discuss the performances of their troops. All were generally pleased. Coach Minturn had a boy on the C-team score fifteen points, a totally unexpected performance. Romero leaned in and told Miles that maybe he would steal the kid so that the JVs could score. "We can defend but not many of my boys can shoot." Romero added that the two boys who had played frequently with the varsity in the league were his best players. "That experience is so valuable."

Returning to their suite, Izzy and Allie went over the game until no turnover was left unturned. And it was still only eight o'clock. Allie suggested they go to downtown Laramie and drink a beer. "The coach of the team that beat us told me that lots of coaches go to a place called the Cowboy Saloon to drink and play pool."

A half-hour later, as they sat in a corner booth, still talking basketball, two men squeezed their way next to them. Allie held up her left hand to display her wedding ring. The man held up his left hand to show his wedding ring but said that his wife wasn't in Laramie and would never know. Izzy pushed her way out of the booth, and she and Allie left without paying for their drinks. On the way out, she told the waitress that the two coaches who remained at the booth would cover it. Back in their dorm room, Izzy told Allie that never in her five years as the girls coach had she ever experienced something like what had just happened.

"My husband warned me about just that, getting hit on. Well, at least we won't be doing that again while we're up here," said Allie.

"I think I'll hold team meetings after our last game each night and discuss the proper way for men to treat ladies. Basic gender interaction 101."

"I don't know them like you do, but do you think Romero and Miles would act that way?" asked Allie.

"I can assure you they wouldn't," said Izzy. "Or Sabka either."

A few minutes later, each coach was on her phone, Allie with her husband relating the incident in the bar, and Izzy telling Jorge about the day's games.

§

Still monitoring her seniors' fragile egos, Coach Soto started her seniors in the second game, Curt for Morgan and Bryson for Charlie. Playing against a weaker team from northeastern Colorado, the Pronghorn starters performed well. Moving the ball efficiently against a two-front zone, Mason and Curt found Boyd and Sal open in the lane for good shots, and the team rebounded hard. They had plenty of opportunities, since few of their first shots found the bottom of the net.

Izzy's second unit, Morgan, Nick, Charlie, Atticus, and Benny continued the high energy, but shot better. Benny tweaked an ankle after three minutes and was replaced by Boyd. Sitting next to Coach Soto, Coach Monroe leaned into her ear. "They look good. Is this a preview of next year's starting five?"

Returning from the training room after a quick tape job, Benny played with the first unit. He showed no effects from the turned ankle and scored twice on drop-steps, one from each side. Coach Monroe stood both times, shouting out her enthusiasm. Coach

Soto found out that her team was good enough to beat weak 2A teams that played zone defense.

Prospect View competed in the middle varsity division at camp, a combination of classifications and about where they should have been slotted. Each game was competitive, and the margin of victory or defeat was only a few baskets. Coach Soto was able to vary her lineups and evaluate each boy's abilities with confidence. After each game, she and Coach Monroe critiqued the team's performance, and at night they sat with each boy to answer questions and point out areas for improvement. It became clear to the coaches that the team's previous coaching staff had never done this.

"Well," said Izzy to Allie as they lay in their beds on Saturday night, "it appears as if we've discovered one of the weaknesses of the previous administration."

Allie laughed at the term "administration." "Yep. A couple of the seniors seemed a little uncomfortable doing that on Friday, but okay with it tonight. Thanks for letting me lead with Boyd and Benny."

"As I said, they're your kids, and they have to know that." Izzy paused. "Interesting. Our forwards and centers are improving rapidly, the positions we played during our careers, but we're weak at the guard position, especially the point. Do you think . . .?"

"No, I don't," said Allie. "I think we're starting from a real place of weakness there. Mason, Morgan, and Curt were only average JV players to begin with."

Izzy interrupted. "Mason was a varsity player last year."

Allie interrupted back. "As I was saying, Mason was only an average JV player when you got him. The guard crew has a lot of catching up to do." She paused. "And we have our work cut out for us there."

"By the way, the tournament we were going to play in next weekend got cancelled, so tomorrow's game is our last one for this summer. I'm going to run practices a couple of times each week for the boys who want to keep at it, but we're about to run into vacations and fall sports. Besides, unlike you and me who never experienced burnout, we might have a few boys who might want to take a break."

"Izzy," said Allie turning on her side from her bed, "you've got me all fired up for this coaching gig. When I signed on, I wasn't sure how it would go, especially with boys, but I'm really having fun. Whatever you have planned for the rest of the summer, I'd like to be included."

The women remained silent for a moment before Izzy arose, turned on the table lamp, and sat down at the small student desk with her legal pad. With her phone, she googled a calendar for 2006. Allie watched silently. Izzy created a calendar on her pad for July and August, beginning on Saturday, July 8, today's date. She wrote notes over certain dates and then picked up her phone again and entered a number. It was fifteen minutes past midnight.

"Romero, it's Izzy. Hey, when will the weight room be open for the rest of the summer?' Getting her answer, "Thanks. Go back to sleep." He told her that Coach Minturn and a few of their boys were still awake talking over the games. She scribbled a few more thoughts and then turned to Allie, who was propped up on one elbow in her bed.

"We have about six weeks until school starts. At twice a week, we can meet with some of the boys twelve times, but if we double that to four times each week, we can practice with them twenty-four times. And, I bet, we can get a few of them every time we're there." Izzy smiled as if her simple math had somehow been the solution to a calculus problem. "Romero or one of the football coaches will have the weight room open every morning early. We can schedule drills for, say 8:30, which would allow the boys to get their weights done and then just walk out to the gym."

"All voluntary?"

"Yes." As if a light bulb came on over her head, "I won't expect you to be there, but this is what I'm going to do. I'll tell all three teams tomorrow just before we load the vans."

"Again, we're going to have to revisit my pay." Both women laughed.

§

Tanya called Sunday night to compare team camp experiences.

"Izzy, the girls played awesome! We lost two, but one of those was my fault. I drew up the wrong inbounds play, and we didn't get a shot at the end of the game. I had Maggie throw it to Lauren, and she just dribbled until the clock expired. And, the Adams State coach is really interested in Bailey for next year."

Who isn't, thought Izzy? *The Western State coach is too and has an in on Bailey.* How did the young ones play?" She purposely did not ask a question about the varsity girls.

"They did good too. Sabka's crew also won five and Georgia's little girls won three. Everyone was super excited about the upcoming season." Tanya deferred again. "You've given me a great program, Izzy." Then, "How did your teams do?"

"Mostly good, especially skill wise. They're getting it, but just have a long way to go. We won four and lost four in the varsity league which was a mixture of classifications. We're probably a year away. I still can't find a leader though. I keep thinking Morgan will be it, but he's reluctant, maybe because he doesn't see himself as a basketball player. Football's his main sport and then baseball. With the baseball playoffs coming up, I don't expect to see him much for the remainder of the summer. He also told me that his family has an extended vacation planned between baseball and the beginning of football. It seems like this team's leaders were the boys who didn't come out . . . or transferred."

"Then maybe not having a leader yet is a good thing. You've been generally pleased with the behavior of your team, haven't you?" said Tanya.

"More than pleased. I'd prepared for the worst. Romero and I had plans for when that behavior arose, and we never once had to deal with it. Even if one or two of those seniors come out in November, I think the past is now the past.

"Would you even want them, Izzy?" asked Tanya.

"If they come with a good attitude, I would. If not, no."

The two coaches continued to tell little stories about team camp before Izzy asked, "Do you want your girls to work out in the mornings with the boys? I'm going to be running skill drills Monday through Thursday at 8:30 for the next six weeks. Right after weightlifting."

"I'll tell them, but I don't want them getting in your way. I've scheduled informal practices on Monday and Wednesday afternoons. My schedule works better at that time. I'm taking a four-week workshop at UNC beginning next week. Edgar will be running the practices."

Izzy laughed aloud. "When did you start calling Sabka by his first name. I don't think in my five years I ever did. *Edgar*!"

§

As the summer wound down, Izzy expressed her optimism to Allie that their team could be a little better than she first expected. The late-summer numbers had been a bit higher than they predicted, and most of the seniors hadn't attended often, but the strength of the team, Charlie, Atticus, and Wes, made every drill, plus they were religious in their conditioning. Hiring Coach Romero was paying big benefits to the program. Boyd and Benny had "fallen in love" with Coach Monroe, and her energy was transferred to them. Boyd's mother called Izzy to apologize for her early skepticism and promised to work on his *growth*. As important as any development was Nick Patterson. Charlie started calling him "Sponge," a reference to his desire to learn not only his position but the responsibilities of the forwards and centers. As the only *varsity* guard who regularly attended the morning drills, he was rapidly growing past the upper classmen. Allie Monroe had been correct in her earliest assessment of Nick.

§

The principal called Izzy at 6:00 pm on Thursday, the day of her last summer practice with the boys before the fall semester began. Izzy was making another list, a depth chart of her new team, while she ate dinner.

"Izzy, this is Dr. Kerrigan. There's been an accident. No fatalities, but it's bad. Real bad."

CHAPTER 6

From miles away, she wrapped her arms around her friend.

"Where is she? Can I see her?"

"North Colorado Medical Center in Greeley. Her family is with her, but they're not allowing any visitors yet. We'll have more information in the morning," said Dr. Kerrigan. "Why don't I schedule a meeting at 11:00 for the team in the gym." Kerrigan provided Izzy with as much information as she knew, but details were sketchy.

"Who have you called so far?"

Izzy snapped her phone shut but remained seated. She pushed her plate toward the center of the table and dropped her head. She swallowed hard and began crying. In a few minutes, she raised her head, wiped her eyes, and opened her phone. After calling five people, the coaching staffs and Jorge, she decided that she would drive to Greeley to sit in the hospital, to be near the parents. She could get information first-hand and make calls from there. Realizing that she still wore her workout clothes, she thought about showering and changing, but decided against that. *Get in the car, Iz, and go. Oh, Tanya, I'll be there as soon as I can. Hang on.*

§

Entering the NCMC waiting room 45 minutes later, Izzy hugged Tanya's parents first and then her boyfriend. She sat with them and listened. "Her car is totaled; t-boned on US-34 just west of Greeley. She came over to take a final exam. Lots of cuts. Her hip is broken, and she has other broken bones as well. Internal bleeding. She was awake at the site is what they told us, but she's in surgery now. All we can do is pray."

They had been allowed to see Tanya briefly but were being kept apprised by the staff. The parents held on to each other, but Jeremy, while sitting next to them, kept his hands clasped between his legs. He was tall and athletic looking. When Tanya introduced him to Izzy two years earlier, she whispered to Izzy that he was the one, only he didn't know it yet. Izzy put her arm around Jeremy's shoulders and rested her head there but remained quiet.

In time, Izzy's phone began to buzz. She would look to see who the caller was and then snap it back shut. Word was getting out. When Bailey called, Izzy walked out of the waiting room into the hallway and answered. "Hey, Precious," she said so softly. "I'm at the hospital with Tanya's parents. She's in surgery."

"Is she going to be all right?"

"We don't know much, but she's getting special care. The doctors said she'll live, but she's got some bad injuries that they're treating right now. She's going to need your prayers and your teammates' prayers. Where are you now?"

"I'm home with Rosie and Lauren. Some of the others are coming over. Can we come to the hospital?"

"No. Remember when Rosie was in her accident and you couldn't see her? I don't want you driving over and then just crowding the waiting room. It's best you're all together at your house. I'll stay here tonight and then tell you what I know in the morning at the meeting. Make sure everyone gets the word about meeting at school at 11:00." Izzy's words were spoken gently but confidently. "If I get any new reports, I'll call you. I'm going to trust you to be the point person here. Make sure no rumors get out. Coach was in a bad accident, but she's receiving excellent care, and we're hoping for the best." Izzy paused. "Can you do that, Bailey?"

"Yes, I will."

"I know you will. Tears and hugs will be good tonight. If I know Coach, she'll feel badly about making you guys worry. She's a toughie." Izzy closed her phone but stayed in the hall. One of the people Izzy had forgotten to call was Bianca. *Maybe,* thought Izzy, *I need to call Bianca more for me than for Tanya.*

"Hey, Bea, it's me, Iz. I'm at the hospital in Greeley." One of the many things that Izzy loved about Bianca was that she knew when to listen and when to talk. Bianca understood that tonight was a night to listen. Izzy told Bea the details, but then wandered off into random thoughts about friendship and destiny, about their old teammates, especially Rosa, about how much Izzy loved her teaching and coaching and Prospect View, that she and Bianca didn't get together often enough, and that Molly hadn't called her in over a week.

When Izzy slowed down, Bianca asked, "Will you go home tonight?"

"No, I think I'll stick around just in case Tanya can feel my presence somehow."

An hour later, around 9:00, Bianca and Adam arrived at the hospital with blankets and pillows and sandwiches.

§

Still wearing her workout clothes and without makeup, Izzy stood before nearly 80 students in the Prospect View gym. Many of the students were not basketball players, but students in Ms. Hatton's math classes. Next to Izzy were Ms. Kerrigan and several colleagues. Virginia Polis handed Izzy a microphone and stepped back.

"Thank you all for coming. I've just come back from the Greeley hospital, and this is what I can tell you. Tanya, Ms. Hatton, is out of surgery and her life is no longer in jeopardy." An audible sigh emanated from the students. "I haven't been able to talk to her, but she was awake for a few minutes early this morning and spoke with her parents and fiancée. Evidently, she was worried that she might miss the opening day assembly next week." The students laughed. Izzy pinched her nose and curled her lips inward, then covered her mouth with her hand. "I'm sorry. I didn't get any sleep last night, so I'm a little weak." Clearing her throat, she continued. "I know you have lots of questions, but I don't have much to add to what I've already said. The accident occurred yesterday afternoon. Evidently, the other car blew through a stop sign and slammed into Ms. Hatton's car. It wasn't Tanya's fault in any way. I think your prayers really helped. I know she heard them."

Izzy stepped back and handed the microphone to Dr. Kerrigan who informed the students that counsellors would be available to answer questions now and all next week. The principal said that Ms. Hatton's classes would be covered until she was healthy enough to return. "For her calculus classes, we've contacted Harvard to see if one of their mathematicians is available." After a little laughter of relief, Dr. Kerrigan told the students that several teachers would hang around the gym if anyone wanted to talk, and the counsellors were in their offices.

Bailey Rockwell, who was sitting on the lowest bleacher, rose quickly and went to Izzy for a hug. "Most of the girls stayed the night at my house. I never knew how things like this wear you out."

All Izzy said was, "Yeah." A few other girls asked Coach Izzy about Coach Tanya, but Bailey kept an arm around Izzy. As the crowd dispersed, Izzy told the varsity girls that she would call them when she heard new information. "She's going to make it, I promise." Izzy looked into the eyes of the six girls surrounding her and saw concern, not confidence.

Rosie swallowed hard. "This isn't like my accident, is it?"

Izzy shook her head. "No, it's much worse, but Coach will pull through now." Izzy's thoughts went back to a night when another coach had to tell her players that their coach would survive a life-threatening stroke. Coach Gloria was also shaken by a sudden turn of events, hurting too, but composed herself enough to reassure Izzy, Molly, Bianca, Rosa, and their teammates that Coach Summitt would survive. "I promise. Why don't we go up to my room and talk, just us."

Sitting on the thinly carpeted floor with their backs braced against the wall, six players and their coach talked. Lauren began. "At Bailey's house last night, we cried. It was such a helpless feeling, not being able to do anything, just waiting for another call." Her friends nodded. "Rosie told us of her hospital experience, and that helped."

"It was sort of the same," said Rosie. "I knew I wasn't going to die, but I thought I might lose this and everything. It was scary, but then the nurses told me that all of you were out in the lobby praying for me. That helped, so last night we said a group prayer."

Izzy smiled. "I'm sure that helped."

"Coach Hatton is different from you," said Maggie.

"How so?" asked Izzy.

"Maybe because she's been our JV coach for our time here, she seems younger, almost like our friend," said Maggie. "This summer, it was more like we were all just hanging out rather than really practicing basketball. Not in a bad way, but just different."

"Coach and I are the same age."

"A bunch of times, she would use you when she gave us instructions or called a play during a game," said Tracey. Her friends nodded. "It was like your ghost was flying above us."

"Ooooow," said Lauren raising her hands and wriggling her fingers, and the girls laughed.

Bailey was bumped up against Lauren with her head on Lauren's shoulder. She straightened herself. "All of us except Rosie played JV as sophomores, at least we did by the end of the year. When we scrimmaged your varsity, you would get so mad at us for not competing, telling us we couldn't back off."

"We were afraid of you that year," said Maggie.

"Coach Tanya would try to comfort us after those scrimmages or drills, but we were scared of you," said Bailey. "And then that one practice just as the year was coming to a close you coached us and had Coach Tanya coach your girls. You demanded that we not back off, kept saying, 'AGAIN' over and over, and we got after it. I think we beat the varsity that day. After practice, we all went to Dominos and talked about it."

Maggie broke out laughing. "Bailey made us do a pinkie pledge never to back down again." Her friends all giggled.

"And you never did," said Izzy. "It's always about accountability."

"You gave me and Lauren varsity uniforms for the conference tournament, and we vowed never to let you down. And we got minutes every game, not many, but a few."

Lauren dropped her head on Bailey's shoulder like Bailey had on hers moments earlier. "We were still scared of you. During practices and games, you were always so intense."

"Was?" added Bailey. "Are! I missed that this summer. That's how you're different from Coach Tanya.

Izzy smiled and tilted her head. "Tanya would have been that way when the season started; she just didn't want to seem like she was being phony. We talked."

"She's really going to be okay?" asked Grace.

"Yeah, not for the next few months, but she's too tough not to be," said Izzy gently.

§

Later that afternoon, Izzy laid on her couch and crashed. She slept for three hours before being awakened by a call from Dr. Kerrigan wanting to know if Izzy needed anything. There was no new information about Tanya, the implication that no new news was good. Stabilized. The principal asked if Izzy was planning to drive over again. "She'll need additional surgeries."

"Not tonight. Romero and his wife asked me over for dinner. Don and Donna. So, I'll do that and then come home and start next week's lesson plans. School has snuck up on me."

Kerrigan agreed on her end. "Summers are always short, and you've been busy, Izzy. We're going to need a replacement for Tanya, at least for the first semester and possibly for the whole year, and I want your thoughts on that. It's really doubtful she'll be able to do any coaching either. I'll be interviewing math teachers immediately, and I'll ask if any of them can coach basketball. I'm so heartbroken over Tanya, but I need to hire a replacement, at least for a semester."

"We have some time to get a good coach. If you don't get one right away, I can monitor open gyms and work with Carl on the pre-season schedule. Have you had any indication from Tanya's parents that she knows she won't be working this year?"

"No," answered Kerrigan, "I've only spoken briefly with them and only about their daughter's condition."

Izzy rose from the coach and walked to her patio door. "I'm going over to hopefully talk with Tanya tomorrow. I won't say anything, but I'll see if her parents have a sense."

The conversation ended, but Izzy continued thinking about

Tanya's parents. *Nice people. Farmers. Four sons and Tanya, their youngest. Six years after the last son. They have to be in their sixties. Weathered faces.* Izzy turned and went to shower before heading off to have dinner with the Romeros.

§

Coach Romero didn't know Tanya well despite the fact that they were colleagues for the past four years, and his wife didn't know her at all. While Izzy's social life for her five years in Prospect revolved around Prospect View High School, Tanya's did not. Izzy had moved to Prospect just a week before she began her teaching in 2001. Her parents helped set up her apartment, bought groceries, kissed her goodbye, and drove back up to Oro Hills. Her parents had to work the next day. Prospect View became Izzy's galaxy. Tanya grew up in the area and had several friendship groups from there: high school classmates from nearby Frederick, the Grange because her family were farmers, and a Denver rat pack from her first two years of college at Metro State. The dinner conversation was gentle, and the Romeros listened to Izzy more than talked. They allowed her to tell stories about her friend, most of which circled back to basketball. Mrs. Romero kidded Izzy about not having a life beyond basketball, sort of like her husband and football. Izzy told them about Tanya's boyfriend, especially about how he was staying near her in the hospital, missing his work in Boulder. Donna Romero asked if Izzy had a boyfriend.

"You don't have to answer that, Isabella. Donna tends to pry into places she shouldn't sometimes," said Romero. His wife's expression suggested he didn't understand her.

"No," said Izzy with a smile. "It's okay. I'm seeing a guy from Ft. Meade. Not really a boyfriend, at least so far. Mostly we just talk on the phone a couple of nights a week. Taking it slow, and I've been so busy this summer." Izzy told them a little about Jorge's background, that he was also a teacher, but not a coach, and that he didn't know much about basketball. Romero interjected that the relationship didn't have much of a future given that small piece of information. Izzy laughed.

"I didn't really date in high school; my dad was very protective. In college, both my serious boyfriends were on the basketball team, and the one guy I was serious about here in Prospect was an ex-jock, so you could be right, Coach." Izzy paused and smiled before going on. "Jorge's a little bit of a jock about soccer, but more of a musician and reader.

"He likes books?" asked Mrs. Romero.

"Yeah, he teaches literature, not writing skills like me. He gave me a book this summer, and it wasn't about basketball."

"What's the title?" asked Mrs. Romero.

"*The House on Mango Street*. He uses it in his class."

Donna Romero nodded. "That's a wonderful book. How did you like it?"

Izzy grimaced sheepishly. "I haven't started it yet. Too busy." She bit the inside of her lower lip. "When we talk, Jorge doesn't ask about how many points one of my players scored, but he wants to know what my kids are like."

§

"Hey, I talked about you tonight at dinner." She paused there on her end of the phone to let Jorge consider her statement.

On his end, he nodded. "Remember when you told me about your first paycheck? What was the first thing you bought?"

"Nicer frames for my high school team's championship pictures. I have them hanging in my apartment by the table. What did you buy with your first check?"

"A new couch for my parents' house."

§

When Izzy arrived at the Greeley hospital around noon, Tanya was sleeping, heavily sedated and calm, but still in the intensive care unit. Izzy was allowed to stand next to her for five minutes, to whisper in her ear and squeeze her friend's hand. Before leaving she leaned over and lightly kissed Tanya's bruised and discolored forehead. Izzy wiped her eyes and went out to join Mrs. Hatton in the waiting room.

The two women hugged again, and Mrs. Hatton retold Izzy of Tanya's prognosis. Full recovery, but it would be slow, and she would need long-term rehabilitation. Several weeks, at least, in the hospital. Fortunately, Tanya's school insurance should cover everything. Izzy asked about the condition of the driver who hit Tanya. "Hardly a scratch. Drunk in the middle of the day. We plan to sue the hell out of him. He's sitting in jail now." Izzy changed the subject and asked about how Jeremy and Tanya's brothers were handling this.

"We're farmers and it's a busy time," answered Mrs. Hatton. "But I guess there's no good time for an accident like this. Jeremy spent the night here last night, but I sent him home when I arrived. He's hurting. He's a good man."

No, there is no good time for an accident like this. At least no one has said, 'She's lucky.'

§

Izzy prayed extra hard at church on Sunday morning. From there, she went to the workout center to spin, and she peddled extra hard there too. She and Tanya worked out together frequently; they had bought memberships when it first opened and had been faithful to their thrice each week schedule. She put the finishing touches on her lesson plans for the week, just three days for the first week of the school year. Jorge called again to see how she was doing, and he told her about losing a high school buddy in a car accident a decade earlier. Jorge had been in the car and suffered only minor scratches. His tone told her that he still hurt over the loss and that he hurt for her now. She drove to the grocery store to re-stock her depleted refrigerator, and then came home and cooked a decadent shrimp scampi. She treated herself to wine with dinner, just a single glass, and then cleaned the kitchen. Finally, she sat back at the small dining room table with her legal pad to help her think. Around 8:00, she put her tongue in her lower lip, nodded, and called her principal.

"Dr. Kerrigan, this is Izzy. I hope it's not too late."

"No. Isn't it about time you started calling me Avery?"

"Avery. Can I have your permission to talk with the assistant coaches about Tanya's job?"

§

Izzy met with Romero after the initial teachers' meeting in the auditorium. The department meetings were scheduled for an hour later, at 11:00. In his PE office, she asked, "How's football practice going? The state sure doesn't give you guys much time to prepare for the first game, does it?"

Romero waved off her second question. "We're all in the same boat, and we had a great summer. What is it you're really down here for?"

"I want you to know how much I appreciated dinner the other night, talking through Tanya's . . ., well, and how much I respected the work you did with my JVs this summer. Between the league and weight room, I thought the younger boys really improved." She paused when he nodded, but he didn't say anything. "I know you're not going to move over to the girls head job, I wouldn't let you, but what would you think about Miles filling in for Tanya?"

Romero moved his head as if agreeing that might work. "There are several options for the girls coach. What about moving Coach Sabka up? He's paid his dues, and from what I've always seen, he knows his stuff."

"Yes, he has, but when I told him of the accident and that Tanya won't be back this year, he was adamant that he wasn't going to be the head coach. He sort of read my mind even before the topic came up. And Georgia is fine just where she is."

"Yeah, I think Miles would be a capable replacement. Unlike me, he has that gentle side that I think the girls are going to need this season."

Izzy smiled and stepped into Romero, giving him an awkward hug. "You just bury your feminine side. I know better." She kissed him on the cheek and left to meet with Miles Minturn.

She found him in the counselling office looking up student records. His department meeting was going to be held in town at Wendy's, a working meeting with lunch, so he only had a dozen minutes before he had to leave.

She sat at a circular table designed for intimate meetings in a less than intimate setting, and invited Miles to sit too. "Dr. Kerrigan will be interviewing candidates to fill Tanya's teaching position, and she'll be asking about the candidate's interest in also filling Tanya's coaching vacancy. I don't want just anyone occupying that role. Lots of teachers in need of a job will say they'll do it, but I don't want that. I was thinking, you would do a great job." She paused before adding, "Besides, you're a Western State alum and we Mountaineers need to stick together."

"To be honest, I thought about it. I think I could do a good job, so Franny and I talked. We decided no. Her pregnancy has been hard, and her due date is right at the start of the season. That comes first. And, Coach, I'm really happy where I am, given the home situation. Franny's just a little frail. Tanya's position will hopefully be for just one year. If not, maybe I think about it next year, but not now. What about Coach Sabka?"

Izzy shook her head no to Sabka, understood Miles' reasoning for not applying for the opening, and told him how happy she was having him on her staff. "I didn't know Franny was having trouble. Do you need to step away from the sophomore job?"

"No. With Allie on board," he paused to get assurance that Allie was going to help during the winter, and then went on. "With Allie on board, I assume she can help you if I need a practice off every now and then." Miles stood. "I gotta go. I really appreciate your thinking about me for this."

Izzy stayed seated for a few minutes. Her department meeting was about to begin too, but she thought about Miles' suggestion. "*Allie.*"

§

Shortly after Izzy left the coaches' office, four boys met with Coach Romero. "Everyone's worried about the girls, Coach, but we've got something good going on."

§

Foregoing lunch after her English Department meeting, Izzy headed for the main office to see if Dr. Kerrigan was available. She wasn't there, but Izzy had Ms. Finkle page her. Ten minutes later, Kerrigan returned and met with Izzy.

"Dr. . . . Avery . . . what about Allie." When Kerrigan lowered her brow, Izzy realized the principal didn't know Allie. "Ohhhh." Izzy stopped.

Kerrigan could see Izzy processing. She smiled and waited. Finally, "When you get this sorted out, come back. We'll talk."

Instead of leaving, Izzy sat down on one of the iron-framed, cushioned chairs in the outer office. After working with Dr. Kerrigan for four years, Izzy realized that Kerrigan probably wouldn't hire a non-certified teacher for the position of head coach. Besides, Izzy hadn't even spoken with Allie about the job. Still, as Izzy Soto perched on the front of the chair, she knew what she wanted, or at least what was needed. It wasn't Allie or Tanya that primarily concerned Izzy, it was Bailey and Lauren and Rosie and Maggie. Izzy stood, and without asking the secretary for permission to see Dr. Kerrigan, Izzy pushed through the swinging security gate and lightly rapped on Kerrigan's door.

"Allie worked with me this summer. She has a college degree in art and played college basketball, but she doesn't have any teaching credentials, so . . . I get it. Even though you haven't said anything, I get it." Izzy's words seemed to outpace her thoughts. Sometimes, decisions in life are made for a person, and that person is simply hitching a ride. As Bianca Acero would say before mounting her horse Departure, "Saddle up and giddy-up!"

The principal remained quiet but rapt, measuring Izzy's proposal, watching as her young teacher chose the road. When Izzy had worked herself through the plan, she stopped talking, as if saying, "Your turn."

Kerrigan nodded. "I'll need to get with Carl to work out finances and get Ms. Monroe some sort of certification. Is it Miss or Mrs. Monroe?"

"She's married but keeps her maiden name, something about being an artist. I don't really know."

"No matter." Kerrigan smiled, because this plan was not really about Allie, but about Izzy. "I'll let you contact Ms. Monroe and get her fully on board, and then bring her in early next week to meet me. You're going to be a very busy woman for the next seven months, but I'm confident you can do it."

Avery Kerrigan couldn't put a word on Izzy's expression when she received her principal's approval. The younger woman seemed to already be preparing for the next step, to be implementing her plan. Izzy pivoted and left. Kerrigan lifted the receiver on her desk phone and punched the AD's number.

Coach Soto went directly from the main office to her own room to make a call. From there, she returned to the PE office to find Romero. A note on his door indicated he was in the weight room, already guiding some of his players through their lifts. *Amazing guy,* she thought. *Amazing work ethic.*

Seeing her standing next to Morgan Rexford as he performed his bench press routine, Romero yelled out, "It's football season now, Coach. Don't be confusing Morgan with strategies for breaking a full-court press." He smiled and waved her over. "I thought I told you no."

"You did, but you have to remember who you're working for." Izzy gave Romero a faux-authoritarian look. "Sort of."

CHAPTER 7

Dr. Kerrigan hired a retired teacher from Boulder to teach Tanya Hatton's math classes. Kerrigan rehired Isabella Soto as the basketball coach for the girls and hired Allie Monroe to be the assistant head coach for the boys team. Izzy would continue on as the head coach. She would assume the duties and responsibilities for both programs. In Dr. Kerrigan's extensive discussions with Izzy before making her final decision, Dr. Kerrigan came to understand Coach Soto's sense of ownership to both programs. Izzy had given her word in the spring to take over the boys program and put it on a firm foundation. She wasn't going to allow it to slide back to where it had been the previous season. For her girls, and they were still *her* girls, she could not allow them to be coached by an interim coach, especially when they were dealing with the trauma of Tanya's accident and with the chance to win a championship. Dr. Kerrigan understood and respected Izzy's motives and then accepted her proposal.

On Thursday evening, Izzy drove to the Greeley hospital to tell her good friend that when she was healthy again, she could/would resume her duties, that Izzy would step aside. Izzy was not sure if Tanya heard her, but her parents were also in the room and could repeat Izzy's words when their daughter awoke. Kerrigan reduced Izzy's teaching load from six classes to five, giving her both 1st and 7th periods off and no extra duty. Izzy protested, but Kerrigan reminded her who the boss was. "You'll be putting in five extra hours every day after school, so you'll need two planning periods to remain effective."

§

Members of the basketball teams plus those students who were interested in trying out come November were instructed to meet for brief meetings during 6th period on Friday afternoon, boys in the gym and girls in band room. It had been a week since Coach Hatton's accident. Izzy decided to meet with the boys team first, since no personnel changes would be effected. About forty boys sat in the bleachers as Coaches Soto, Romero, and Monroe addressed them.

"It's been a difficult week for the Pronghorn family," said Coach Soto. "The good news is that Coach Hatton is improving. Most of you don't know her, but those of you who do know what a special teacher she is. The coaching staffs of both the boys and girls teams have been in close discussions with Dr. Kerrigan and Mr. Porter to hire her replacement. In a minute, I'll let Coach Romero and Coach Monroe give you more details and answer whatever questions you have. Let me just say that your staff will remain the same. I will remain as the varsity coach, continue to be your coach. We came a long way this past spring and summer, and I expect you will continue to grow and develop. Open gym will begin on Monday, September 18, at 7:00 o'clock. If you're out for a fall sport, that's your priority. Check with your coaches to see if they will allow you to play at open gym. Now, I have another meeting to attend, so Coach Romero will answer your questions." With that, Izzy left the auditorium and hurried off to the band room.

Coach Romero stepped forward looking at the boys. "Lots of lessons here, men, but the one I want you to focus on today is being proactive. When you want something, speak up. Romero looked directly at Curt and Mason, held their eyes, and nodded approvingly.

§

Casually conversing with about 35 girls, Coach Sabka told them to take a seat as Izzy entered. She began with the same line as she had used ten minutes earlier, but in a gentler tone. These girls had been constantly monitoring Tanya's progress. "It's been a difficult week for the Pronghorn family." She lifted her eyes and noticed one senior bring both hands to her face, covering both her mouth and nose. "After long talks with Coach Sabka and Dr. Kerrigan, I asked to become your coach again, and Dr. Kerrigan agreed." Izzy was interrupted, surprisingly, by Coach Sabka.

"To be clear, Coach Soto asked me if I wanted to take the head job, but I declined. I like coaching the feeder system, and I don't want the limelight."

There was a smattering of noises indicating several things. Izzy continued. "I talked with Coach Hatton last night in the hospital and assured her that when she was able, she could return and take the reins. As I told you last spring when I was asked to become the boys coach for the good of Prospect View, it was the hardest decision I had ever made . . . to step away from you. This move is not difficult at all; I'm returning to my first love." The girls broke out into applause to welcome their coach back. Many had worried about who might be hired as Coach Hatton's replacement.

Izzy went on to explain how the process unfolded and that she would also continue as the boys varsity coach, "sort of like the manager of a major league baseball team. Coach Monroe, whom some of you met this summer, will be the assistant head coach, and whenever there is a scheduling conflict, I will be with you, and she and Coach Romero will assume the duties for the boys." She instructed the girls about weight training, open gym, and classroom behavior. "This setback with Coach Tanya is not going to slow us down. We are not going to miss a beat; you will make her proud of your efforts and intensity every day. Finally, expect me to be tired and cranky a lot, and so, I intend to yell and nag a lot too." Izzy smiled with tight lips, and the girls understood. "Now, get back to your 6th period classes and find out what you missed."

Several girls touched Coach Soto on their way out. A few hugged her. Four girls lingered until all the others left. Bailey spoke for them. "At my house a week ago, when we stayed all night, we hoped you would come back, but we didn't think it would happen. We didn't think you'd quit the boys. We never thought of this solution. We were scared about who might be our new coach."

"Be careful what you wish for," joked Izzy. Then, quite sincerely she said, "Thank you. We've got a State Tournament to prepare for, remember."

§

"Izzy, what did you just do?" yelled Molly. "I just got off the phone with Bianca."

"I didn't *just* do it, Mol. If you'd call more often or check your email, you'd be up to date. I signed up at the end of August. We've been going full steam with open gyms for over a month." Izzy took her dinner, a bowl of yogurt with fruit, from her small apartment kitchen to a circular dining table and sat down.

"Both teams?"

"Yeah. Wanna quit that little college job you have and come be my assistant? I can't convince Bianca to give up her vet job and help out. By the way, are you going to be good again this season?"

From her end in California, Molly laughed. "In our conference we will be, but we're so far behind the major conferences." Molly had always willed herself to excellence, ever since high school, but now she was battling universities with histories of winning and with bigger recruiting budgets. "Bianca told me about your assistant coach's accident; I'm so sorry."

"She's shown so much improvement. No lasting mental damage. That's what we were all afraid of. I'm helping with her rehab every Sunday afternoon. She's back at her parent's home."

Molly quickly turned to the subject she always turned to. "Do you still have that dynamite point guard, Bailey? She hasn't signed below her talent level yet, has she?"

"Oh," laughed Izzy, "so this call isn't really about me. It's a recruiting call."

For the next fifteen minutes, the two former high school teammates and now forever friends chatted about basketball. Molly and Izzy had gone from high school basketball to college basketball to coaching. At each stage, Molly performed on a higher platform, but as Molly always reminded her friend, not a more important level. Still, Molly was the one who would tear a competitor's eyes out to win. "Are you going to be good this year?" asked Molly.

"My girls will be. We're better than I thought we might be after losing three starters from last year's team, but the reserves had a good summer. If we don't make it to State again, I'll be shocked. My boys, though, oh lordy." Izzy paused. "For the past few years, their reputation did not revolve around their basketball prowess. That's why my principal asked me to coach them, to bring discipline to the team. Well, when the rowdies found out I wasn't going to let them run amok, they all quit, so now I have the nicest bunch of kids in Colorado. Their skills have taken a major leap forward, but they wait for me to tell them what to do on every possession."

"Do what Coach Summitt did. Have film sessions with your point guard three or four nights a week. He taught me how to be a leader, that's for sure."

"That's NOT going to happen, Mol. I'm a 28-year-old woman living alone. I won't be inviting teenage boys up to my apartment for any reason."

Molly laughed again. "My guess is they all have major crushes on you anyway, *la bella y encantador* Isabella Soto."

"Cut it out."

Still laughing as a tease, Molly went on. "Do you have a point guard though?"

"I do. A sophomore who's growing up fast, but he's a move-in and really defers to the two senior guards. The good thing is they're both out for football, so Nick has every open gym to do that growing. His dribbling is exceptional."

"Can he shoot?"

"Not like you or me."

"If I remember, you couldn't shoot as a sophomore, but someone taught you and you put in all the hours. I can't think of anyone better to teach shooting than you, Iz. Get to work."

§

Coach Soto understood that the first practices for an experienced team returning after a very successful season are structured differently from the practices of a team made up mostly of juniors with no history of winning. Still, the emphasis on fundamentals remains, and the teaching of physicality starts with the first drill on the first day. Coach Romero warned Izzy about the daily transition from the talent-rich girls team to the talent-average boys team. "It will take true discipline on your part to turn that switch on and off."

For that reason, Izzy scheduled the boys practices immediately after school and would bring in the girls at 7:00. The staff might have to trim the varsity and JV squads by a few boys, but they decided to do that after the first week of practices, and these cuts would be only for the seniors and juniors who obviously did not have the skills for that level. Romero convinced a young, volunteer football coach whom the boys liked, twenty-three and eager, three years younger than Miles, to help Coach Minturn with the C-team. Sophomores, except for a handful who had previously demonstrated their abilities during the summer and open gyms, would start out in the auxiliary gym at the same time as the varsity and JVs were practicing in the main gym.

As she had done for five years with her girls, as she had been taught by Coach Summitt ten years earlier, Izzy began with teaching the boys not only how to take a charge properly but also its necessity. She and Coach Monroe demonstrated the proper positioning and how to fall, with Coach Monroe taking the charge and falling to the floor after being hit by Coach Soto. Izzy wanted to say, "If women can do this, so can you," but she allowed the demonstration to speak for itself. Every boy had to take and deliver five charges.

The second drill was diving on the floor to capture a loose ball, another painful drill, especially if done improperly. The third drill, and a variation of which she would use every day in practice, was boxouts. "If you miss your assignment, I'll go ballistic." She looked over to Coach Romero. "And if I go ballistic, Coach here will climb in your jocks." Izzy delivered the line in such a way that no boy laughed, which is how Coach Soto intended it to come across.

Izzy, Allie, and Romero scripted this first day's schedule by the minute, while allowing a few extra minutes for blockouts to get a certain message across. Romero noted that the guards, led by

Morgan, seemed to relish the violent contact of charges and diving on the floor for loose balls, so that rebounding contact was simple continuation. "Where was this energy during football?" he admonished his fall season athletes. The skinny forwards were less eager to hit the floor for any reason, giving Coach Monroe her first opportunity to "participate." Izzy lowered her head so as not to allow the team see her grin.

Allie stopped the drill. Shaking her head, she stepped between Atticus and Charlie. "I saw this coming this summer, and I will not allow it to continue. Taking Atticus' arm, she put him ten feet from the hoop, supposedly in an offensive position. "Charlie," she said as she moved him into a guarding position, "this drill is all about contact. BIGS, WHEN THE BALL GOES UP, YOU HIT SOMEONE!" She had Atticus simulate a shot and move to rebound, and then she, not Charlie, hit Atticus in the chest with her forearm while simultaneously lowering her butt and pivoting onto his thighs. Atticus responded by retreating from the blockout. "Your courtesy to an older woman is noted, Atticus, but get over it. Out here, I'm just Coach Monroe." She turned to Charlie Sampson. "Now, remember that on every shot, the defensive man has to be the aggressor; you have to make and keep contact when you're inside ten feet, to out aggressor him." Allie nodded to Izzy that the drill could continue. For the next fifteen minutes, Coach Monroe and Coach Romero, with raised voices, coaxed and encouraged the forwards and centers to wage war under the basket, while Coach Soto insisted her guards do their part in the battle.

The second half of practice consisted primarily of four-on-four drills, with lots of instruction, both offensively and defensively. Each coach brought a different persona to practice, but the combination infused electricity into the gym. Romero moved among the players, taking them by the elbow to get them positioned properly, always talking in his football line-coach voice. Allie stood on the baseline close to Boyd and Benny and two boys who would end up on the JVs teaching technique with infinite detail. "Set the screen and then roll to the basket. Find the ball! Anticipate the next pass. Benny, you can never allow an uncontested cut to go unpunished.

Get that armbar up!" As the practice proceeded, Izzy was sure the boys had never experienced this kind of intensity to detail, but she was sure by their behavior, that they loved it. As did she.

Romero and Allie put the boys through conditioning drills for the last ten minutes, while Izzy sat at the scorer's table scribbling notes. Two boys ran to the trash can and threw up. After the last suicide, the team gathered at mid-court. Izzy looked to Romero for any comments. He simply said, "It's a start. We've got a long way to go, but it's a start." She turned to Allie who rubbed her jaw where Wes's wrist had hit her. "I hope you boys are quick studies, or I'm going to get lots of bruises demonstrating." There was some laughter. Allie closed. "I saw lots of good things out there that we can build on. Also, lots of mistakes. Don't make the same ones tomorrow. Remember what I said at the beginning of practice; out here, there is no varsity or JV distinction. We are one team growing into one family." Izzy added a few necessary housekeeping comments and then gathered them together with high hands to yell, "Pronghorns".

She thanked Romero and Allie for their help and the trio exchanged perceptions about the two-hours-plus practice. Coach Romero informed Izzy that very few boys wore jock straps anymore. "Designer underwear." They were in general agreement that the time had been productive. Romero left to talk with Coach Minturn about his first practice, to see if any of the "young'uns" might make the JVs. Allie commented on how tired she was but asked if she could observe the first few minutes of the girls practice.

Coach Soto had a half-hour to rest and transform into Coach Izzy. From her briefcase, she pulled out a sandwich and energy drink. She tucked her boys notes into one side and withdrew a folder containing her practice plans for the girls. She offered half her sandwich to her co-coach, who accepted it, and then went silent as she studied her plans.

§

Coach Sabka knew Izzy's routine. He rolled out the ball rack, reset the clock, collected paperwork from girls who hadn't turned it in at the pre-season meeting, and began moving the girls into their pre-practice stretching. The ultimate assistant, "Sancho Panza" had been with Izzy since her first year. Coach Izzy wandered among the girls as they lay on the floor doing those stretches, talking, and exchanging high-fives. These girls knew their coach and the bond was obvious; they were happy to have her back. Bailey Rockwell also walked among the team, having already completed her stretches. Unlike the boys, this team had its leader. She knew it and embraced the role, and her teammates knew and respected her for her dedication to them.

In the stands, Allie Monroe watched closely. For the earlier boys first practice, after a few brief words to the entire group, Izzy had split the boys into two gyms, and she or Romero would run over to the aux gym occasionally to check on the underclassmen and the new coaches. For the girls, all of them stretched together in the main gym and then began ball-handling drills together, juniors and seniors pairing up with the newbies to teach them the "Pronghorn Way." Once the drills began, the noise level increased to a productive buzz. For fifteen minutes, none of the three coaches blew a whistle or yelled out a command. Georgia paired with the odd-numbered girl, while Izzy and Sabka offered enthusiastic instructions to encourage the sophomores. At the end of the Bailey-led drills, the entire group began clapping in unison and moved to center court. When they were all gathered up, their hands went up and the team yelled, "Pronghorns!" and they sat down quickly to listen to Coach Izzy.

"Friday, December 1st, is our first game. We have three weeks to get ready. As always, I will expect us to be the hardest working team in the state. No compromise on that. Rosie, what's the first rule on defense?"

"Communicate!"

"Lauren, next."

"The ball stays out of the middle!"

"Maggie, third."

"Never ever foul the outside shooter. Contest, but don't foul!"

"Grace, fourth."

"Block out!"

"Tracey, fifth."

"GO GET IT!"

"Sophomores. These are your defensive commandments. Memorize them. Coach Georgia will be testing you beginning tomorrow. You run sprints if you don't know them." Coach Izzy pulled a note from her pocket. "This is from Coach Tanya. She wants you to know that she's doing fine and will be coming to some games as soon as she can. Specifically, she says, and I quote, 'Bump all cutters!'" The girls who had played for her last year all laughed. Tanya had been the queen of *bumping the cutters* in demonstrations. "All right! Charges, loose balls, and blockouts. Juniors and seniors on this end; sophomores on that end." The best battle on the boards featured Maggie versus Grace. Coach Izzy called the sophomores to the varsity end to watch, to see how it was done.

§

The Romeros served dinner to the entire boys coaching staff on Saturday after practices. Donnie and Donna, Miles and Franny, Allie and her husband, Miles' young assistant Will Stoneman and his date, and Izzy. Franny was in her ninth month and was uncomfortable all night, but she laughed at herself frequently. Around the table, the coaches discussed personnel, as the time was drawing near when a starting lineup would need to be determined.

"The battles are really between Wes and Atticus at forward to go with Charlie, and at the point," said Allie, directing her comment to Izzy. "Morgan's the physical leader, and he's got everyone pumped up on that side of the ball. At some point you're going to have to go with Nick as the other starting guard."

Coyly, Izzy held her wine up and inspected its color. Satisfied, she smiled at Romero and said, "Coach Romero and I have always known that. We've just been waiting for you to get definitive about it."

Allie tossed her napkin across the table at Izzy. "Now, now, girls," said Donna. "They'll be no fighting at the dinner table." The table laughed.

"So, how will Mason take it?" asked Allie.

"Not well, he's a senior who thinks that entitles him," said Izzy, "but he'll have to accept it. He's a very capable backup, but he's been beaten out. Nick and Morgan are a good match and have specific roles, whereas Mason likes the two-spot better, even though he knows he won't replace Morgan there."

"And at the forward spot?" asked Allie.

"Who do you like?" responded Izzy.

"I don't think we have to decide quite yet. Those three will surprise a lot of teams this season. We're only a week in, but it's all coming together. Boyd's been a little gimpy since Wednesday; what about starting all three forwards?" asked Allie.

"That will happen at times, but I think Boyd will be fine. When he is, our lineup is decent." Izzy smiled sarcastically. "Except for that one little thing."

"What's that?" asked Miles.

Romero answered. "That little thing called defense. Only Morgan gets it. This is the first year Prospect View basketball has been asked to play it." Izzy cocked her head at Romero like a mother scolding her child for an obnoxious misstatement. "Okay," he corrected himself, "BOYS basketball."

"Yeah, the girls gave up an average of 28 points per game last year"

"What about your girls this year?" asked Donna Romero.

"Solid," answered Izzy. "I'll start three or four seniors, and there'll be no issues about that. Plus, I have Bailey."

"And if she goes down with a sprained ankle or something?" asked Donna.

"Then, I give Allie the girls, and I work exclusively with the boys. Needless to say, without Bailey, we won't be playing in the State Tournament. I hit the jackpot when her family moved to Prospect."

§

Tanya's brothers constructed a mini gym in the garage to facilitate her rehabilitation. Her most serious injury was a broken pelvis. She discarded the wheelchair in early November and the walker a few weeks later, using crutches or a cane depending on how far she needed to travel. Izzy worked out with Tanya on Sundays, especially on recovering her upper body strength. As the two women moved through their hour-long workout, the obvious topic was the basketball team.

"I have greater respect for Rosie now that I have to do these tedious exercises," said Tanya.

"Hush. Talk when you're the spotter." Izzy guided the bar as Tanya grunted. "Good! One more. Come on, you can do it," commanded Izzy.

Completing her bench presses, Tanya smiled up at Izzy. "As I was saying, I have more respect for Rosie. How's she holding up?"

"No restrictions, and I haven't seen her act like there's any lingering pain or anything. She's her old self, which means she's the second hardest worker on the team." Izzy's reference to Bailey was obvious. "We're ahead of schedule, but the top six are good. We might not be able to get Broomfield in the opener, they're scary good again, but we'll go into their gym and compete."

Izzy helped Tanya move from the bench to a stationary bike. "Easy. Still the lowest setting?"

While Tanya peddled, Izzy went through the lineup. "Bailey and Tracey, Rosie, Lauren, and Maggie, with Grace as the first sub for all of them. She's really relishing her role as sixth girl. We're not as deep as last season, but we'll be as good or better through these six."

"Sabka will develop a good bench for you."

Izzy nodded. "For us. He always does."

§

Coach Soto stood with Mason at the mid-court line. She had just subbed in Nick for him, and Mason had reverted to his pouting stance, a posture obvious to the coaches and his teammates. She had moved back from the half-court scrimmage to speak with her disgruntled guard, allowing Allie and Romero to guide the other players.

"Want to get it off your chest?" said Izzy.

"Not really," mumbled Mason.

Izzy allowed that to sit for a moment. Looking straight ahead and resisting the urge to correct a poor pass by Wes, she replied. "Sometimes a person is asked to play the role the group needs instead of the part that person wants or expected." She paused again. "This team needs you; we're better with you, but not as the starting point guard. It's not your natural position anyway. Last season, you played more two, a really good rebounding guard and solid defender. Coach Miller had a couple of seniors who handled the ball most of the time. Your time came at the two."

"I played some point."

"I've watched lots of last year's film. I know you did."

"You're still holding it against me and Curt that we didn't come to open gyms right away. You still think we resent you."

"Actually, Mason, when you came to the Memorial Day tournament each day and supported your teammates, you erased any lingering thoughts I had about your commitment. Since then, I haven't given it any thought. I've been evaluating you on your skills and effort. You've given a hundred percent."

"It's my turn to be a starter."

Izzy let Mason think about his last statement while she considered her next words. "You started at free safety as a junior. Should you have come off the bench to give a senior your position because it was *his turn*?" It was a rhetorical question and Mason stayed silent. "Several things that I do in my system demand a pure point guard. I could modify that if we didn't have one, but it wouldn't make us any better. As my first guard substitute, you'll get lots of minutes, some at point and some at the off-guard and occasionally at the three. This team needs you, but not the you from the last two days. We need the Free Safety Mason, the one that Coach Romero and the football team counted on the last two years. You're a good player. Don't let Morgan and Curt and Bryson and your other teammates down." Izzy didn't allow Mason to stew any longer. "Go in for Morgan and keep Curt off the boards."

Coach Soto stepped back towards the perimeter players to demand greater attention to the offensive cuts and the defensive denial of those cuts. Mason did not allow Curt to get another rebound or take an unchallenged shot.

§

The second Saturday of the season, Thanksgiving Saturday, was a full-blown intrasquad scrimmage day for both the boys and girls. Bailey and Rosie arrived at 9:00 to chart the boys scrimmage; they had volunteered. Area officials, mostly the young and inexperienced ones, came in without pay to work the cobwebs out of their bones and be monitored by a few older refs. Coach Soto coached one group of five while Coach Monroe coached the other, and as the makeup of the teams altered over the course of the morning, the players received instruction from both coaches. After the first fifteen minutes, the JVs took the court. Fifteen minutes on the court, fifteen minutes off for a critique, and then they would go again. Two hours. In the auxiliary gym, Coach Minturn did the same thing, albeit without refs. At the conclusion of the scrimmages, the boys shot free throws and then ran suicides. Then, they sat in the bleachers for the review.

"We are an inconsistent bunch, that's for sure. You had some excellent stretches out there, but some stagnant minutes too." Izzy knew that whatever group was headed by Nick performed more consistently than any group headed by Mason, although Mason played very well as the two guard alongside Nick. Reviewing Bailey's statistics as she spoke, Izzy recognized what she intuitively knew: this team didn't turn the ball over much. Shooting woes aside, they had taken to the staff's directives to be shot aggressive and to "shoot it before you turn it over."

Coach Monroe focused on the inconsistent offensive flow. "We're here to run, make or miss." Her bigs came under the microscope most critically, especially the forwards who seemed to have thin skin and needed "to toughen up." With Boyd and Benny, she was gentler. They had the most to learn, the greatest distance to travel if the season was to be successful. Still, they had not been immune to her temper at times. "You guys have the farthest to run in transition, baseline to baseline and then turn around do it again, but you've got to sprint to the backside to get that rebound! That's where you're going to get your most offensive rebounds."

Romero always shook his head at his two partners after these talks. "You think you're giving the boys heat during these talks, that a slightly raised voice is showing your temper. You need to come to a football practice when I have a handful of mask and am four inches from their face."

The scrimmage had gone well, except for the very last session when Romero's starting JV five played the varsity underclassmen for one quarter. The JVs didn't win, but the score was closer than expected, due to poor shooting. Fatigue played a part, but Izzy was not allowing that to excuse poor effort. Coach Soto blasted her boys for playing down to the level of their opponents. "This is why you seniors are so important to this team!"

Two hours later, at one in the afternoon, the girls held their scrimmage. The chatter while the clock was running was all business. "Watch the screen, I got your girl!" "Ball, ball, ball!" Bailey's voice could be heard over every other girl's voice, and her words were directed at both teams. Pointed, direct, instructive, but never demeaning. She was Coach Izzy's coach on the court, almost as if she had adopted Tanya's role from the previous season. Charting this practice were Nick, who had been lingering after the boys practices to study Bailey, and Charlie, a whose classroom interest in analytics transferred to the intricacies of shot value depending on the spot and which shots were most easily rebounded by the offense.

Unlike the boys team, which had ten players more evenly matched so that scrimmages could pit even teams, the girls top six dominated. Izzy wanted to give her starting five time as a cohesive unit, but needed to divide them into two teams of three with lesser quality players to round out the five to be competitive. It was her principle worry as she headed into the season, that her starters were not being tested during practice.

At three, the girls shot free throws and ran, while Izzy went over the positives and negatives with Sabka and Georgia, and when the girls gathered up to hear about their performances, none of the coaches "got in their faces." Izzy knew that it wasn't a gender thing, but an experience-inexperience thing, a difference in the makeup of the coaching staffs, and the difference between a team coming off a

State Tournament run and one that had never had a sniff of the air at a State Tournament game.

When Izzy dismissed the team and after all the equipment had been put away, she saw Charlie's aunt sitting in the bleachers. "Waiting to clean up?" asked Izzy.

"You put in a long day. I'll have to recommend you to Dr. Kerrigan to take my job when I retire," said Virginia Polis patting the plastic bleacher seat next to her. When Izzy sat down, the custodian opened a cooler and handed Izzy a diet soda. "Kerrigan said you drink a lot of these, no doubt to keep you from getting fat like me." Izzy noted that Virginia didn't have an ounce of fat on her, that she was simply a larger woman.

"So" asked Izzy, "did you notice anything we can improve upon?"

"I couldn't watch the girls until the very end, and you really don't need any advice for them. They're a well-oiled machine. But those boys, well, they're coming along just fine."

"Thanks. Charlie's really made strides."

"He's loving it and can't wait for the first game. He wants to show Brooks Danson what he's missing out on."

Izzy corrected Virginia. "No, it's the girls that are playing Broomfield. The boys get the new school north of Broomfield. Coal Creek."

"Haven't you heard, Coach? Brooks transferred again . . . to Coal Creek. Guess he couldn't get along with the Broomfield coach either, so daddy moved him again."

CHAPTER 8

Don't ever forget what it took to get to this point.

Basketball season! With the girls first game just five days away, Coach Soto moved their practice time up to 5:45, immediately after the boys finished. This would give the girls extra time to sleep, but Izzy had another motive. Her girls played at Broomfield on Friday, while the boys played a second-year school, Coal Creek, at home on Saturday. The boys had originally been scheduled for Friday also, but Izzy convinced Carl Porter to move it back a day so as not to conflict with the girls, so she could be on the bench for the boys first game too. The boys were ready, had grown as planned, and needed a game, but Izzy wasn't sure about her girls. All weekend she had an itch that couldn't be scratched. Really good, but . . .

"We'll be putting an untested bunch on the floor against Broomfield," said Izzy to Georgia and Sabka after the scrimmage on Saturday. "Bailey's our only returning fulltime starter, and you know Broomfield will put that all-state, 5'10", whirling dervish on her."

"And double-team her whenever possible," added Sabka. "And on defense, Bailey will need to cover their little point guard."

Now, sitting over a salad on Sunday evening, she compared Bailey to Molly, two terrific point guards separated by a decade but joined by passion and ability. Both of them practiced against inferior teammates; Izzy chuckled about her own feeble attempts to guard her friend back then, about her inability to keep Molly out of the lane despite Coach Summitt's best instruction. *Molly certainly made you a better player, Iz, made you all better players, put you all on her back and charged into battle.* Those practices and games continued to be vivid memories for Izzy. *Face it, Iz, you don't have any girl on your squad that can imitate the Broomfield stud. You don't have a Stevie. Bailey will have to learn as the game goes on.* Izzy rested her chin in both hands, her elbows on the table, while staring at a computer screen with vacant words on it. Eventually, she moved her eyes back to her legal pad and wrote down a line-up that might be able to defend Bailey.

§

Fresh off their Saturday scrimmage and a day off, the boys practice was crisp and sharp. Today's emphasis was on transition, both offense and defense. Allie coaxed the wings to get out fast and wide. "Touch the sideline, Charlie! Your first look is long, Boyd. You'll have time to find Nick after that first look. Keep the defense on its heels!" Izzy countered. "Deny that strong-side long pass, Curt. Make Boyd throw it to the corner, Bryson. Contain, contain, contain!" Coach Soto emphasized making the opposition go against a five-man defense. "No odd-numbered breaks." Still, Charlie and Nick had figured out what their coaches were preaching. Attack! And Boyd was learning that the only real mistake was passivity.

This week would also include lots of shooting. Twenty boys on six baskets, perimeter players on the main baskets, bigs on the side with Allie and Romero. The coaches' voices were louder than what Izzy demanded of the players. "On that inside-out pass, Nick, get your feet in the air. Ball in the air, feet in the air." She was just as adamant about the passes. After observing two weak passes, she put the perimeter players on the line for punishments. Then, they resumed shooting with greater attention to her pet peeve. She called Morgan over.

"Do you and Bailey ever shoot baskets together?"

Morgan blushed slightly. "No, but she's always talking basketball."

"Do you think you could guard her if you played one-on-one?"

Morgan squinted as if that was a stupid question.

"Would you mind sticking around after practice for a little bit of the girls practice. She's too good for her teammates, and she needs to be pushed around and taught a bit of humility." Izzy hadn't been sure whether Morgan would be willing, but his eyes lit up and he agreed. With Morgan on board, Coach Soto recruited Nick, Jimmy, and two JV forwards to scrimmage against the girls. All underclassmen and all under six feet tall.

A half an hour into the girls practice, Coach Izzy put the five boys on the court to defend her girls. Lots of giggles and talk, but that ended on the first possession when Nick stole Bailey's first entry pass intended for Lauren on the wing. As the scrimmage continued, Morgan refused to allow Bailey to get a return pass from her teammates, so the girls offense sputtered to a halt. Morgan Rexford was not only an all-conference running back, he was an all-conference linebacker. He relished defense. Early on, Bailey was forced to turn her back to Morgan to protect the ball, but little-by-little, she regained her confidence and had some successes. To Morgan's credit, he understood what Coach was looking for, so he used his quickness and savvy rather than his strength to guard Bailey.

When Izzy switched the girls to defense, Bailey guarded Nick. Left-handed and quick, Nick had focused on getting his team easy baskets since his arrival in late-May. Coach Soto commented to him that she had found a player who hated turnovers as much as she did. Bailey struggled to contain Nick, to keep him out of the lane. For some odd reason, Jimmy found his three-point shooting touch and made several on kick-outs from Nick. Coach Monroe, knowing what Coach Soto had planned, stayed around to help the bigs on the baseline. The thirty minutes demonstrated to the girls that they were not State Champions yet.

When the scrimmage ended, Izzy called her boys together and thanked them. She asked if they would be willing to do it again on Wednesday. They consented. Izzy spoke to Morgan as the other boys dispersed. "That wouldn't have worked if you hadn't stepped forward. I really appreciate it."

"I probably wouldn't have agreed to do it a year ago. It was fun, and I won't let Bailey hear the end of it." Izzy was surprised at Morgan's revealing statement. He had always kept his emotions, except competition, hidden.

§

Izzy and Allie ordered pizza on Thursday after practice. They thought it ironic that the girls game would pit two State contenders, while the boys' game would be played with two teams at the opposite end. "Yeah," kidded Allie, "but one of them won't be come February."

Izzy picked the olives off her side of the pizza and deposited them on Allie's half. It just dawned on Izzy that Allie had practice on Friday with the boys, the first one that Izzy would miss. "You'll be driving over, won't you? I want you behind me on the bench."

"Of course. Jake's picking me up at school and we'll hustle down. I should be there by halftime of the JV game. How are your JVs going to be?"

"Probably won't be close. Broomfield's a big 4A school with freshmen. We won't have our freshmen in the building for at least one more year, until they finish the new classroom wing. We're scheduled to move up to 4A after next year. Our league is a 4A/3A mixture, and none of the teams have Broomfield's talent. Only Elgin and Windsor Christian and maybe Lyons Creek are even close."

Allie smiled. "That bodes well for you in the league though."

"It does. By the way, Jorge wants to meet your husband, said he needed to start meeting my extended family if we're going to keep hanging together."

§

Waiting for her at the office on Friday morning just as like the previous five years was a bouquet of roses from the Mountain Matrons who had continued to love Izzy and the other Cheetahs over the years. "Good luck, Izzy, for both your teams" read the card. Izzy knew these flowers came from Queenie and Mercedes, but the other Matrons helped when they could afford a little extra. Doris Finckle handed Izzy a tissue as she read. "Wouldn't want you to smudge those eye lashes," kidded the secretary.

§

Broomfield's fans were among the loudest and rowdiest in the state for both girls and boys games, a rarity in most schools where regardless of the records of the teams, boys contests were better attended. Both teams were well-coached and talented. Despite having gone to State the previous three seasons, Prospect View had not beaten Broomfield in their pre-season games. "Sure," Coach Izzy would tell her team, "they're a 4A team while we're just 3A, but it's still five girls versus five girls, and they put their uniform shorts on one leg at a time, just like we do." Then, to herself she would say, *as do Diana Taurasi and Sheryl Swoopes.* Still, each year, Prospect View had gotten closer.

Both sub-varsity teams lost by substantial margins, often an indication of how the varsity game would play out. But not on this night. From the opening tip, it was clear that the next 32 minutes would be highly contested, a battle between two teams likely to be playing on the last weekend of the season three months later. Coach Soto's decision to bring in boys from the varsity to scrimmage her girls provided Bailey and her teammates a taste of what they would see on this Friday night, quickness and size superior to their own.

Broomfield led by three heading into the fourth quarter, but Maggie rebounded a miss by Lauren and powered it in to cut the lead to one. Rosie intercepted an entry pass which led to a three-on-two break for the Pronghorns. Bailey fed Grace on the left side and her layup put Prospect View ahead by one. Broomfield retired its plan to double-team Bailey since her teammates used the resulting mismatches against the Eagles to effectively attack the basket. The final minutes were played straight up player-to-player defense on both ends, and that gave Bailey the edge she needed to penetrate Broomfield's defense and score two late layups giving Prospect View the win.

Two hours later, Izzy charted the game, even though she intuitively knew her girls had kept the turnover number low and prevented Broomfield from getting extra shots. Those were the two statistics she hung her coaching hat on, as any keen observer of her practices could attest, and her players would confirm. "Don't miss a blockout assignment or the whole team runs!" Around midnight, she replaced the game tape with a practice tape of the boys scrimmage from the previous week. *Nick will take care of the ball, Iz, but our defensive rebounding needs more work. But be patient, girl, it's coming.* Izzy yawned. *You're not going to change that tonight or tomorrow before the game starts. Go to bed, Iz.* She didn't, of course. She analyzed the boys scrimmage for another hour.

§

Two Saturday morning practices. The girls were in at 9:00 for an hour-and-a-half to go over their mistakes, give scrimmage time to the girls who hadn't received many game minutes the night before, shoot free throws, and condition. It was a giddy bunch celebrating a win over a quality opponent and eager to play two games the next week. At 11:00, the boys came in for a shoot-around, to review inbounds situations, and shoot free throws. Since the game was on a non-school night, the sophomores would play at 4:00 rather than concurrently in the aux gym at 5:30 when the JVs played on the main floor. Coaches Soto, Monroe, and Romero sat the boys down at noon to emphasize two points. Izzy's words focused on "first game jitters, trying to do too much too soon." Then, she stepped back to give Assistant Head Coach Monroe the floor.

"Not only is this your first game, but mine too. Well, we've all played games before, but you know what I mean. I like our practices and I believe we're ready for tonight, not March ready, but certainly December ready. I do have one concern, though." Allie let that statement hang in the air for a moment. "Some of you may think tonight's game is against Brooks Danson." Again, she slowed her cadence. "From what I understand, he's a big trash talker, one of the leaders of last season's misbehavior. I don't expect him to have changed simply because he changed schools. Let me be clear. You are playing Coal Creek, not your former teammate, and we will not tolerate any trash talking from you or any body movements designed to bring attention to you or to disrespect your opponent. Our crowd, especially many of the boys who played with Brooks on the football team, will want to stir things up. If any of you buy into that, you'll find your butt sitting next to me and Coach Romero, and it won't get off the bench for the rest of the night." Allie looked specifically at her seniors. "Do I make myself clear?"

§

Coal Creek High School, located west and south of Prospect and closer to Boulder, was in its third year of existence. So far, they had suffered the pangs of a new school competing against established, larger schools. This would be the first meeting between Prospect View and Coal Creek, both 3A schools, and neither with a history of basketball excellence. Unlike Friday's contest at Broomfield, the crowd at Prospect View only filled about a third of the gym, and there were no flag wavers or percussion groups or the band, just the cheerleaders. Pre-game music was recorded and pre-screened rap. As if scripted, Brooks Danson warmed up wearing a red headband, a bandanna really, tied behind his head, just as he had done when he played for Prospect View as a junior. He heard the calls from the Prospect View crowd, many still his friends, and waved his arms to rile them up. For the pre-game introduction of starters, Coach Soto intentionally had Coal Creek's players introduced together rather than alternated with her starters, so as not to give Brooks a stage at the beginning of the game.

Gathering her squad around her before the tip-off, Coach Soto kept her words brief. "Run! Run! Run! Ball pressure on D! Hit the boards!" She stacked their hands and in unison, they all yelled, "Pronghorns!" Nick, Morgan, Boyd, Charlie, and Wes moved to center court. Atticus had tweaked his ankle, but was ready, as were Mason, Curt, Bryson, and Benny.

Izzy remembered a moment from her first home game as a junior in high school, when Oro Hills' opponent was a small school with inferior talent, and her team demolished them for their first win of her playing career. She smiled and hoped.

After a predictable first quarter for both teams, and a low score of 6 to 5, Coach Soto's squad found its pace and raced out to a 22-13 halftime lead. Only once, midway through the second quarter when Prospect View started to pull away, did an incident develop. Brooks intentionally knocked Nick down as he drove to the basket and then stood over him glaring down. Morgan forcefully, but calmly, moved in front of Brooks and helped Nick stand, then they both walked away from Brooks. Nick sank both free throws. While the Prospect View crowd razzed Brooks, the team stayed composed. The second half was more of the same, much more of the same, and Prospect View crushed Coal Creek 59-34. Brooks Danson, last season's second leading scorer for Prospect View, didn't score while Morgan guarded him, and only got his points late in the fourth quarter when being guarded by Jimmy Yang.

When the gym had cleared and the players gone, the coaches sat in Romero's office sipping sodas and smiling.

"A sweep," said Romero. "All three teams by double digits. A good start."

"Let's enjoy it tonight, because next week's opponents won't be like Coal Creek," said Izzy.

Romero responded. "No, but this was good for the boys . . . and us. Every team did some good things, and our boys behaved as they should have. Our crowd has some learning to do, but I was proud of Mason and Curt, in particular. Danson tried to get under their skin, but they didn't bite. Their coach was a jerk too, seemed like he was encouraging Brooks' behavior. Did you see the look he gave you late in the game when Charlie dunked on his kid?"

Izzy nodded. "I noticed. Yeah, he approved of Brooks' behavior. Sad."

"I think Morgan set the tone early by shutting him out," said Allie. Changing the topic, "I'll be curious about the stats. *My bigs* dominated the glass, and your little guards took care of the ball."

"Fool's gold," said Izzy. "We'll get a better gauge next week."

§

Izzy hadn't asked, but she wondered at what time Virginia Polis did arrive at school each morning. Nick checked with Coach Romero at Monday's practice to see if the Shoot-Around machine could be left up so he and Jimmy Yang could come in on Tuesday morning to get some extra three-point shots up. Nick didn't want the netting to get in the way of PE classes the next day. As it turned out, Polis had let Nick and Jimmy in at 5:30 and said she'd be responsible for them until Romero arrived. Romero left the balls in his office, and the two sophomores shot until 7:00 when they both hit the weights.

Both teams played on Tuesday, so it necessitated Izzy to relinquish the boys to Allie, Romero, and Minturn. She had mixed feelings about it, not about her assistants' abilities, only her possessiveness, but kept them to herself. The Boulder area prep school would be a much tougher opponent than Coal Creek. Izzy's girls were at home against another 4A school, Brighton, who would not be as talented as Broomfield, but still a test. She met with the boys squad after school to review again the situation, which they fully understood. After they boarded the bus, she realized that it was she who needed the meeting, like sending your child off to school on that first day. Letting go. Allie promised she would call immediately after the game with the results and a quick run-down.

§

Bailey and her teammates quickly gained the upper hand against Brighton's girls. Using a more aggressive press than they had in the first game, Prospect View frustrated the visitors from the first possession. In the second half, Coach Izzy was able to give her backup point guard, sophomore Josie Touslee, minutes with the juniors, while letting the seniors cheer from the bench. The Pronghorns gained a solid win, and Izzy realized she had not thought about the boys until her cell phone rang a half-hour after her game ended.

"Lost a close one. Five points," said Allie. "Peak Prep packed it in and dared us to shoot from the outside. We threw up some bricks. How did the girls do?"

"We won easily. We were able to work on some things that we couldn't against Broomfield," said Izzy. "Who played well?"

"The boys all defended well against a cautious team. We held them to 41, but we just couldn't put the ball in the hole. Charlie had eleven, I think, to lead us, but Morgan and Nick played well, and Mason came off the bench and did some good things. As I said, that tight zone just dared us to shoot, but we couldn't rebound against them effectively or throw it inside. I think Nick made our only two threes. I kept thinking you might have an idea on how to attack that zone differently that would help us." Allie sounded like she could go on all night, but she had a bus to catch. "Romero's boys won. He's got them defending all over the court like wild animals."

Izzy remembered another team of wild animals who defended like that. "I'll wait for you at the gym and we can talk," said Izzy.

"Do they deliver pizza to the school?"

§

The following morning, Dr. Kerrigan fielded a call from a man, who remained anonymous but whom she assumed was a parent, that Coach Soto needed to coach one team or the other, but not both. It wasn't fair to short-change one squad by having rookies coach them. Dr. Kerrigan listened politely before thanking the man for his input. She never told Izzy about the call, nor did she give it any consideration after she hung up.

§

Izzy resumed her spot on the boys bench on Friday, another away game, this time against a 4A Loveland school that had terrorized its conference in the nineties, but had fallen on hard times. The Thompson Valley coach, persistent to the point of stubbornness, pressed the entire game, but Nick and his teammates handled it effectively, scoring layups by the bundle. Defensively, Morgan led the Pronghorns, and Izzy and Allie saw the beginnings of what could become a "tough-ass" defense, to use Romero's description. It wasn't there yet, but it had potential, albeit it was using "skinny-boned" kids, this time Allie's adjective.

On Saturday, the girls mauled a suburban Denver team, a game that Izzy evaluated as a glorified scrimmage against her JVs, a game that did not move her team forward on its path toward March. She criticized them for sloppy play in the second half and then closed the book on the game.

Three games under both teams' belts, the boys stood at two wins and a loss, while the girls were undefeated, with the one solid win against a quality 4A team. Two more non-league games remained next week before league play began the week before Christmas break. Izzy's girls were on track, but she still didn't have a feel for her boys yet. Their two wins came against weak teams. Only Peak Prep might compete in the Corridor League, but she wasn't sure. Jorge had attended two of her games and assured her that the Prospect View boys could beat his school, but then again, he wasn't a basketball virtuoso.

§

When filling out the non-league schedules in the fall, Izzy chose different paths for her two teams. For her girls, she chose a four-wheel drive road, tough competition that might bring a defeat or two, but that would prepare her girls for league competition. They were traveling on a road whose final destination was Denver in March. For the boys, she scheduled paved country roads with a lower speed limit . . . also, teams that were still available, still looking for games after the ranked teams were already taken. Izzy wanted her boys to get wins or at least be competitive. No blowouts. They had experienced enough of those the previous year and over the summer. However, the last two non-league competitors were unknowns to Izzy, but she hoped they would test her boys beyond what they had experienced in their first three games.

Prospect View's girls played in the Jeffco Summer League, 4A/5A teams at the highest level of competition: talented, well-coached, disciplined, experienced. The inexperienced Pronghorns had held their own, winning just over half their games: Tanya's team playing the schedule Izzy had established. Having graduated three-and-a-half starters and not having Rosie because of her accident, they took their lumps at times as they retooled, but Izzy spoke often with Tanya about trusting the process and was pleased with the results. Two of those summer teams, both of which had split with Prospect View, were now the next two opponents. Tuesday at Golden and Friday home versus Lakewood, a 5A school and a 2006 State quarterfinalist.

§

Golden leaned its big-bodied girls against the Pronghorns all night. It was a push-and-shove game for 32 minutes, but the Demons couldn't contain Bailey's quickness, nor could they close out on Prospect View's wings, leaving them free to shoot threes. Still, for three quarters, the Demons kept it close, but they finally succumbed to the Pronghorn press. When Izzy addressed her girls on the bus, she raised four fingers on one hand and a fist on the other to signify their record. Her girls all hooted and flashed their Pronghorn hand sign, similar to the Texas Longhorns. Izzy responded in kind.

Far to the north, Prospect View's boys played Northridge, the third large school in Greeley, another town undergoing significant demographic changes in the 21ˢᵗ century, although at the opposite end of the economic spectrum. Nick was pestered early and became frustrated, confused by Northridge's multiple defenses. Mason had no more success. Once Prospect View got across the timeline, the triumvirate of Charlie, Atticus, and Wes had some success, but Northridge's guards bested Prospect View's guards and won by ten.

"Coach," asked Izzy on the bus ride home to Prospect, "how'd you do?"

"Lost by ten," answered Allie. "What about you?"

"We won. Wore them down. Tell me what happened?"

"Northridge played to its strength, quickness, and to our weakness, inexperienced guards. Nick got flustered early and got no help from Boyd or Wes or Atticus. I think he can do what you're asking of him, but he kept trying to include his teammates, and they backed off leaving him all alone with the ball against their attack. He settled down some in the second half, and we made a run, but it was too late. All the boys kept looking to me for answers, and I didn't have enough to give them. Overall, we were too tentative."

§

Career Day. Wednesday morning classes were cancelled so students could attend "Plan Your Life Day" in the gymnasium. Teachers were expected to be available so students could discuss with them any opportunities they may have just sampled. Sixty booths, everything from the military to dentistry, plus several colleges and universities. Izzy and Romero sat on the bleachers together, an occasional student joining them to ask a question that a presenter might not have answered.

"I don't remember my school ever holding one of these," said Romero.

"Ours did, but it wasn't like this. Lots of local businesses and just a few colleges. The military groups had kids do pullups, as if that was how you got into the Army." Izzy thought back to Oro Hills. "I never thought ten years ahead, Coach. Heck, I never planned for anything past high school."

Romero turned in order to see his colleague easier. "A drifter?"

"If you mean by that that I just sort of got what came next, then yeah. My family was poor, not dirt poor like some others in Oro Hills; we had a house with three bedrooms, one for me and my little sister, one for my two brothers, and one for my parents, but we rented, and we never bought a new car. One bathroom for all of us. I was going to graduate from high school and then get a service job something like my parents worked. College was never an option, so I didn't plan for it."

"Sports, huh?"

"Yeah, basketball. My junior year, we get an old man coach who was retired, but for lack of a better description, *got it*. He devoted his whole life that year to our development. At the time, I thought he was just teaching us basketball, but it was never just about that. He somehow joined forces with a bunch of ladies, friends of his wife, who were successful in town." Izzy and Romero were interrupted by a student needing a signature from Coach Romero.

Romero signed a form and then pointed the student in the direction of a computer booth. "Continue."

"Well, anyway, these women were amazing. They decided we, meaning the girls basketball team, were worth something, so they began funding all our endeavors. If we needed shoes, and several of us did, they suddenly appeared. Jackets? Same. They were both our rich aunts and fairy godmothers. Then, it became college tuition.

My cousin was able to attend college when it had never been considered. As it turned out, I got a scholarship, but the women still covered some of my other expenses. As I look back on it, though, I think my attitude changed because of that coach. All of us know that our lives would have turned out differently—and less successful—without basketball. Those two years gave us, I don't know, validation maybe. Certainly, it provided us opportunity beyond small town poverty."

"Is this the Morgan Summitt that I always hear about?"

"Yep. And something else. The Molly you also hear about discovered that she was truly special, and she, maybe subconsciously, pulled the rest of us along. She was Bailey times three, an outsider in the sense that she belonged on the big stage her whole career, the best player in the state regardless of classification. A coach and a teammate."

Romero nodded. "I don't remember any teammate doing that, but I did have that special coach who took me under his wing. Probably didn't quite present himself like your Coach Summitt did, but he made sure I worked my butt off to get a football scholarship. And keep my nose clean. My family picked beets. I had very little chance of being anything but a picker, but Coach Moore saw something. He got me into college, where I proceeded to screw up my freshman year. Joined the Army and then went to CSU and finished what I started, what he pointed me to."

"One of those ladies that I just referred to owned a bar. She kept a big pickle jar next to the cash register for tips to fund various needs of ours, and patrons gave what they could. I always thought that said something about my town." Izzy smiled at Romero. "None of our kids here are poor, at least none of our basketball players. Prospect is upper middle-class and rising."

"Doesn't mean they don't need you just as much, just in a different way."

§

During Wednesday's practice, particularly in the scrimmage, Coach Soto frequently stopped play to advise Mason and Nick about certain aspects of the offense. Allie stood on the baseline with her bigs waiting for play to resume. When the boys shot free throws, Allie and Romero spoke to Izzy. It was Romero who spoke first.

"Do you do that with your girls too?" he asked.

"Do what?" asked Izzy.

"Stop the scrimmage on every mistake."

Izzy started to reply and then stopped herself. Then, "Did I just do that?"

Allie answered. "Yeah. While you're helping Nick and Mason, everyone else is just standing."

Romero broke in. "We've watched you with your girls, and I know the answer to my question. You don't. You trust them with occasional mistakes. Maybe Bailey's earned your trust, but you need to stop coddling your guards."

"All your boys," added Allie.

Izzy blew out hard. "They've got so far to go."

"You've brought them a long way already," said Romero, "but this is still school, and we're supposed to allow them to make mistakes sometimes." He smiled. "You're all business with the boys, like you have a checklist."

"Izzy, they're not going to rebel or behave poorly during a game. You took care of that problem this summer. These are really good kids who respect you and listen to you. But we think you need to loosen your grip a little now and allow them to flow." As Allie spoke, Romero could tell she was uncomfortable, but she continued. "When Morgan threw that pass to Benny on the block and it was in the wrong spot, you stopped play to ask him where the pass should have gone. He knew it was off target; you didn't have to stop play to tell him. Just say 'baseline side' and keep the play going. You don't get to stop play during games to correct them, so manage scrimmages the same way, the same way you do with your girls."

Romero wondered how Izzy would take the advice. She looked at her practice plan, which called for a fastbreak drill, nodded, and looked up at her two assistants. "You're right. Thanks." She blew her whistle and then tucked the pink lanyard into her shirt. When the boys were circled around her, she said, "Okay, full court varsity scrimmage. JVs, stand on the sidelines and watch carefully. Coach Monroe, take Morgan's five. Coach Romero, you have Mason's group. Put them in whatever you think your guys need to work on the most." She addressed the team. "I'm going to sit up there," pointing to the bleachers behind the scorer's table, "and scout you. You listen to only your coach and each other. Especially each other. Don't glance up at me." Izzy looked for something of which she wasn't sure. "Mason's team, go brown. Morgan's team, go red. Now, get after it!"

§

Standing in front of the bench watching her girls battle Lakewood, Izzy gave instructions to her team through Bailey. While the clock moved, she mostly just offered praise and encouragement. This game was the test Izzy had hoped for, the last non-league game before heading into Corridor League play, another talented, undefeated team trying to find weaknesses in the other squad, trying to impose its will when opportunities arose. 5A Lakewood was willing to play a 3A team only because its coach knew Izzy. Coach Russell had married Gloria Fawkes the summer after Gloria had coached Oro Hills to their State Championship back in 1997, had taken the reins when Morgan Summitt suffered his stroke. She coached that one magical season and then moved on to marriage and children. Now, Gloria assisted her husband, and games between Lakewood and Prospect View were family affairs both during summer league and pre-season.

The Lakewood crowd knew nothing about the friendship between the coaching staffs; they just wanted another victory. Izzy had piled her varsity boys on the bus with the three girls teams for the 30-minute trip to west Denver. They sat behind the Prospect View bench, and along with the parents, were the only supporters in a sea of orange and black.

On paper, the Tigers were taller than the Pronghorns, but Lakewood's all-conference center sat with the flu, and a forward seemed a bit weak, going to the bench early. Still, Lakewood had depth to call on, and in a non-league game, reserves would get a golden opportunity to show their talents. Izzy's teams had a reputation for discipline, able to play tenacious defense without fouling, so her top six played most of the minutes, and they were better than Lakewood's starters without two of their top kids. The Pronghorns prevailed in a tight, high-scoring affair, after which Izzy hugged Gloria and Ron and their two children.

§

At Saturday's game, Izzy sat except when Nick or Mason ran over to get dead ball instructions to pass along to their teammates. She had instructed Allie to put a hand on her shoulder whenever she started to stand, to keep her from being a micro-manager. Competing against a nearby 2A team with slow guards, Nick, Morgan, and Mason played with confidence, finding the bigs early and often, as Romero said. The win pushed the boys record to three and two as they headed into league play the next week. All three coaches conceded that the boys had won the three easy games and lost the two hard ones, and they didn't know how the league season would play out.

CHAPTER 9

Preseason, Conference, Districts, State. The Path.

Conference play. The Corridor League, named for the I-25 corridor north of Denver and south of Ft. Collins. All eight schools were within twelve miles of the interstate, and all except two had rural underpinnings. All were in a period of rapid growth in the early 21st Century; some, like Prospect View, more than others, and most of the schools had moved up at least one classification in athletics over the past decade. Six had remodeled or rebuilt their schools to accommodate this growth, and all except Ft. Meade were overwhelmingly white demographically. Prospect even renamed its school: Prospect View. Press coverage was provided by the *Boulder Camera*, which had reported on area high school sports for decades, and by a few of the local weeklies, such as the *Prospect Times*. Fourteen games over two months interrupted by the Christmas break with its no contact/limited contact rules. The *Camera* had predicted that "Coach Izzy's" girls team, based on its strong run in the previous season and its current 5-0 record would be the top team in the conference. The Pronghorns also were ranked fourth in the state. Conversely, "Coach Soto's" boys were not expected to achieve much, maybe battling Firestone and Ft. Meade to stay out of the Corridor League cellar.

Both teams would play Longs Peak the week before the holiday break, the girls on Thursday and the boys on Friday. The Lions were the most stable school in the conference, a 3A school with the oldest gym, a 1960s model with bleachers on only one side and a noise level that horrified audiologists. Both Longs Peak teams expected to be in the middle of the pack at the end of the season.

Izzy subscribed to both newspapers as well as a Denver paper, although with her time-consuming schedule, she read only the relevant stories in the sports section, clipping them out and placing them in a well-organized folder. Unlike previous years when she and Tanya would grab a fast-food meal and hop in her car to scout conference teams or "possible opponents down the road," she hadn't had the time with her two-team assignment. Also, unlike Tanya, all her assistants were married and not anxious to drive up and down the Front Range on school nights. Alone in her apartment on Saturday night, Izzy graded essays, trying to get that part of her professional requirements out of the way so that Sunday evening could be pure basketball time. Her phone's vibration alerted her to the incoming call. She turned down the music and answered Bianca's call.

"Hi, Bea. What's up?"

"Are you out on a date? I don't want to interrupt if you are."

"No date tonight. School work."

Bianca laughed. "Well, I hope Jorge is there rubbing your feet or something."

"No, not tonight." Izzy hesitated. "That's sort of on hold for now. He thinks I need to be available a bit more than I have been of late. Don't know what will happen."

"Oh, Iz, I'm sorry. He seems like a good guy."

"He is, a real good guy, but I'm so busy, and when I'm home, I just sort of collapse. I fell asleep on him over dinner a couple of weeks ago. What are you calling for?"

"Adam and I want you to come for dinner tomorrow. We had to put an old horse down at the clinic last week, so Adam's making a stew." Both women laughed.

"That's sick. Funny, but sick. What time and what can I bring?" asked Izzy.

"Nothing, we have it covered. Or you could bring Jorge maybe."

§

After church on Sunday, Izzy drove to the Hatton ranch to work out with Tanya, as she had nearly every Sunday since her friend had been released from the hospital. Tanya's mom fixed lunch and then sat with the two sweaty women at the kitchen table.

"I called Kerrigan Friday," said Tanya, "to tell her to rehire my replacement for second semester. My doctor thinks I still need another month or so before I put a full day on my hip, much less full weeks. My broken arm and shoulder are getting close to one-hundred percent, but this darned hip has a mind of its own."

Mrs. Hatton put a hand on her daughter's forearm. "Sort of like the rest of you, my dear."

Offering no sympathy, Izzy replied, "Well hurry up. I'm getting worn out doing all your work for you. All of the game programs list you as the head coach, but I'm doing all the grunt work."

Tanya appreciated Izzy's sarcasm and also understood that on this first week of conference play, Izzy was fully invested in coaching both teams—and fully capable of doing both well. Tanya knew that her best friend could wear both hats, filling the roles that her school needed this season, emergency roles in a sense. Tanya also worried about the toll the season might take on Izzy's stamina.

§

Izzy called. "Hey, stranger. Want to go to dinner with me up at Bianca's and Adam's house in Ft. Collins?"

On his end, Jorge smiled, "Only if I can pick you up and not just meet you at their place."

Izzy accepted, and when the call ended, she smiled in anticipation.

§

Prospect View's girls swamped Longs Peak on Thursday, closing December with an unblemished record. Izzy believed her girls could go undefeated in the conference if they stayed focused, which meant practicing with a purpose and developing her younger players to provide depth and competition for her top six. All doable. Coach Sabka's JVs had lost three to the bigger schools, but his girls might be able to win a dozen conference games. Her program was on solid grounds, and much of the credit belonged to Tanya. Izzy felt good about her friend's recovery, wanted it to happen sooner, of course, and couldn't wait to have her back.

The next night, Izzy guided her boys to a double-digit win against Longs Peak. Each boy performed his role well: Charlie and Atticus scored, Morgan defended, Nick ran the offense with only two turnovers, Boyd led the team in rebounds, and the six others all contributed. It was a good sendoff game for the boys, one that would sit well for the Christmas break, for the two weeks before their next game.

The coaching staff went to Izzy's apartment after the game to eat pizza and have a drink or two. Izzy joined the conversation late, having to call in the team's stats to the newspapers.

"We can watch film," she suggested seriously, but her offer was met with a chorus of boos. Not tonight. While the first topic was the game and the progress of the team, it moved on to holiday plans.

"Are you going to hole up here for the holidays?" asked Donna Romero. "If you are, I'll send Donnie over to drag your butt to our house for Christmas dinner."

Izzy held up her hands and laughed. "Nope, I'm leaving tomorrow to go home. I'm going to let my mama pamper me for a few days."

"What's Christmas like at your home?" asked Donna.

"Well," smiled Izzy, "tomorrow afternoon, my dad will make a couple hundred tamales, and the whole family will help him. Everyone will be gathered in the kitchen laughing. I'll get teased for not being married and having kids yet. I hope to do a little shopping at some point; I already have presents for my parents, but I need one for the name I draw out of a hat when I get there. Just a cheap one. On Christmas eve, we go to midnight mass, and then open presents on Christmas morning. Dinner is a pretty traditional Mexican feast."

Miles, who slightly knew Izzy from college, smiled at her account. "How did the two of you end up at all white Prospect View?" he asked referring to both Izzy and Romero.

They looked at each other to see which one should answer. Romero accepted, drawing out his answer. "Well, Miles, it's kinda who you know. We both had to swim across the Rio to get into the country and then work in the sugar beet fields to earn a little bit of money to go to college. We only got in because of Affirmative Action, and then this district hired us to show how forward thinking they are."

Miles flipped Romero off, and everyone laughed. "No seriously."

Donna Romero answered. "Romero and Soto are Latin names, but it never came up for Donnie when he applied. They just hired a football coach who played at CSU. Yeah, most of this town is white, but we speak the language." She winked.

Izzy gave Miles a more serious answer. "My high school was mostly Hispanic, but basketball sent me to Western State. I just applied for the job here, got an interview, and was hired. It never came up. I'm third generation American. When people back home ask where a person is from, they mean your last home. For me, I was born in Colorado, and I lived in Oro Hills most of my life. My great grandparents came to Arizona from Chihuahua, Mexico, to work in the copper mines. My mother's side of the family is from California." Izzy paused. "How about you, Miles? How did you end up here in Prospect?"

§

Bailey Rockwell's flu hit like a tempest three days before Christmas, sending her to bed for nearly a week. She ordered her father to get the season's game tapes from Coach Izzy and then had him set up a viewing screen in her room, a room crowded with trophies from her early years, pennants of her favorite teams, and posters of Jason Kidd. She allowed none of her teammates to visit her to prevent them from getting what she had, and she studied game films as if she was the chief scout for a D-1 university preparing for the NCAA tournament, mostly tendencies of her teammates and herself. *Lauren is more effective on the right block. Rosie comes late on the help backside. Tracey turns her back when she's pressured. Maggie clogs the spacing by staying too long in the lane after her cut, but she does get offensive rebounds that way. Grace doesn't want the ball late in the game. And you, girl, you're taking yourself away from the play on your first cut! Get back to the ball quicker. Remember what Coach Izzy taught you—one pass away at all times!* Bailey stayed sequestered for one extra day so as not to spread her flu to others, then went back to work on her conditioning and skills. She told Coach that her Christmas present was getting the flu when she could afford to, when there were no games or regular practices.

§

Coach Soto's other point guard, sophomore Nick Patterson, came early and stayed late for the post-Christmas practices mostly working on his three-point shooting. Romero rebounded, passed to Izzy, who then passed to Nick. Accurate, crisp passes followed by a quick comment on footwork or hand positioning. Charlie was correct, Nick was a *sponge.* At one session, he commented to his coaches how different they were from is coaches in Illinois.

"They yell more, like they have to win to keep their jobs, even the lower-level coaches."

Romero understood. "My coaches in high school and college were all screamers, both for football and basketball. Coach Izzy says she never experienced that." He flipped the ball to her. "Pampered, I guess."

Izzy tilted her head, tossed her hair, and raised her eyebrows as if to say, "Of course," even though she had tolerated two years of a loud coach in college. Then, she asked Nick if the old style bothered him.

"No, I guess all coaches do it their own way. It was sort of how my old coach was. When I met Coach Romero last spring, I imagined he'd be the same way. I didn't think I'd be playing varsity this first year."

"When did you start seeing yourself as a varsity player?" asked Izzy.

"Not until we started in November. I kept thinking there were some guys who hadn't played over the summer who would be coming out. I expected there would be players here as good as the ones from my old school, but that was unrealistic. Colorado basketball isn't as good as Illinois basketball. No offense, but a school of

2500 will be better than a school our size."

Romero grunted in the way football coaches do when something is stuck in their craw. "Wouldn't have mattered; you would have beaten them out."

Later that day when the kids had all left the gym, Romero asked Izzy about point guards, in particular, her two starters. "Back when, we just called little kids guards, not making the distinction between the two players at that position. But it matters. Morgan is not Nick, and they play a different position. When did that labeling start?"

"I teach writing, not history." Izzy laughed. "I don't know, but I do know that my high school coach knew. We had three guards, a point guard, a defensive specialist like Morgan, and a shooter. Me. And we were none of us the same, like we were raised in different countries with different cultures. No doubt about it though, the point guard was the key. For my time as a coach here, that's how I look at my team's makeup. Where's the point guard? Every other position can be massaged. Other coaches can be successful in other programs without making that distinction, but I can't. Sort of like yelling, I guess. Good coaches win using their unique styles. You've toned yourself down a little from your football persona, but you correct mistakes quite differently than me. And it works, especially on the defensive side of the ball."

Romero nodded and rolled his tongue between his teeth. "Speaking of defense, have you been watching Atticus closely?"

CHAPTER 10

Let no careless error go unpunished—even when you're ahead by 20.

With their win on Tuesday, January 30, 2007, the Prospect View girls league record climbed to 8-0, and they were two games up in the conference race. Defensively, their opponents tried every trick to slow Prospect View down: multiple zones, box-and-one, triangle-and-two, even a triangle with a double-team on Bailey. Izzy's girls responded effectively to each one. The Firestone Farmers even tried fouling every time Prospect View passed the ball inside, sending Rosie, Maggie, Lauren, and Grace to the free throw line rather than allowing them to shoot layups. The game lasted beyond the normal length of a high school basketball contest, making it a long and boring ordeal. The Farmers' coach later explained that he felt it was their only chance, that it would test Izzy's forwards' ability to make free throws rather than allow easy shots. Five Farmers fouled out and Prospect View made 60 percent of its 45 free throws and rebounded several of the misses. Still, it provided Prospect View with another test. Only two opponents played the Pronghorns straight up player-to-player defense, the Windsor Christian Eagles, who sat in second place, and the Ft. Meade Diggers, whose quickness matched Prospect View's. Because the Corridor League teams' abilities couldn't match Izzy's girls', she challenged her team to win every quarter, to be consistent for all 32 minutes of every game.

When Izzy's boys returned after the New Year's break, Morgan told Coach that he didn't want to scrimmage against the girls any longer. When asked why, he said that he was uncomfortable guarding Bailey, that "they weren't a thing any longer." Izzy understood, but by then, her second team had improved enough to challenge the starters. Bailey told Coach that the breakup was no big deal, that Morgan was just a junior and that they had never been serious anyway. In the bigger picture, Coach Tanya attended all four of the team's home games. Izzy wanted Tanya to sit next to her on the bench, but Tanya's doctor ordered her to sit two rows up just in case an errant pass sent a diving player crashing into that bench. Izzy kidded her friend about being "a step slower" since the accident. Regardless, Bailey and her teammates were ecstatic about the return of Tanya to their bench. Six games remained, most of the second round of conference play, with important meetings with Windsor Christian, Lyons Creek, and Elgin, three teams capable of pulling an upset.

Coach Soto's boys' league record sat at five wins, three losses, putting them in fourth place. Prospect View had an upset win against Longmont East, but a disappointing loss to Ft. Meade, the seventh-place team in the conference. Still, their progress put them in a position to finish in an advantageous position for the District Tournament at the beginning of March . . . if they could continue along this path. Izzy and Allie used all ten of their players, but eight of them played key roles in critical minutes. Each position had a valuable backup: Mason at both guard spots, Wes at both forward spots, and Benny behind Boyd at the center position. Allie's work with the bigs had reaped enormous gains, and Nick's extra shooting in the mornings gave the Pronghorns a three-point threat at the top of the key. Izzy and Allie designed meticulous practice plans in an effort to steal an extra win or two to move their boys into that third spot in the conference and away from top-ranked Elgin in the District Tournament. They believed that one of those upsets would have to come against either Windsor Christian or Lyons Creek, the numbers two and three teams in the conference. Both had beaten Prospect View in the first round.

§

During games, while Coach Soto usually stood, she reserved a seat next to the boys on the bench. When she made a substitution, that player was to come to the bench and give every other player a high five and then sit next to Izzy in order to receive a quick word of praise or a piece of advice on how to make a particular play. Izzy had Allie sit on her other shoulder so that the two coaches could bounce ideas off one another as the clock moved. Romero sat at various places on the bench depending on which player he wanted to speak with . . . or yell at. Friday's boys game pitted Prospect View against the sixth-place Firestone Farmers in their gym.

"Coach," said Izzy to Allie during the JV game, "it's time. You make the calls even when I'm here now. No more of this dual coaching role as we head toward the playoffs; this is your team now, and I'm your assistant. You sit next to the boys and make the substitutions and call the defenses." Izzy would not have made this move, this stepping back, if the boys and girls games were always played on different nights. She would have continued to be the head bench coach for both squads, but as the season moved toward the tournament, she felt in necessary for Allie to be seen by the boys as the coach, so they would have complete confidence in her.

Allie smiled. "Thank you."

"When the boys are dressed and we give them their instructions, I'll just make the announcement. They need to hear it so there's no question who they look to. Really, it won't be a big deal since you've been their game coach half the time anyway. But as we head for Districts, this is the way it needs to be. I won't be with you then."

Two women standing at the end of the gym away from the action on the court exchanged a meaningful hug, one that resembled a hug given a decade earlier when those same two girls who had just battled for a District Championship then walked through the congratulatory line, and the loser of that game received a hug from each player on the victorious team, a measure of the respect gained through competition.

Romero's JVs continued their winning streak, now up to five, defined mostly by aggressive defense and rebounding. His squad took more charges than the boys and girls varsities combined, and each time one of his players hit the floor, he stood to smite his chest, a symbol for taking the collision in the chest, and a sign of unselfish courage. On his statistics sheet, a charge was not labeled as a C, but with BB for butt bruise. Three juniors and nine sophomores were willing to sacrifice their bodies for "The Bricklayer." After his post-game talk with his team, he stood with Izzy in front of the bench while Allie spoke with the officials before the varsity tip-off.

"I know we talked about it, but it was still hard for you. I'm very proud of you, Isabella."

Izzy continued to look out onto the court. She nodded slightly and curled her lips inward. She reached into her pocket for a tissue. "Got something in my eye."

Prospect View's pressure, led by Morgan Rexford, prevented Firestone from executing their half-court offense, and by the end of the first quarter, Firestone's guards wanted nothing more to do with handling the ball. By halftime, the game was decided; Prospect View had imposed its will on the Farmers, and they were sent back to their fields to plant next year's crop. When Izzy called in the score to the *Boulder Camera*, she learned that Lyons Creek had lost, which meant Prospect View's boys were now tied for third in the league standings, five spots ahead of where they had been picked in December before any game had been played.

§

Saturday's home and away games with Elgin went as expected. Izzy's girls hammered the fourth place Impalas, while Allie's boys played even with Elgin's first place boys in the second half after falling behind by a dozen in the first half. The loss moved the Prospect View boys back into fourth position, but it was an anticipated loss, so third place was still a possibility. To pass Lyons Creek, the boys would need to win four or five of their last six, including beating Lyons Creek at their gym.

The following week, playing on Tuesday and Thursday because of wrestling districts, both Prospect View teams swept their opponents. Against Ft. Meade both Izzy's guards had been bumped and hacked with enthusiasm by the Diggers' guards, so she did an unusual thing; she cancelled practice for the girls on both Friday and Saturday. Bailey, who had rolled her ankle in the third quarter, objected, as Izzy knew she would, but Coach held her ground, telling Bailey to come in after school and get with the trainer to rehab. For all her girls, it was four days to rest and mend. For Bailey, it was the longest weekend of her senior season. "I don't have hobbies; I play basketball!"

§

As the Basketball Gods would have it, the boys would play meaningful games the last two weeks against Windsor Christian and Lyons Creek, the two teams in front of them in the standings, and against the number five team, Longs Peak who still could pass Prospect View in the standings. Coach Monroe and Coach Romero held intense practices, pushing their boys to find another gear, to push past their fatigue. When Allie would encourage the boys with a "You can do this!" phrase, Romero would holler, "Suck it up, boys, it's going to get even tougher!" Izzy tried to be more "Sabka-like," but occasionally she would shout out her frustration over a mistake that one of the coaches had just recently corrected. "Darn it, Charlie, Coach Monroe just told you! Don't pass up that shot! Boyd's moving into position to rebound as he should. He has to know that you'll take that shot and not pass to him in a crowd."

§

As she frequently did, Allie arrived at school during Izzy's free seventh period to plan practices. "You have my complete attention, Coach," said Izzy, "since I don't have a girls practice to make."

Allie handed Izzy the practice plan, a diet soda, and a deli sandwich, knowing Izzy had probably skipped lunch again. "I watch you," began Allie. "When did you learn to be such a fierce competitor? I don't remember you so much in high school; it was Bianca and that little turd, Molly. Maybe a little as seniors when you kept sticking threes, but that to me was talent more than competitiveness. Maybe it was because I never guarded you."

Izzy smiled as she popped the tab on the can. "Fierce? I'm not sure anyone ever accused me of that."

"I mean it as a compliment. Sincerely. In practice, if the kids mess up because of laziness or lackadaisical play, the veins in your neck almost pop out. Quicker than Romero can say, "Get you butts on the line," you've already jumped into their comfort zones. Boys and girls. They know the next few minutes will be painful."

Izzy raised her pop can to Allie. "As a junior, I was just happy to play. When my coach subbed for me, it was okay. It was usually my cousin or a good friend, so I was fine with it. He always used me as an example of supporting my teammates and understanding my role, but Molly got so mad at me at State that season. I remember her coming into my room in Colorado Springs after the quarterfinal game and almost screaming at me that she needed me on the court at crunch time." Izzy shook her head, as if remembering. "She was the first person to hold me absolutely accountable for my play, and that meant for my practice habits and conditioning."

"I can imagine Molly doing that."

"Yeah, it's a vivid memory. I pooped out in the semifinal game and we lost. Not very effective at the end, and I felt like I let my team down. I vowed never to have to come out of a game again because of fatigue or because I was soft. Losing . . . and fearing Molly's wrath, I got in the best shape I could, and when we scrimmaged on Coach Summitt's driveway that summer, I learned to *battle*. That's a word my coach used to motivate us, but I finally got it."

"Well," said Allie, "your girls certainly have your mentality. They know when to step on their opponent's neck. They have your killer instinct. I learned that hard work and even attention to detail wasn't enough to win the championship. That final step requires an inner drive. I know now that in high school, your two teammates had that and were the toughest pair at the State Tournament. I see that in you." Allie arrived at the place she wanted to get. "Now, I need to instill that in the boys. We need to."

"Let's lean on Charlie, Morgan, Mason, and Nick at practice this afternoon. Tell Romero to lean extra hard on the defensive side."

§

Both Windsor Christian boys and girls teams were good, both held second place in the league, but the boys were more dangerous, at least in Izzy's mind. That didn't minimize its girls' chances of upsetting Prospect View if the Pronghorns weren't focused, but the margin of error for the boys was less. The boys needed to play their best and hope for a few fortunate bounces, or as Coach Romero said, "WIN THE 50-50 BALLS!" The boys were also playing away, on *The Hill Where Eagles Soar*, the motto of Windsor Christian. Conversely, the Prospect View girls were playing at home, a place where they hadn't lost in over two years.

Before boarding the school bus to take her boys north toward Ft. Collins, Allie reminded Izzy of another girls team from a decade earlier that had a long, home court winning streak that was shattered by a team on the rise. "Don't allow that to happen to you!" Coach Izzy's girls must have heard Coach Allie's warning. Scoring the first twelve points, they raced to a 22-point halftime lead. In the first minutes of the third period, they "stepped on Windsor Christian's neck" and broke the Eagles' spirit.

Up on The Hill to the north, Charlie Sampson imitated his favorite NBA player, Tim Duncan. Without fanfare, Charlie played his best game allowing his team to stay close, to have a chance at the end of the game. With four minutes left, Charlie seemingly scored his twelfth field goal and 30th point on a driving layup to give Prospect View the lead, but the referee ruled it a charge, and Charlie fouled out, done for the night, replaced by Atticus. Coach Romero almost got a technical but was restrained by the head coach. Down the stretch, her boys battled. Atticus refused to allow Windsor Christian's best player to touch the ball. Boyd and Wes corralled every defensive rebound, and Nick hit a three from the top of the circle to cut the deficit to one with 25 seconds left. Both Allie and Romero jumped from the bench to call timeout as Nick's shot swished the net.

Crouched in front of her boys, Coach Allie nodded and smiled confidently at them. "We have one timeout left. I'll use it if we need it, but if we get the ball in transition, just go. Don't foul right away; we have about ten seconds to try and get a steal. Mason, check in for Boyd and keep their big center from acting as the pressure release on the inbounds pass. Morgan, keep #22 from the ball. Atticus, great job out there. Don't switch, Nick, but if Morgan is screened, stay with #22 until Morgan can recover." She pounded her fist on Nick's knee. "We don't want him with the ball or shooting free throws. We're in Scramble for ten seconds to get a steal and then go Red and foul." They stood together with their hands held high.

Coach Romero smote his chest and yelled, "All heart, boys! Chest to chest!" Allie yelled "Pronghorns" and sent the boys out onto the court.

It took eight seconds. Windsor's point guard tried a spin dribble to get past Nick, who anticipated the move and tapped the ball ahead where Atticus seized it. He passed to Nick, who glanced briefly at his coach. She pointed at him and then swept her finger forward, and Nick headed up court. Well-coached, the Eagles assembled their half-court defense and dug in. Nick dribbled right with his right hand, then suddenly crossed over to his strong hand to get past his defender and into the lane. With the clock ticking down, he hit Mason on the opposite wing for a fifteen-foot jumper.

Fifteen minutes later, Allie literally screamed into her cell phone to Izzy. "Coach, we won!"

§

With their victory over Windsor Christian, the girls clinched the Corridor League championship, an important goal, but just a stepping-stone goal. Their ultimate goal was the Gold Ball, the State Championship. Coach Izzy made sure during Wednesday's practice that her girls stayed focused. "We're currently ranked third. A single loss either in league or at the District Tournament will hurt our seeding for State. We want one of those top three seeds." Then she and Sabka nit-picked the details in four-on-four shell drill, reminding them that there were still areas in which they could improve. After practice, sitting with Sabka, she laughed.

"Want to know a secret, Coach? "she said to Edgar Sabka.

"What? That you only do this for the money?"

"Well, yeah, besides that. Each year I schedule a week like this where nothing the girls do can please me. I criticize every little thing. I call it *bitch week*. Tanya knew that it was all an act, but the girls didn't. Always that battle with complacency."

Sabka gave Izzy a high-five. "I can only imagine what it would be called if Romero scheduled such a week for the boys."

§

As the girls closed out an undefeated regular season, the boys needed a win in their final game to get the number three seed for the District Tournament. While the girls would be hosting their tournament, the boys tournament would be held at Elgin by virtue of its league championship, so Thursday's game would be the boys last home game. Their record stood at nine-four in league, twelve-six overall, a marked improvement from the previous year, in fact, the best boys record in a decade. For the first time, Prospect View boys basketball was on the map, and realistic thoughts of a State Tournament appearance were permissible. Still, the common message from the coaching staff was, "Don't get ahead of yourself. Lyons Creek is in the same boat as we are. They aren't going to roll over for you because you have a good feeling about yourselves."

In her pregame directives, Coach Monroe covered matchups, keys, and variables. Then, owing to her coaching inexperience, she turned to Coach Soto for the final words before sending the boys out onto the court. "You and Lyons Creek are evenly matched, so I expect a close game. I've had this peculiar feeling that one team might jump out to a big early lead, but then the other team would show its mettle and close the gap, that the game would come down to the last few possessions. Against Windsor Christian, you showed that you can handle those last minutes. Keep in mind what we've been preaching all year, 'attack, attack, attack.'" She paused and let the silence introduce her final thought. "We," and here Izzy, putting her hands on the shoulders of both Allie and Romero, "couldn't be more proud of you. You have exceeded our early expectations, and now it's time to take the next step. Be brave. Be warriors tonight."

Izzy's premonition had been accurate. The Pronghorns jumped out to an eight-point lead in the first quarter, but Lyons Creek methodically reeled them in before half. The game stayed close until mid-way in the final quarter when the visitors concentrated on stopping Charlie, leaving Nick open at the top of the key for two threes and enough separation to claim the victory. Rather than head straight for the locker room after walking through the congratulatory line with Lyons Creek, Coach Soto told the team to stay on the floor and mingle with their classmates. "Soak it in and enjoy the moment."

Romero put his arm around Izzy as they stood before the bench watching. "How did you know how this game would play out?"

Izzy smiled and giggled. "I didn't; I just made that up. I wanted to give the kids some confidence in case Lyons Creek jumped out to a big lead, that we could come back."

"You dog you," said Romero.

"You know, don't you, that I haven't thanked you enough for helping me this season. You were the key to getting this done."

Romero scrunched his nose and shook his head. "You just admitted to lying about the game premonition and now you're making up another story." He paused, then gently put his arm around Izzy and gave her a shoulder-to-shoulder hug. "Thanks anyway. It's been fun."

"We aren't done yet."

Out on the floor, Izzy's girls joined the celebration with the boys, sharing the victory that gave the boys a third-place finish as if it was as meaningful as the girls' first-place trophy. And on this night, it was.

The Playoffs awaited: for the girls, the challenge, for the boys, a reward.

CHAPTER 11

We determine the terms of the conflict!

On Sunday after the regular season ended, Tanya hosted a pre-tournament party for the women coaches and male coaches' wives on both staffs plus Bianca Acero, "who has enough sense to avoid coaching and lead a normal adult life," and Jorge, "who will act as Izzy's secretary today so they can fit in a little time together." Basketball geek that she was, Izzy brought construction paper and magic markers so that while she filled out the master brackets for both teams for the District playoffs, each woman could make a copy to take home.

Donna Romero, lifting her mimosa in a toast, said, "Congratulations to you all, not so much on your game accomplishments, but for putting up with my husband all winter. Really, I should be saying thank you. In the past, he couldn't stand the off-season, and he drove me batty with all his little projects." Donna looked to Izzy. "How do you keep the two teams separate?"

Allie Monroe broke in with laughter. "She doesn't always. Every so often, especially when we would be putting a practice plan together, her drills wouldn't match up with mine, and I would realize she had the girls on her mind. The boys numbering system, like for positions and presses, are the same, but I'd be talking about Charlie, Atticus, and Boyd, and she's thinking Maggie, Lauren, and Rosie."

Izzy smiled. "The only things that saved me from going completely off the rails were, one, lots of the games were on the same night, so I could focus on just one team at a time, and two, Allie bought in so quickly to what I was trying to do."

"And what was that, sweetheart?" asked Donna.

Bianca and Izzy laughed at the same time. Izzy had to cover her mouth so as not to cough up her muffin. She motioned to Bianca to tell the group why they were laughing.

"Allie's heard this story in parts, but back in high school, and we went to a very poor school, a group of ladies, not unlike this group in some ways except they knew nothing about basketball, sort of adopted our team. The leader of that group was a big, black woman from the South . . . she was a lawyer . . . named Queenie, and she called everyone 'sweetheart.' We haven't heard anyone else use that term, unless we use it to each other to kid."

Izzy broke in. "We loved her, and she and her partner continue to support us, not just Bea and me, but the other six girls from that team." Izzy grasped Bianca's hand and they smiled at each other. "Anyway, Donna, to get back to your question about what I'm trying to do here, it's not complicated. I want a consistently winning program that represents our school in a positive manner. And I want to help our players grow into upstanding adults." She paused. "The same thing your husband wants too. That's one of the reasons I wanted him as my assistant."

"Well, that, and he could whip those boys to behave," said Donna. "I personally think that's why some of them didn't come out. They're afraid of him."

Tanya's mother served another round of baked goods and refilled the empty glasses.

"The Corridor League," explained Izzy, "has both 4A and 3A teams, so while it's still a league tournament, it's mixed up for how the state determines seeding in the round of 32. Because the girls won our league and because of our high ranking," everyone clapped, "we're automatically into that round. For the boys, it's not so simple. But for today, we're only going to fill out the brackets for District." As she wrote in the school names on her poster, she made comments about the strengths and weaknesses of each. She even warned about how eighth place Firestone, her girls' first round opponent, could give the girls problems, although none of the other coaches agreed. The boys tourney was to be held at Elgin, and number 3 Prospect View would play number 6 Longs Peak, a 4A team that had not lived up to early expectations. Allie added that Longs Peak probably had as much talent as Prospect View, and because they were taller, could cause real matchup problems.

That afternoon, Izzy and Jorge went to a movie, and then for the first time, Izzy ate dinner with Jorge's family.

§

Even though Izzy might not be the boys lead bench coach for any post-season games, an observer of these post-season practices wouldn't know it. While Allie coached the bigs and Romero exhorted the boys to make contact, to "knock somebody down," always preaching defense, Izzy paced the perimeter, almost as if she were playing, as if each directive might make the difference in the next game.

For the girls, Izzy focused on her Five-Out motion offense. "Cut hard! Get to the basket! You're spacing is too tight!" And always, for both the girls and boys, lots of shooting. "Game shots at game speed." Each team, both boys and girls, benefitted from excellent coaching staffs dedicated to their craft, coaches knowing exactly what their squads needed to be focused on. At the helm of both, however, was a woman committed to preparing both teams for post-season play at the highest level.

Both teams practices were cut to an hour-and-a-half, but the increased intensity reverberated off the walls of the gym. "The time is now, ladies! Drop your butts and get into the passing lanes!" For Izzy's girls, her voice was the only loud exhortation; Sabka and Georgia used classroom tones. For the boys, adding Coach Minturn to the mix, any one of the four might point out an area for improvement or congratulate a good play with voices reaching into the rafters.

One player on each team, however, heard a different voice, Bailey Rockwell and Nick Patterson, one an all-state player, the other a sophomore who might receive a couple of votes for all-conference. They heard the same message, however: "It's your team; every possession is your responsibility," but delivered as if two physicians were discussing the best way to successfully perform an operation. Coach Soto would lean into Nick's ear and ask him if the shot his team just took was taken too early, "Did you move the defense?" Coach Izzy would stand in front of Bailey, her back to the rest of the team, and say, "Try to get Lauren more involved on this next possession; she's kind of wandering on the perimeter. See what you can do." And when practice ended, after she had addressed the entire squad, she would collect both the starter and backup point guard on each team and remind them that they must have big shoulders, but also that she would not have allowed them to play this most important position if they hadn't demonstrated their mental toughness and earned her confidence.

Wednesday's boys practice held a different vibe for Izzy than the girls practice. She believed her girls would run through the District playoffs, but the boys faced a tough game in each round. They could be eliminated by one bad quarter, and she wouldn't be on the bench to prevent it from happening. Because of a car accident five months earlier, it couldn't be avoided, and she hoped the boys and their parents understood this. Izzy believed in Allie and Romero, but she was the one who had taken the reins of the team last spring. In her mind, in her heart, these boys were her team. *Yeah, yeah, yeah, Iz, the boys won fourteen games and finished third, the best they ever have, but they could have gotten one more and been seeded second. So, don't get too high on yourself.*

Jorge called on Wednesday night to wish her good luck and to remind her to get some sleep, and to tell her he would be there. Izzy apologized for being so busy, but Jorge brushed it off, saying "it was playoff season." She called Tanya, who had inexplicably missed practice, to check on her. Tanya assured Izzy that she would be at the gym for the pre-game discussions and sitting behind the bench when the game started; it had just been a little ache in her hip that she wanted to rest. Bianca called to wish Izzy luck, but laughed that she wouldn't need it for her girls. Allie called, thanking Izzy for trusting her and giving her this wonderful opportunity, promising Izzy that she wouldn't let her down. And finally, after Izzy had sat down with a salad and glass of wine, her phone buzzed one last time.

"Hi, Coach. Isn't past your bedtime?" she asked.

"The missus retired a while ago, but I wanted to wish you good luck. I was just making some notes on my pad, and it occurred to me that I didn't know who your second game would be against."

"Boys or girls?"

"The girls first? You get one of those 4A teams, don't you? Be careful about that one; they'll each have a little momentum from winning their first-round game, so they'll have some of that mojo."

"We won't look past anyone, Coach. Promise."

"Your boys have done very well. I expect Charlie to have a big tourney." Coach Summitt knew every player on both of Izzy's teams, his basketball gene never going away.

"I think it's our defense that will carry us. Morgan has been a stud there."

The conversation went on for a few more minutes before Coach Summitt told his girl that he was proud of her, something he always said at the end of each call. And Izzy closed with what she always told him. "Thanks for calling, Coach. Luv ya."

§

Prospect View's boys, as the third seed, played the second game at Elgin which was scheduled at 4:30. Coach Monroe suggested that if all went well, meaning if they won, they could dress quickly and get back to Prospect to cheer on Izzy's girls who would play at 6:15. Izzy nixed that, saying that she wanted the boys to live the tournament, to soak in the atmosphere and breathe post-season air. She didn't want them to perceive their game in any way as less important than the girls game. Izzy met with the team as they boarded the bus during last period, patting each boy on the shoulder as he boarded. She told Romero not to come back if they lost, and when Allie was about to get on, Izzy slipped a colorful ribbon into her hand. "It's too girlie to wear, but it's always brought good luck to me."

§

Longmont East played well early and led the entire first half. Prospect View hung close despite some poor shooting, but the boys minimized their turnovers and defended like bulldogs. The press began to produce results in the third period, and when Morgan hit a layup after a steal and Charlie cashed in a three on a nifty pass from Nick, Prospect View had its first lead. Playing from behind, Longmont East reverted to the disinterested play that it had exhibited during the regular season. Prospect View won by seven, advancing to the semifinal round to play Windsor Christian on Friday.

Bailey Rockwell "rocked the gym" in Prospect, leading her Pronghorn girls in scoring, assists, and rebounds. She sat the entire fourth quarter, giving Josie Touslee tournament experience that would carry over to the next season. While Coach Izzy stood, Bailey sat next to Coach Sabka, both demanding that the younger girls defend. Now, Prospect View would play one of those 4A teams in the semifinals that Coach Summit warned Izzy to be wary about. She called Allie immediately after the game to get the boys results and then informed the girls that Prospect View had two teams in the District semifinals.

§

Bianca and her husband Adam attended Friday's semifinal game and sat with Tanya, her parents, and two of her brothers behind the Prospect View bench. Heeding Coach Summitt's words, Izzy did not allow her girls to look past this game. Showing their separation in talent and preparation, the Pronghorns' press struck early, giving Lyons Creek no breathing room. Rosie and Maggie stole pass after pass, and by halftime, the game was no longer in doubt. Prospect View was living up to its number 3 ranking in State.

Thirty minutes away, the boys did not have it so easy. Morgan picked up his third foul early in the third quarter sending him to the bench, allowing Windsor Christian's leading scorer a little breathing room. The Eagles were trying to settle a score from just a few weeks earlier when the Pronghorns had marched into their gym and "stole one." Returning to the floor at the beginning of the fourth quarter,

Morgan slowed down the Eagles' attack. Nick did his best point guard imitation of Bailey Rockwell, and Prospect View stormed back to send the game into overtime. After Wes hit a follow-shot to give Prospect View the lead, Morgan picked up his fifth foul on a questionable reaching call. The Eagle coach decided to double Prospect View's sophomore point guard, Nick Patterson, to force Coach Monroe's squad to run their offense through Mason. When her team struggled, Coach Monroe took Coach Romero's advice and countered by moving Mason to a forward spot and turning the ball-handling duties to 6'3" Charlie Sampson. The experiment early in the summer of playing Charlie at the point guard posi-tion—before Nick came on board—paid dividends now, eight months later. Windsor was forced to end its double-team on Nick. The game was decided on Nick's three-pointer and a "man-sized rebound" by Boyd Smith on Windsor's last shot.

All the women inked in their brackets with two Prospect View finalists.

§

Saturday morning shoot-arounds for both the girls and boys teams; game shots-game speed, free throws, power layups, and then reviews of inbounds plays. Izzy did not add anything new, since the girls had never needed to use an end of game special to get a basket. Allie used one of Izzy's to add to her repertoire. Both teams played at 7:00, the girls at home versus Windsor Christian, while the boys traveled back to Elgin to play Elgin, the league champion. Since Elgin was a 4A team, the boys had assured themselves of at least one additional game in the Round of 32 by being the highest 3A team left in the League tournament. If they could somehow beat Elgin, a tall mountain to climb, they might even get a top eight seed.

It was a relaxed morning. The coaches of both teams, including Tanya whose hip was better, sat in the bleachers drinking coffee or sodas. Izzy waved Virginia Polis over to sit with them, but Virginia declined, holding up her wide broom and smiling, indicating that some people still had work to do. She and Izzy had shared many moments of conversation over the past months about the boys team. At 11:30 Coach Monroe brought her boys over to give them the bus schedule, their instructions for eating, and remind them they would be wearing their away uniforms. When the boys dispersed, Coach Izzy called her girls in.

"We're 21 and 0, but . . . we haven't been tested since the pre-season, so be aware. Every team now is capable. This isn't an elimination game for us, only a State seeding game. Also, we have two straight District championships; let's make it three tonight. They stacked hands, yelled "Pronghorns," and left the gym.

The coaches remained, except Sabka who had a four-hour shift to perform at his job. It was Romero who brought up an interesting dilemma. "You know, don't ya, that we have three head coaches sitting here?" Only Izzy understood immediately what Romero was referring to, even though he had been asking in jest. He continued, "I never had a woman coach, never coached with one, so this has been an eye-opener for me.

Izzy reached over and hugged Romero around his shoulders. "Awww, can't wait to do it again, can you?" Then, she wiped her left eye carefully. "We've certainly had a good time, haven't we? The game gives us electric moments, like lightning strikes. Practice, though, gives us friends, like a river being enlarged by tributaries, some large and some small." She opened her eyes wide to control her tear ducts. "Thank you all."

§

At 7:00 o'clock at two gyms 30 minutes apart . . . really, at dozens of gyms across Colorado . . . referees tossed a basketball between two players wearing different colored uniforms starting championship games. At Prospect View, the girls lost the tip and fell behind 2-0. Bailey hustled the ball down court, passed to Maggie on the wing, cut hard ball-side, received the return pass in the corner, and drilled a three, wiping out Windsor Christian's only lead of the night. Windsor had demolished Ft. Meade on Thursday, winning by 54 points, and then edged Elgin in overtime on Friday. A good team and well-coached, the only private school in the conference, it tended to look down from The Hill on the surrounding schools, especially those on the east side of I-25, at least that was their reputation. Jorge, usually stoic about Izzy's teams' games or about basketball in general showed his "Latino passion," as she laughingly explained it to Allie, and encouraged Izzy to run up the score on Windsor if they had the chance. "It hurt our girls to lose by 50. It was totally uncalled for!"

Prospect View won its 22nd straight game in convincing style, its last loss coming in last year's semi-final game at State, but Izzy refused to run up the score. The margin of victory would not influence the basketball committee that determined seeding for State. Winning by 24 or 54 would not matter, so Prospect View's starters sat most of the fourth quarter. Ironically, Windsor Christian's leading scorer had to be carried off the court with less than a minute to go, apparently with a broken ankle.

At the Elgin Impala gym, more drama was occurring. Staying within striking distance most of the second half, Prospect View's boys scratched and clawed but couldn't get over the hump. The bigger and more experienced Impalas fought off each Pronghorn run. Charlie endured the bumping and pushing throughout the game, the obvious target of Elgin's defensive plan. "Bottle up their big gun." Boyd and Benny gave up about twenty pounds of muscle to Elgin's bigs and wore down. Time and again, Nick dribbled past his defender only to find the lane clogged with another Impala. After the game, upon receiving their second-place plaque, Coach Monroe expressed her pride in their effort and reminded them that they would have another game . . . or more . . . beginning on Thursday. "Keep growing. We still have our future in front of us!"

As they rode home on the bus, Romero patted Allie on the shoulder and said, "By the way, Coach, where else would our future be?"

§

"Seeding Sunday" for the Round of 32, or for Sub-regional, or the First Round of State, or whatever it's called. The suspense for Prospect View was not on the girls side; it was all on the boys. Coach Izzy's girls would get a 3-seed if the newspaper rankings were to be believed and then receive two home games on their journey back to the *real State Tournament*, the Final Eight. The boys most likely would fall in the nine to sixteen range which could give them one bonus home game, and if they won, a second game on the road on Saturday. The state association would announce the pairings in the afternoon, posting them on their websites at 3:00 o'clock. Bailey had arranged a party for her teammates at her home; the boys decided to meet at McDonald's at that time to learn their fate.

Izzy's Sunday schedule did not alter, at least for the morning. Church, work out at Tanya's, and phone calls with family, but then she and Tanya would join the girls at Bailey's house for the announcement, since the girls pairings were to be released an hour before the boys. She would leave the girls and head over to McDonald's to join the boys. Hopefully, Allie and Romero would already be there.

Arriving at Bailey's just as Tanya drove up, Izzy asked her if she had showered after their workout. "I'm thinking you should ask your doctor if you can move to the front row now."

"I've missed it more than you know, Iz. I can't say as I was lucky, but it certainly could have been worse. I might not have recovered or . . . yeah, worse. I've had such a wonderful support group in you and the girls."

Mrs. Rockwell greeted the coaches at the door and ushered them to the den where all twelve players were gathered. Rosie had the website up on the large computer screen. It was Bailey who asked who Izzy thought they might play on Thursday night.

"Hopefully not the Lakers. Maybe the Nuggets though since we'll be hosting," said Izzy. Two soft chairs had been reserved for the coaches with TV trays in front for soda and popcorn. Settling in, listening to the buzz of the girls about basketball, the laughter that would break out in the various little groups, watching a healthy Tanya out of the corner of her eye, Izzy knew she occupied a corner of Heaven surrounded by angels.

The tournament pairings for the girls appeared on the screen at 3:15. To everyone's surprise, Prospect View got the number 2 seed behind Bishop Machebeuf, the only other undefeated team in 3A. Denver Christian, last year's State runner-up, but loser to Machebeuf in their District finals, slipped to number 6 and was on Prospect View's side of the bracket along with number 3 Holy Family. By virtue of gaining the number 2 seed instead of number 3, the Pronghorns would not have to go through the gauntlet of the three private schools in the Elite Eight, because HF and DC would meet in that first round of the Elite Eight. Every team in the group of eight would be tough, but beating Denver Christian, Holy Family, and Bishop Machebeuf on three consecutive nights could have been a major obstacle. *Yep, Iz, you got a little gift today.* But those teams were a week away, Prospect View would host number 31 on Wednesday and the winner of the 15-18 game on Friday. Izzy had supreme confidence that her girls would not lose to either of those teams. Her girls' destiny was in the bright lights of Denver beginning in eleven days.

"All right, ladies, I need to find out about the boys' seed, so you and Tanya can break out the champagne now, just don't let me know about it." Izzy excused herself, thanked the Rockwells for their hospitality, and drove to McDonald's.

Two of her boys, Benny and Curt, held part-time jobs at the fast-food restaurant and had a link established to the state association's website. At 4:00 the pairings began appearing on the screen, beginning with the top seeds. Number 1, Kent Denver versus number 32. Number 2, Eaton versus number 31. And so on until the eleventh seed was listed, number 11 Prospect View versus number 22. A home game on Thursday. Izzy and Allie briefly hugged, and then Coach Soto stood to address her team.

"Congratulations! Wow, the eleventh seed; that's quite an accomplishment! You're the first Prospect View boys basketball team to make it this far. You're the foundation for future years of excellence, and you deserve this for all the hard work you've put in. Mason, Curt, Bryson," Izzy stopped to allow the team to clap for these three seniors. "I couldn't be happier for you guys who stood with us when some others bailed. I know you got a lot of grief from some of your friends about, well, you know, playing for a coach that was, well, . . . a football guy." Izzy looked at Romero and everyone laughed. "Let's not be happy with being in the Round of 32; let's keep moving forward. Thirty-two, sixteen, Elite Eight." She paused again. "And beyond."

CHAPTER 12

*What happens in practice is more important
than what happens during games.*

The schedule remained the same; boys practiced early and the girls late. Izzy tried to remember her practices in high school. She and her teammates loved practices, dreaded their ending. It meant the return to the real world of poverty. Practices were pure joy. They had alternated with the boys, some weeks early, some late. Now, Izzy set this current schedule to facilitate her assistant coaches. Sabka worked and Georgia taught at an elementary school, so practicing late made it easier for them. Romero and Miles were in the building. Allie's schedule was flexible. Izzy never had to check her schedule to see when she was with whom. Boys early, girls late. Except for those two seasons at Western State before it made a coaching change and the new coach installed a new system, Izzy loved practices. She had considered them when she took the job as the boys coach; she even made an agreement with Dr. Kerrigan that if after the summer season, she couldn't stomach the boys, Kerrigan would find someone else. It was in practice where culture was established; games were only displaying that culture.

Two weeks left in the season . . . if the post-season played out as she hoped. The girls opened on Wednesday at home; the boys played on Thursday, also at home, a bonus game at home for them. She never dreamed they would have progressed this far this first season, maybe a Round of 32 game, but not at home, and even that had been doubtful three months ago. As she watched them stretch for this first practice in the "boys' post-season era," she smiled proudly. She watched Allie wander around the circle of boys asking about their day, kidding them about one thing or another. Romero did the same, but slapped hands and shoulders more often. His work out of sight had been one of the keys. The boys were stronger and tougher, and his gruff personality brought a certain macho-ness that the boys bought into. *Certainly*, thought Izzy, *Allie and I didn't bring that characteristic.*

"Three practices, young men. How much better can we get in three days?" Coach Soto walked around the perimeter of the circle of boys like an army *officer* rather than their sergeant. While she had relinquished the game coaching duties to Allie, she had not given up the role she signed up for. Head Coach. Allie constructed the rough draft for these practices, but Izzy fine-tuned them. "What are our *everydays*?" she asked. "Blockouts," the boys answered in unison. Coach Soto smiled and looked to Romero as if to say, "Well then, what are you waiting for?" This rebounding drill had become the team's signature drill, partly because the coaches gave them enthu-siastic responses for their successes. Lots of contact, some blood, but team building at its best. "This is who we are, men!" Romero would yell, and he would fire up another bad shot sure to produce another rebound. "The Bricklayer," the boys called Coach Romero. *Yes, he is*, thought Izzy.

Allie stayed for the girls practice, something she had been doing more and more as the season moved toward a conclusion. For the girls, Allie took on Romero's role, but without the colorful phrases to question their toughness; demanding, yes, but no "off-color references." When Allie had said that over drinks one evening, Izzy and Tanya could not stop laughing. Her coaching staff, so different between each team, but fully committed to building young men and young women, all in on winning . . . and winning big! Tanya's presence completed the circle. Per doctor's orders, she was not allowed in the contact drills, but she toed the edge of those orders. Four women and Sabka coaching twelve young ladies who had a chance to win it all.

With this group, much more than with the boys, Izzy was senti-mental. All twelve were Prospect girls, not a single move-in during the high school years, no girls who lived in another small town and transferred into Prospect View. Izzy was not just their coach, she was family; they were her children. When practice ended, she gathered them at the center circle as she always did and asked her assistants for any comments. Mostly, these focused on certain basketball techniques. Then, Izzy would move beyond the fundamentals and relate what they were doing on the court to life. Tonight's question: "What do Rosie and Coach Tanya have in common?"

The answer was obvious. They had both been injured in car accidents caused by drunk drivers. Mama Izzy continued. "I don't know if you heard about it, but there was another serious accident near Prospect this weekend involving alcohol. Every time I read about one of these, I shudder. Sometimes we can't control this, like Coach Tanya's accident, but sometimes we can." Izzy looked at Rosie and nodded. "Sometimes we can," she repeated. "Just a reminder that getting into a car with someone who's been drinking is stupid. As always, you can call one of us, no questions asked."

When she let a moment pass, she returned to the task at hand. "One more practice. All shooting and reviews. Then, we lace up our sneakers on Wednesday and get game one of the five. We treat every team like a champion that needs to be overthrown. We look past no one."

§

Girls team number 31 came to Prospect's Prospect View High School sporting an 11-11 record. They left 11-12, beaten in the first quarter by a herd of Pronghorns on a mission, "the fastest animal in America."

§

Boys team number 22 would arrive the next evening with real hopes for an upset. Plainview High School, a school with a similar name as the Pronghorns, reminded Izzy of Ft. Meade, a poor school district with a majority Hispanic student body, serving a town that had once had a large meat-packing plant east of Greeley. Plainview was on the northern end of the 1930s Dust Bowl, and its basketball reputation was to play fast and reckless. When Izzy researched

Plainview, she got a bad feeling about the upcoming game, not one that she shared with the coaches or players, just a vibe that made her uncomfortable. Plainview's mascot was the cheetah.

Adam answered Izzy's call on Thursday night and handed the landline to Bianca. "How come you didn't answer your cell?" asked Izzy."

"I misplaced it somewhere. I probably ought to give you Adam's number. What's up, Iz?"

"Anxiety pains about tomorrow's game."

"Don't you have those before every game?" asked Bianca.

"This is different. It's like a premonition, like a sinking feeling that I can't control."

"Unless I'm missing something, Iz, the game hasn't started yet. Your boys are playing well and should be the favorite. Did something happen to any of your players?"

"No, Bea, nothing like that. We're playing a team that runs and presses like us, but their mascot is the cheetah. They're the Plainview *CHEETAHS.*"

When Bianca stopped laughing at her friend, she asked, "Is Molly Rascon on their team?"

"Don't be stupid, of course not. It's just a sinking feeling I have."

"Oooo, the ghost of high schools past. Get some sleep and go get a win. Adam and I will be there, and we'll chase off these cheetah apparitions."

§

Prospect View versus Plainview. The Pronghorns versus the Cheetahs. The prey versus the predator to Izzy's way of thinking. She had never had a feeling like this before, but she kept it to herself, although Romero noticed her anxiety.

"What's up, Coach?"

"Just nerves, I guess. I so want our boys to win, to taste this playoff experience. They've worked so hard, and I don't want to let them down."

Romero shook his head. "You've created something special here, Coach, and they're ready. No guarantees, but I like our chances."

Coach Monroe sent her usual starting five onto the court: Nick, Morgan, Charlie, Atticus, and Boyd, while Coach Soto reminded the reserves to be ready. "The tempo will require you guys to play lots of minutes. Pick out the guy you'll most likely be covering and study him. We're going to need everyone tonight!"

Indeed, the game was played fast. At the end of one quarter, Plainview led 23-21. It seemed to Izzy that the only starter who couldn't be replaced was Nick, because the Cheetah's press was too tough for Mason when he handled the ball. Izzy and Allie agreed that Prospect View's sophomore point guard would have to carry the load. Izzy recalled something Nick had said to her eight months earlier, that the pressbreak his team in Illinois used was like what she had installed for them. He could do this. At a timeout, from the bleachers just three rows behind the varsity, Bailey Rockwell yelled to Nick, "Take him off the dribble, Nicky, and attack the paint." With every possession, the young guard seem to gain confidence, and Charlie's baseline jumper at the buzzer gave Prospect View the halftime lead, 47-45.

Coach Monroe's words in the locker room echoed Nick's confidence. "You've figured out their press, now execute. Once we get into our half-court offense, storm the boards. That's our strength. Boyd, Wes, Atticus, Benny . . ." she looked for their eyes, "now's the time to take advantage of all those times when Coach Romero was yelling at you. You're his kids this half." Allie and Izzy gave a few more pieces of advice, but the message had been about rebounding.

The second half belonged to the Pronghorns. Nick handled the pressure, Charlie shot lights out, and the bigs dominated the smaller frontcourt players for the Cheetahs. 91-72, and Prospect View was into the Sweet Sixteen.

Bianca hugged Izzy after the game. "Hey, Iz, there's only one true Cheetahs team. That's us, and no one will ever take that away."

§

With the staggered schedule, games seemed to run onto each other, which in some ways, they did. For a head coach with two teams, Izzy not only had a game in the evening, she held a practice in the afternoon, ate a snack, coached, returned home to lesson plans, slept five hours, taught five classes, and then would hold practice again. With the number 15 seed due to arrive at 6:00 o'clock, for a game with her girls, Izzy decided that she would only stay a few minutes with the boys after school. It would be a shooting practice for the most part. Allie came by Izzy's room during seventh period to go over the practice plan and brought Izzy her snack and soda, but remarked that the head coach might want to dab a bit more undereye makeup on to hide the dark rings there. "When the State Tournament is over, I'm checking you into a spa for several days," joked Allie.

"When I was considering Dr. Kerrigan's offer last year, I never even thought about this. I think I'm running on adrenaline. Having two teams in the Sweet Sixteen is a powerful drug."

Allie smiled and motioned for Izzy to eat. "Well, if it is a drug, then let's take another hit tonight. Your girls will do great." Allie stopped talking to let Izzy eat. Then, she asked, "Did you ever do drugs, Iz?"

Izzy shook her head and smiled. "No. You're looking at the most strait-laced coed ever to attend Western State. My dad would have killed me if I had, but more than that, I'm kind of a chicken. All those tv ads scared me. You?"

Allie smiled back. "A little during my last year at UNC when I couldn't play basketball anymore, but not much." She smiled a broader smile. "I thought artists were supposed to get out-of-body experiences, so I experimented for a few months. My paintings looked like crap, so I stopped. A college experiment, I guess." Allie returned to basketball. "I'm heading down to get the balls out for the boys. I'll see you in a few."

Sitting alone in her classroom, Izzy thought about this interesting path she and Allie had taken to get here. Certainly, Allie came from a wealthier home, a private school, whereas she had come from an economically struggling home . . . and Oro Hills. *It was all basketball experiences, Iz. Without those, the two of you would never have crossed paths, but competing against each other gave you a common bond. All your best friends, Iz, have that basketball gene that draws you together. Allie, Tanya, Bianca, Molly, Stevie. By the way, Iz, when was the last time you called Stevie?* Izzy took her phone from her purse and punched Stevie's number. "Hey, girl, it's Friday, which means my team's playing, so you need to come up and watch. You can sleep over on the couch. Bianca will be here too."

§

The basketball gene must have contacted more of its kin, because Bianca brought Rosa to the game and Stevie rounded up Cindy, so the bleacher rows behind the Prospect View bench filled up with several 28-year old women all wearing colorful ribbons in their hair. Cindy brought the ribbons thinking that Izzy's team might need a bit of luck. Allie could only shake her head at The Miner Girls, but she did get a hug from each one of them. Allie also remarked that if her high school, Academy Prep, could pull an upset and beat the number 7 seed tonight, Prospect View would play Academy Prep in the first round at State next Thursday.

The success of the two basketball teams had transferred over to Prospect View's student body and the town. The gym was packed, the band was loud and unruly, and several of Romero's football players wore antlers on their heads. "Reindeer antlers left over from Christmas, Coach. The best we could do on short notice," said Romero. "Besides, nobody knows what Pronghorn antlers look like anyway. It was Mason's idea."

Bailey and her teammates brought the show. Leaving nothing to chance, they jumped out to an early lead and extended it throughout the game. The Pronghorns did not resemble Oro Hills of the nineties in size, being taller and stronger, but still possessed lots of quickness, and they played with the same passion and exuberance for one another. A good pass was noted with a hand slap or a pointed finger from across the court. The bench jumped up in support on every charge taken or basket scored. Prospect View's un-drama Queens put the game away with a 12-0 run midway through the first quarter, but the crowd stayed for the entire game cheering for the girls in their last home game. When the buzzer sounded ending the rout, Izzy's girls sincerely congratulated the losers for their effort. It was a tradition that Izzy had instilled in her program from her first year; "Walk slowly through the end-of-game congratulatory line, make eye contact, and shake hands. No simple hand slaps. Find the girl who guarded you and make a point of saying something positive to her." And on this night, Coach Izzy kept her team on the court long after the game ended to mingle with their classmates and remember their careers in this gym.

§

A dozen and a half coaches, spouses, and former teammates ate at the local pizzeria celebrating the Pronghorns victory and return to the State Tournament. It would be their third straight appearance in the Elite Eight, but the goal was to win it this year. Not an easy task with the loaded field, but certainly they would be one of the favorites. Allie noted that Academy Prep had been beaten, so there wouldn't be a rematch between her alma mater and Izzy's. The crew toasted all the coaches with both serious and goofy comments. Several parents, also at the pizzeria celebrating, paid the bill for the coaches. Near midnight, Tanya rose to make a final toast. The table lifted whatever beverage glass each had and waited as Tanya wiped her tears. "All season long, the program," and here Tanya held up a Prospect View program, "has listed me as the head coach of this team. That has meant the world to me." She wiped her tears again. "But tonight, as we celebrate our win and begin preparations for the final leg of this journey, I want to toast the real head coach." Tanya raised her glass a few inches higher. "We love you, Iz."

§

Later that night, in the dark of Izzy's apartment, Stevie yelled out to her friend Isabella Soto, "Did you ever imagine any of this, Iz?"

§

Bailey brought her team to the gym on Saturday morning, each girl bringing a handwritten letter for each one of the boys before they boarded the bus to Buena Vista, the number 6 seeded team and Prospect View's Sweet Sixteen opponent. The letters offered support and encouragement. Several of the girls wanted to ride the bus with the boys, so Izzy allowed it despite the three-hour bus ride each way. She wanted her girls to rest, rehydrate, and recharge, but maybe the girls could provide a little support for the boys in a hostile gym. Twelve players, four coaches, three student managers, the Activities Director Carl Porter, seven faculty members, eight varsity girls, and the head custodian Virginia Polis, piled into the bus for the Prospect View boys first trip this deep into the State playoffs. Just like the night before, a victory would send another Pronghorn team to Denver as one of the Elite Eight. Buena Vista agreed to hold the game at 4:00 o'clock to facilitate a safe return at a reasonable time for their guests.

Buena Vista won the boys State Championship in 2001 and was a powerhouse in several sports in the mountain region. Along with Eaton and Roaring Fork, Buenie was one of the three non-religious schools in the top eight, and a legitimate contender for the championship. Prospect View would need to play its best to have a shot, and even then, it might not be enough.

§

Arriving in Buena Vista at 2:30, the team ate energy bars and walked around the outside of the school. At 3:00 they dressed out, stretched, and read over their coaches' scouting reports. At 3:20 they went into the gym for leisurely shooting. At 3:35 the boys returned to the locker room for Izzy's, Allie's, and Romero's last words. At 3:45 they ran onto the court and began shooting layups, full speed.

When the Prospect View bus had arrived, it was met by the Buena Vista activities director, who informed Porter that a dinner reservation had been made for the Pronghorns at a local restaurant after the game. The BV coaches met with Izzy and her staff, each side congratulating the other for a fine season to this point. Around 3:30 a dozen or so cars arrived from Prospect bringing family and students to support their sons and fellow students, about fifty people in all. Carl Porter had called ahead to see if BV would rope off a section for about fifty to sixty fans behind the Pronghorn bench. The rest of the gym filled to the rafters with locals wearing red.

"Those guys are huge," said Benny as the team returned to the locker room for the coaches' last words.

"Speed kills," Romero reminded the boys.

"Buena Vista will be in a zone, a different zone each trip," said Coach Soto. "Treat whatever zone it is the way you've been taught. Odd front, Wes and Atticus, align yourself with Nick. Even front, we go one-four to enter, then make your slides." Each coach in turn added more advice, but the messages were similar. "Battle!"

BV's big zone gave the Pronghorns trouble, especially with penetration, and the Demons took the early lead, stretching it to a dozen at halftime. Back in the visitor's locker room, Izzy scribbled a few diagrams on the chalkboard, with Allie pointing out the gaps to her bigs. "We're going to miss shots, so we've got to go to the boards harder." Romero challenged the bigs to be the difference in the second half. Izzy closed with these words, "One bite, one step, one possession at a time." The boys understood what this phrase meant. "They've had their half, this second one is ours. Nick, Charlie, be shot aggressive. Morgan, Mason, Curt, get those long rebounds. BVs guards don't block out. Don't wait for them to set up in their zone; race the ball and get it on the glass. Then, do what we do best."

The second half turned into a track meet. BV lost control of the tempo, and by the middle of the fourth quarter, Prospect View had tied the game. Still, BV was an excellent team on its own mission, and their coach challenged his kids to win each battle in order to win the war. When Mason rebounded Nick's errant three and dished a nifty pass to Boyd under the basket, the Pronghorns had the lead. BV had one offensive possession to advance or stay home; Prospect View needed one stop to seize the victory. Izzy and Allie had used their last timeout to set up their last basket. Now it was BV's turn. When both teams returned to the court, as the crowd turned up the noise to Rocky Mountain levels, Izzy recognized BV's play. It was hers and she knew where the shot was going to come from and who was going to take it. She screamed as loud as she could, but her voice was drowned out by the Demon crowd. BV's shot found nothing but net.

§

The locker room atmosphere differed, it seemed to Izzy, from her girls' losses at State the previous three seasons. Yes, it was a tough loss. Yes, it hurt. But it seemed more like a locker room from four years earlier when her girls had also lost in the Sweet Sixteen. Not quite a relief, but the feeling that it was nowhere near what every previous season in these boys' experience had been. They achieved; they were respected; they had played for reasons beyond . . . fun. None of the boys cried, or at least if they did, they hid it well. Ten boys played, with eight getting the most minutes. Nick never came out, nor did Charlie. Morgan picked up a couple of cheap calls and had to sit for substantial minutes, but Mason was a stallion. Boyd and Benny stood toe-to-toe with BV's post players in the second half, and in the end, the game came down to a single possession. A one-point loss on the road. 17-7 for the season. Only three seniors, none of whom were starters, would be gone from this team. "When can we get started for next season, Coach?"

Izzy was too tired to cry. Romero and Miles didn't cry either, but Allie did. She tried not to, but it had been years since she had participated in such a meaningful game. She had joined late, mid-summer, but jumped into the deep end and gave every bit of her energy to this team. Like every game since the new year, Izzy had stepped back and let Allie be the bench coach. Her team had lost, and she felt she had let them down somehow.

The post-game words, a nice dinner at a family restaurant, lots of Buena Vista fans stopping by their tables to say what a valiant effort they gave, a long bus ride home in the dark. As the bus turned for the last leg of that journey, about fifteen minutes from the school, Morgan walked to the front of the bus and sat with Coach Soto and Coach Monroe. "I don't know what your practice plans call for next week, but if you need some of us to come in to scrimmage the girls, we can be there."

CHAPTER 13

Izzy arose early on Sunday to attend Mass, then returned home and went back to bed. She had called Tanya from the bus to tell her not to expect company for their workout, but that she would see her later on Sunday. Izzy had several offers for dinner: Bianca, Donna Romero, Tanya's mother, even Dr. Kerrigan had called to invite her to her house, but Izzy accepted the one from Jorge. "It has to be early, around four. I'll drive over so I can stop off at Tanya's on the way back. We need to plan for some little thing coming up later in the week." Jorge understood . . . finally.

When Kerrigan had called, Izzy asked if it would be acceptable for her to take a personal day on Monday; she had so much to do and at that moment on Sunday, Izzy was exhausted. Kerrigan told her that of course it was. "I'll need coverage on both Thursday and Friday too, at least for my afternoon classes." Izzy slept until 1:30, a four-hour nap, as much sleep as she got on a few nights. She fixed herself a bowl of yogurt and called Allie.

"How're you doing?" Izzy asked.

Allie breathed hard into her cellphone. "I'll survive, but you didn't tell me how emotionally involved I would become in this job. I'd forgotten." Allie paused and Izzy waited. "I haven't cried over a basketball game since losing at the State Tournament ten years ago."

"Yeah, the kids kind of bury themselves into your heart and become a part of us. Hey, since you don't have anything else to do now that the season is over, why don't you help Tanya and me this week?"

"I was going to call you and ask if I could."

"Do you remember how to get to Tanya's farm? I'm meeting her there around 6:00 to put three days of practice plans together and make some calls to get information about our opponents, especially Centauri. You know they were State champs last year?"

"Yeah, I was on the website this morning. Does that qualify me as a basketball dweeb like you now?"

§

Early in December, Centauri had played a non-league game with a Colorado Springs school, so early Monday morning, Allie drove two hours to the Springs to get the tape. She was back before noon, and she, Izzy, and Tanya charted the Falcons' tendencies. "Be careful that we don't focus too heavily on early season successes against a weak team. I think Bailey will be better able to handle their press," said Izzy. "But those three guards are quick, that's for sure." Allie had also secured a roster that included sizes and experience for Centauri.

"Not real big and kinda young," said Tanya. "Sort of like Ft. Meade in that sense.

"All us Latins are quick," teased Izzy.

"Don't I know it," laughed Allie. "I still have nightmares about you and Molly and Stevie."

Being the second seed, Prospect View drew the second game of the first round on Thursday, 4:30, so Izzy scheduled practice for that time on all three days leading up to the tournament. "Body rhythms." Coach Sabka and Coach Georgia would ride the bus down to the Coliseum with the kids on Thursday, allowing Izzy, Tanya, and Allie to arrive early in order to watch the entire first game at 3:00. They would also stay after their game, assuming Prospect View won its first game, and watch the two late games. "Find a weakness, learn a tendency, something to gain a basket or two, leave nothing to chance." Also, Carl Porter's preparation showed his professionalism, making sure that Izzy and her team would not be inconvenienced or surprised by non-basketball issues. Romero told—not asked—Izzy that he would be riding the bus with them, and that he would be standing behind the bench during the game. "If anyone asks, I'll just tell them I'm security."

"I suppose you'll be at practices then," said Izzy.

"Wherever thou goest, there goest me," answered Romero, "or something like that. Irregardless, I signed on as your assistant for the year, and most of your girls have been in the weight room, so we've got another week."

"There's no such word as irregardless; it's just regardless."

"Excuse me, English teach. *REGARDLESS*, I'll goest to practice."

§

The girls completed their stretches by 4:30 and began shooting layups at that time. "This is the routine we'll follow on Thursday. Twelve minutes of shooting to get a feel for the spaciousness of the Coliseum. You know how it feels, we've been there enough," said Izzy proudly. At the same time, eight boys shot layups at the far end of the gym, all wearing red practice jerseys. A purposefulness pervaded the gym, but the atmosphere was also relaxed, with some bantering between the girls and boys, the young women and young men.

At 4:45 Coach Soto brought both squads together. "Coach Romero and Coach Allie will have the boys. They're Centauri. You gals will have Coach Tanya and me. This is a teaching scrimmage, really not much of a scrimmage, but a set of drills. I'll be stopping the action frequently to make points about what we can expect. When the boys helped us before the Broomfield game, it helped us win that game. I think this will yield the same result."

Forty-five minutes later, the scrimmage ended with each team declaring victory, and Izzy sent her girls to the free throw line. "Make five in a row, then go through the Mikans." She thanked the boys and told them they wouldn't use them on Tuesday, also she would expect them to be loud at the game. Izzy walked back to her girls to make points about the Centauri tendencies. Romero herded the boys onto the one row of bleachers that protruded from the wall, sat them down, and talked about their game in Buena Vista.

He told them that he would be assisting with their team again next year, that this hadn't been a "one and done" proposition. "We have unfinished business, and our work starts now."

§

Even though the drive from Centauri to Denver took over four hours, hundreds of Centauri fans made the trip to support their kids, their team. Being the defending State champions does that for a town. Prospect was about 45 minutes away, and more fans would make the trip. Still, both schools were well supported. In the opening game featuring two Christian schools from the same conference, Holy Family beat Denver Christian and would be Prospect View's next opponent, again, if Prospect View won its game. Izzy downplayed Centauri's experience as State Champs, because her team had three years of games at this level and wouldn't be overawed. Centauri's championship team had been a senior dominated team as had Prospect View, so each team had three or four new starters this year. "Where we may have a little advantage is our conference is better than theirs; we might be better prepared in that sense."

The four Prospect View coaches dressed to the nines for this first game, and as always, Izzy applied her trademark eye makeup fastidiously. For the game, she would stand, Tanya and Allie would sit together directly behind her, Georgia would sit at the end of the bench with the underclass subs, and Romero would stand behind the chairs, arms folded. He had been warned by Izzy not to address the officials either directly or with asides. Behind the Pronghorn bench, about 500 adults and students stood waving banners and placards. Included among those were several of Izzy's former teammates.

Game time.

Both teams played fast, wanted quick shots, and then would turn loose their full court press. Having a Centauri film helped a little. Having an all-state point guard helped a whole lot more. As Coach Izzy always told Bailey, "It's your ball, take care of it." Bailey did, and Centauri's press was neutralized. With their primary weapon quieted, Centauri couldn't sustain any offensive runs. They were a layup team, not a perimeter shooting team or a team that executed well against a solid half-court defense. Izzy's team understood half-court five-on-five defense and blockouts. "Give them one contested jump shot and then deny them any second shots." Prospect View's size made a difference, and the Pronghorns secured a twelve-point victory. There would be no repeat champion for 2007. Izzy's girls were into the semifinals for the second straight year, the Final Four, and would play Holy Family on Friday.

Unlike many coaches, Izzy always wanted her point guard in the game at the end of every quarter. That last minute of each quarter seemed like such a momentum moment, so to give Bailey extra rest, Izzy would often sub for her around the two-minute mark, let her get a drink and catch her breath, and then put her right back in. In the post-game comments, Coach Izzy pointed to Josie Touslee, the sophomore backup point guard, for her quality minutes when she took control of the team while Bailey rested. "No turnovers at all, young lady. Way to hold the fort!" Izzy also lauded Grace Oyler for her minutes off the bench.

After the team boarded the bus for a date with a north Denver restaurant, Izzy, Tanya, and Allie sat at the end of the gym in the section reserved for players and coaches critiquing the game. "We played great!" said Tanya.

Allie agreed. "Either they weren't as good as we thought, or we're just that much better. Either way, we didn't do much wrong tonight."

"Our four seniors were just outstanding," said Izzy. "They've grown so much this season. They were sort of like Josie last year, getting a few minutes to back up the starters. I hope our young ones can do the same next year."

Tanya turned to Allie. "She does this all the time in case you haven't noticed. We just won a huge game at State, and she's planning for next season."

Izzy's head nodded. "You're right. It's all about the here and now. Bailey Rockwell, Rosie Peterson, Maggie Butler, and Lauren Chadwick. These four seniors started out on our C-team and now we're here because of them. They're a remarkable group!"

Tanya unshuffled the game stats given to her by the managers. "Look at this, Centauri only got two offensive rebounds."

Izzy's head continued to nod. "Well, as we watch these next two games, let's put them in the perspective of what we do best, our rebounding and care of the ball. We and Holy Family are in; let's see if Machebeuf and Basalt can hold their seeds."

The number 1 and number 4 teams won, setting up a Final Four with the top four seeds: two undefeated teams, a one-loss team, and a three-loss team, a combined 92-4 record. Across town, in the 4A tournament, Broomfield advanced.

§

Coach Summitt and his wife would certainly attend the semifinal game. They would drive down in the morning to their son's house, who now was married, pick up their daughter, and the family would arrive early to get a prime seat as close to Prospect View's bench as possible. Izzy would find him and visit for a few minutes. Last year, Bianca and Adam sat with the Summitt's. This year, Stevie, Cindy, and Izzy's cousin Elena also joined their old coach in the stands. As Izzy conversed with Morgan Summitt, they were joined by the Holy Family coach.

"We go way back," said Morgan about Coach Ronstedt. "He coached boys in the Jeffco League when I did, back in the eighties, so we matched up a few times."

"Let me tell you," said the Holy Family coach to Izzy, "Morgan got the best of me most of the time." Turning to Coach Summitt, "I'll let this little reunion continue, I just wanted to say hi." Back to Izzy, Ronstedt wished her good luck and returned to the seats at the end of the gym.

"He was being nice, Izzy. I'm pretty sure he got me more than I got him. You have your work cut out for you against his girls; they're on the rise just as you are. He coaches with love, so his girls will play all out for him."

Izzy hugged the gauntlet of former teammates and left to get her team and herself prepared. As she walked to the locker room, she thought about what her former coach had said, *He coaches with love.* Holy Family's first game had been a struggle, a contest between another team in the Metro League that they had played three times before. One of their losses had been to that team, the other two to Machebeuf, so the players on both teams bumped and shoved whenever they could. Izzy doubted it would matter tonight; the fatigue would be delayed until Saturday.

Standing in front of her team, Coach Izzy laid out the game plan, noted the best players on Holy Family who would need to be marked, and emphasized her own girls' strengths. "We play to those, ladies. I expect Holy Family will pack it in with their zone and dare us to shoot threes. Don't fall in love with that easy shot. Let's go inside out on those, so we have a better opportunity to rebound our misses." Tanya showed the girls a particularly effective high post screen and roll that Holy Family used and demonstrated how to defend it. They warned against fouls, as Izzy always did, stacked hands, and headed out to battle. Walking out behind them, Izzy remarked to Allie and Tanya that she hoped her being a Catholic would nullify God's favoritism to Catholic Holy Family.

"Well," said Tanya, "you are pretty faithful in attending every Sunday, so it can't hurt."

Allie laughed. "It only matters what religion the Basketball Gods are."

Because of the slower pace of this game compared to the quarter-final game, it was mostly a contest of starters. Holy Family moved the ball up court against Prospect View's press without turning it over but twice in the first half. Methodical. Prospect View relied on Bailey to probe the Tigers' half-court defense. Every point from either team was earned. At half, Izzy's team held a slim lead, but it was a low scoring affair that favored Holy Family.

In the third quarter, Holy Family wrestled the lead from Prospect View when Izzy's forwards took a few questionable threes. The Tigers' defense then collapsed even closer to the basket daring the Pronghorns to cast up more ill-advised outside shots. Still, the score remained close as the game neared its end. Behind by two points with thirty seconds remaining, Prospect View was forced to foul. The Holy Family player made both free throws extending the lead to four. Not wanting to use her last timeout, Izzy motioned to Bailey to push the ball, but the Tigers' defense was set and focused on stopping Bailey. Finally, with just twelve seconds remaining, Izzy called time.

"We're two possessions down. We'll run Carolina on this inbounds to get it to Bailey for a three. Maggie, if Bailey is double-teamed, throw it to Lauren in front of the basket. I know it will be contested but throw it anyway! Lauren, if it comes to you, you have to get it. Then go straight up into the defender's chest. Be strong, Lauren, we need you right now."

Holy Family did double-team Bailey, so Maggie threw a perfect pass just four feet in front of the hoop. Lauren seized it, took it up, and scored. "And one!" Only eight seconds remained as Lauren lined up to intentionally miss. The ball careened off the iron, and in the ensuing scramble, it went out of bounds under the basket off a Holy Family player. Just three seconds remained. Bailey looked to Coach Izzy for an inbounds play, and Izzy yelled "Duke." Bailey nodded, and as she gathered her team quickly for a last word of instruction, she reminded them not to move until she slapped the ball. Holy Family chose not to call time out to prevent Prospect View from setting up a special play. Instead, they defended the play as they had throughout the game, no one covering Bailey and all five Tigers face-guarding the four Pronghorns to physically block any screens or cuts. A three-point shot could beat them.

The referee handed the basketball to Bailey. Instead of slap-ping the ball, she threw it off the back of the nearest Holy Family defender, then stepped in to retrieve it, and powered it up for a basket. As the ball fell through the net, the buzzer sounded. Overtime.

In the huddle, after she quieted her team, Izzy looked them in the eyes. "Now, we play to win. If they sit in that zone, Bailey, dribble to your right and fire up the three. Rosie, Maggie, Lauren, anticipate the shot before it goes up. As Bailey dribbles to the side, get early rebounding position. Then, make or miss, we pressure like crazed animals. Don't foul but fly around!"

Lauren won the tip, sending it back to Bailey. She hesitated only a moment to allow her forwards to move toward the lane, then she dribbled right and shot her first three. It missed, but Rosie was there to rebound and power it in. Tracey tipped Holy Family's inbounds pass, and Bailey picked it up. Again, she hesitated before dribbling to her right. At the same spot as before, she lofted another three-point shot. This one found the bottom of the net. A shaken Tiger threw another weak pass into the hands of Rosie, and as before, Bailey shot another three. It missed but Tracey retrieved the rebound, found Bailey in the corner, who caught the pass and shot again. Inside out, another three. Holy Family called timeout, but the damage was done. Izzy's girls closed out the game at the free throw line, outscoring the Tigers 13-0 in the overtime period. The Pronghorns had tied the game on a courageous play by Bailey, but then seized the win by being fearless in the overtime.

Allowing her girls to shower one another with water bottles for a few minutes in the locker room, Izzy stood to the side with her extended coaching staff. When she finally did quiet them down to congratulate them, Romero whispered to Allie, "She pretends she's a gentle lady only interested in providing a few educational lessons to her players, but underneath, she has the heart of a warrior. She'll rip your heart out if that's what it takes to win."

Allie leaned into Romero's ear and whispered back, "Maybe you need to hire her as the football coach too."

"Well, ladies," smiled Izzy, "you made me pee my pants in this one." The girls cheered before quieting again. "Here we are. One to go. Go out there and study this next game. I'll send you home with Coach Sabka again at halftime while the rest of us scout. Get something to eat, hydrate, and go to bed. We'll meet at school at 10:00 to go over anything we see. Those of you who didn't see many minutes tonight, I want to run you through a little four-on-four half-court scrimmage to keep you ready. The third night of this tournament always demands a little extra effort, but the legs don't always buy in, so everybody needs to be sharp." As the girls began to stir towards their lockers, Izzy spoke again. "I've told you every day at practice that you are many things, only one of which is an athlete." She looked at each girl. "But tomorrow, in this arena, you—all of you—will be basketball players first and foremost. And tomorrow, we play to WIN!"

§

In Friday's late game, Basalt, a small-town north of Aspen, gave Bishop Machebeuf everything they could handle, but Machebeuf won by five, setting up a championship game between the two undefeated teams. When Romero, who had driven his van down with his new harem, dropped Izzy off, he told her how proud he was to be part of her coaching team, that he couldn't wait for tomorrow's game. "You get your sleep too."

Izzy had five messages on her land line, all congratulatory in nature. Four were expected, but one came from a friend whom Izzy hadn't heard from in nine years. "Izzy, this is Penny Mathews. I've been following your team this year, so when I saw you were playing tonight, I drove up to watch you. I saw so many of our teammates near the court sitting with Coach Summitt, but I didn't go down to talk with them. It's been too long. I just wanted to tell you how great your girls played. That last play by the one girl was amazing. Where did she get the audacity to try that? Anyway, I can't make it tomorrow, but I'll be pulling for you. I'm so happy for you." Penny did not leave her number, but Izzy knew someone who might. Even though it was late, Izzy made the call.

"Cindy, it's Izzy. Yes, I know. Thank you. Hey, Penny Mathews left a message on my landline answering machine. Do you know anything about where she is now or what she's doing?"

CHAPTER 14

In the beginning . . . at the end . . . it's about having an opportunity.

Saturday, March 10, 2007, Denver Coliseum. #2 Prospect View vs #1 Bishop Machebeuf for the 3A Girls State Basketball Championship. Machebeuf had won the tough Metro League, maybe the most competitive 3A conference in Colorado, to earn the top seed. The green and gold Buffaloes were, as Izzy told her assistants, "the real deal!" Two nights of watching them win games against Buena Vista and Basalt showed Izzy, Allie, and Tanya that their girls would need to "bring our A+ game," to which Romero had laughed, noting the number of clichés being tossed about. He reminded Coach Izzy that Broomfield was playing in the 4A championship, and they were better than Machebeuf. "Do you remember who won that game back in December?"

A season minus one evening in the books. Sixty-four teams in the classification now down to two, and for this year, unquestionably the two best, one coached by a forty-five-year-old man in his third year at Holy Family, the other by a twenty-eight-year-old woman in her sixth year at Prospect View. To most observers, the game would not be decided by gimmicks, but by which team made a couple more shots than the other, which team had the hot hand, or which team could finally impose its will on the other. Neither team was going to change what brought it to this game.

Once again, Izzy Soto followed a ritual that had developed over four seasons of advancing to State, especially once her team stepped off the bus. While her assistants escorted the team to the locker room, she would head to the stands to meet with her entourage, an extended family that was growing yearly. *A wonderful tradition,* thought Izzy. Afterwards, she and Tanya and Sabka, now joined by Allie, Romero, and Georgia, would discuss any new strategies, great ideas that occurred to one of them on the trip down from Prospect. In short order, as things on this evening tend to advance more rapidly than anticipated, the coaches would sit their girls down and go over keys to the game, offer words of encouragement, and tell them that this was where they belonged, that they had earned this honor. All that was left to be done was to go out and give their best effort. Lift hands toward the rafters, shout Pronghorns!, and play. In another locker room, girls would stack hands and yell Buffaloes!

Introductions. First the starters from the visitors. In turn, Tracey, Maggie, Lauren, Rosie, and Bailey heard their name, jogged to the opposite bench to shake hands with Machebeuf's coach, fist bumped the officials, and then joined the others at the free throw line in front of their bench. Then the Buffaloes would do the same. On this night, the public address announcer introduced Tanya Hatton as Prospect View's head coach, and she met the Machebeuf coach in front of the scorer's table. "It's great to see you've recovered from your accident, Coach. Good Luck."

Subconsciously tightening a colorful ribbon holding her long black hair back, Izzy Soto stepped into her group of twelve and looked around. "Three keys: block out, be shot aggressive, and defend like the Buffaloes are trying to stampede your land. Protect it!" It was trite, and Izzy knew it, but it gave the girls something to hang onto for the first few possessions. As the horn sounded to send the teams out to do battle, Coach Izzy grabbed Bailey by the elbow. "Everything I've taught you about being a point guard, I learned from a teammate who led my school to a State Championship. You have the tools and power. Put this team on your back." And then, Bailey did a unique thing; she leaned in and kissed her coach on the cheek.

The largest lead either team enjoyed in the first half was five points, but when the first sixteen minutes ended and the teams ran to their locker rooms at halftime, Machebeuf held just a one-point lead. The third quarter was contested just as closely, but the Pronghorns had made one more basket and taken the lead heading into the fourth quarter. Eight minutes to determine a champion. Both teams brought over a thousand fans each, and the students from both schools treated the game as a tryout for a television game show. Colorful outfits, clever retorts, and thunderous applause. "The Show!"

Izzy's girls played their hearts out and performed at the highest level, as she later said they needed to. The same could be said for the Buffaloes. Machebeuf had the better overall starting five, while Prospect View had the best player, and indeed, Bailey Rockwell put her team on her back. The Championship came down to the final minutes. No overtime as there had been the previous night, but a seven-point margin determined the outcome. When the trophy was handed to the victor, those girls ran it over to their fans, held it skyward, and danced. The loser took its second-place plaque and headed to the locker room. A thousand fans wearing one color cheered. A thousand fans of another clapped politely and shouted words of encouragement as their daughters or friends passed them on their way to the locker room. It had been a game both squads could be proud of, one that showed toughness, grit, and sportsmanship.

CHAPTER 15

The Championship Game is an important chapter,
but it's not the last chapter.

"If you have a minute after school, Coach, drop by my office. I'd like to run something by you," said Dr. Kerrigan to Ms. Soto as she monitored the lunch line.

Izzy nodded and turned her attention to the two students who had tried to cut in line. "Not today, boys, you'll have to go all the way back there," she said pointing to the end of the line. Even though she was still on a modified classroom schedule, Izzy resumed her duty schedule. "Only fair," she told Romero.

Bailey Rockwell and Lauren Chadwick came running up excitedly. "Hey, Coach, we both made it. All-State!" Lauren was holding the Rocky Mountain News: Bailey on the first team and Lauren on the second team.

"I've known about it for a week. So proud of you both. You deserved it." Addressing Lauren, "Have you made a decision about Western State? They really want you."

"I know, but it's so cold in Gunnison. I'm still considering. They gave me some more time to make my choice."

"Are you still considering UCCS?" asked Izzy.

"I am, but it's so expensive. They want me to walk on, but I really like it."

"Want me to call?" Lauren nodded. Izzy smiled at Bailey. "Coach Rascon called again last night. If she doesn't sign the one girl from Los Angeles, she'll be calling you. She likes your game."

"Do you know when she'll know?" asked Bailey.

"By the end of the month is what she said. I told her she'd be sorry if she missed out on you."

Bailey hugged her coach. "Tell her you'll come with me and be her assistant. You'd like California."

Izzy laughed slightly. "Nah, I'm pretty happy here. This is the level where I fit. Not sure I could handle all those D-1 prima donnas."

"Isn't that what you said about coaching boys?" Bailey smiled and the two girls scampered off.

The two boys whom Ms. Soto had sent to the back of the line passed with their trays. "We missed out on the burgers. Only thing left were the hotdogs."

§

Izzy started her Honda and then remembered that Dr Kerrigan wanted to talk with her. "Dang it!" She turned off the engine and returned through the gymnasium doors. Virginia Polis pushed her wide broom across the floor, collecting a day's worth of dust and sweat. "Hey," yelled Izzy. Virginia pushed her broom in Coach's direction.

"Charlie wants to know when basketball starts again. He's getting pretty antsy."

"I know. He bugs me every morning. His first hour is next door to my room, and he and Atticus are in there together. You can tell him the same thing I do. Soon, probably next week."

Virginia nodded. "When will you know?" she asked referring to another issue.

Izzy didn't answer. She just raised her eyebrows and smiled.

Kerrigan was shuffling papers in her office when Izzy knocked on her door frame. "Come in. Soda?" Izzy nodded and sat in the leather chair across from Kerrigan's. Handing Izzy the soda, Kerrigan leaned against her desk. "Do you know how many little birds fly around this office. Every one of them tells me something." She let that float in the air for a moment giving Izzy time to respond.

"Just one rumor? Huh, I thought there'd be more." Izzy looked up at Kerrigan over her soda can.

"Romero suggested I sweeten the pot, but I really can't

manipulate the salary schedule."

"Oh, . . . that little bird. I'll need to talk to Romero about spreading rumors."

Kerrigan pushed herself off the end of her desk and sat in her chair. "It's nice to see your eyes returning to normal. Looked like you had permanent dark circles tattooed under them for a while. Have you made a choice yet? I know it's hard."

Izzy put the soda on Kerrigan's desk and spun the label around to face her. "It's funny. Every day, both teams dance around in my head. I guess I've already decided, but things happen, and I don't pull the trigger. So, . . ." Izzy paused. She dabbed her eye where the dark circles had been. "A deal's a deal. I told Tanya when she was in the hospital that when she got healthy, the girls were hers. She's healthy and we need her in this building. The calculus kids need her."

Kerrigan stared at Izzy. "You're a good soldier, Izzy." The principal hesitated again. "It wasn't Romero who told me about Ft. Meade. Romero's your guy. If you told him in confidence, I could never pry it out of him. Tell me," Kerrigan asked.

"My boyfriend told me about the opening, and I just looked into it out of curiosity. The English opening includes teaching writing. That's pretty enticing for me. Their teams need good coaching. New challenges, ya know." She nodded, probably more to herself than her principal. "And there's Jorge." She smiled at her boss. "He'd be a pretty welcoming colleague."

"Another one of those little birds told me that too."

"I really considered it. In case you haven't noticed," Izzy laughed at her joke while she stared at the soda can, "I'm Latina. Not many of us here in Prospect, so I talked with Romero about it. He got me to drink an entire beer over at his house while we talked, double my usual intake. He said he didn't want to be the lone Mexican here. He was joking. He said my being here had nothing to do with that, that being here at Prospect View had allowed me to challenge myself. I'd never looked at it that way. I always wanted to challenge the kids, but teaching and coaching were just how I did that." Izzy stopped and breathed in and out heavily, almost like a sigh. She looked up from the soda can to Kerrigan. "I like it here."

"So, you'll be staying?'

"If you'll have me,"

"You won't get the easy schedule like you've had this year. I'll have to add that sixth class to your schedule again. It'll be junior rhetoric and writing . . . creative writing. Think you can handle that?"

"I'll have a few extra hours to plan for it this summer." Izzy smiled. "Since I'll only be coaching boys. By the way, who's the little bird?"

"Oh, he doesn't teach here. A music teacher from another district."

§

Back at her apartment, Izzy decided to fix herself an elaborate dinner. No salad or yogurt, but a real dinner. *You've earned this, Iz.* She changed out of her teaching clothes and put on sweats and slippers, then returned to the kitchen and slipped on an apron. She placed her iPod into the new speaker case and turned it on. Opening the refrigerator, she bent over to explore the shelves, to see what was there. Her inner self laughed at her. *Oh, Iz, there're no ingredients in there to fix. What will you do?* Still holding the fridge door open, Izzy pondered dinner. *Well, I'm not changing clothes and going to the store.* She closed the door and noticed the pizza coupon held there by a magnet. *Why not? You can even go with double sausage and peppers; throw in a salad and maybe some bread sticks.* After she called, where they said it would arrive in 45 minutes, Izzy poured herself a glass of wine and slouched on the couch to relax. The decisions had been made now; she could take a day or a weekend off. Open gyms would start next Monday, so she had five days to herself, at least in the evenings. *Now might be a chance to read Mercedes Spinelli's book. You've had the printed manuscript sitting on your bedstand for over a year, Iz.* Izzy laid her head back and closed her eyes.

The doorbell awakened her. "Pizza delivery boy."

She wasn't lonely as she ate, but she never really was. Something about basketball always kept her company. She stretched to reach her legal pad on the other side of the table. *Broomfield's girls play at our gym next season. That'll be a good one, Iz. Hat will have her hands full. Broomfield will want revenge for their only loss last season. Maybe you could get their boys to come over on Saturday. Make a weekend of this new rivalry. Talk to Porter in the morning and see if he can schedule it.* She returned to her dinner and her eyes focused on her picture of the Oro Hills team that won the championship in 1997. Penny Mathews was missing from that photo. She had run away after their junior year and become a ghost. Izzy and Cindy tried to find her the week after the playoffs but came up empty. "The Penny Mystery" continued, worrying all her teammates.

Izzy ate only half her pizza but finished the salad. After wrapping up the remainder of dinner, she punched in a number on her cell and listened while it rang. She got Molly's recorded message. "This is Molly Rascon, head women's basketball coach for the University of California Moreno Valley. I'm unavailable at the moment, but I'd like to talk with you when I can. Please leave a detailed message and your number, and I'll return your call as soon as possible. Go Gamblers!" *Go Gamblers. So Molly*, but Izzy's friend did receive lots of teasing about that school mascot. "Molly. Iz. Don't miss out on Bailey Rockwell. Call me."

Next, Izzy called the UCCS coach to talk about financial aid for Lauren to offset the huge tuition cost there. Again, Izzy received a recorded message. *Don't these coaches work in the evenings?* She put aside her pad and called Jorge.

"Whatcha doing?" she asked.

"Watching game films," Jorge answered.

"Liar. You're probably writing music scores, not basketball scores."

"You're probably right. Are we still on for Friday?"

"Of course." They talked for a few minutes before Izzy signed off. "Luv ya."

Still early and no longer sleepy, Izzy opened her computer and logged onto the television coverage of their State Championship game. She fast-forwarded to the final two minutes.

Rockwell's basket has forced Machebeuf to call a timeout. They're in a hole now, down seven. Fans, this has been a terrific contest, everything we hoped it would be, but Prospect View has scored the last eight and seems to have won the mental battle for control, or I should say Bailey Rockwell has scored the last eight points and willed her teammates to a probable victory. The Championship is fully in her grasp.

The Buffaloes break their huddle. They need some magic to win this game. Smith inbounds to Carlson. The Pronghorns continue with their man-to-man pressure; it's been a problem for Machebeuf these last few minutes. Carlson passes to Cooper who fires up a three. It's short! Chadwick grabs the rebound. She's been the difference on the boards. Outlets to Rockwell. Machebeuf will need to foul soon if they hope to have any chance. Prospect View is not going to turn it over. So well coached. Rockwell is fouled, but the Buffaloes let too many ticks run off the clock. I'm pretty sure if Rockwell makes one, this game is over. Forty-four seconds remain. It looks like the Machebeuf coach is waiving the white flag; he's emptying his bench, giving some of his young girls a moment on the Coliseum floor. Coach Soto or Coach Hatton, I'm not sure which one it is, is going to her bench now too. Rockwell swishes her first shot, and now the celebration begins. Their fans know it too. The Prospect View Pronghorns will be the 2007 State Champions!

Izzy closed her laptop leaving her hand on top of the computer. The scene of Bailey turning to the bench with that smile of pure joy was what Izzy wanted to see again. *Now,* she thought, *I need to make sure that Nick and Charlie get that same opportunity.*

She reached for her pad. She listed the names of her returning seven varsity players, five of whom were starters. She nodded her head. *Well, Iz, that's a nice place to begin. It won't be easy, Coach, but you'll have a chance.*

And as Coach Summitt taught his girls a decade earlier, that's all any player or coach can ask for.

CHAPTER 16

Full Circle

Tanya Hatton made a full recovery, took over the girls team that spring, and along with Georgia and Sabka (who always talked about retiring but never did), guided Prospect View to continued excellence on the court for years to come. Allie Monroe went back to Northern Colorado to earn her teaching credentials, and after serving as Izzy's assistant for two more years, took a full-time art teaching and assistant boys basketball coaching job in Ft. Collins. Romero assisted Izzy for two more seasons and then took the head football job where he "didn't have to monitor his language so carefully." His teams exemplified toughness and character, and he convinced the school board to return the school's name simply to Prospect High School, its original name until the building had been enlarged a decade earlier. "Roots matter," he told the board, "and we only have one high school in town." He and Isabella remained close friends for the rest of their lives.

Izzy's 2008 team finished with just two losses, its opening game at Broomfield and the championship in an overtime loss on the last night of the season. Charlie, Wes, Atticus, Boyd, Benny, Morgan, and Nick got their huge smiles when they rallied from ten down in the fourth quarter and Charlie made a difficult shot to send the game into overtime, but they missed out on the Big Gold Ball when his last jumper careened off the rim at the buzzer. Izzy, Romero, and Allie had given them their chance. The following year was "Nick's Team," and Prospect View repeated as undefeated Corridor League champs and advanced to the State Tournament as one of the favorites, but Nick sprained his ankle in practice and couldn't play in the opening round. Still, they had exceeded expectations to get that far.

Dr. Avery Kerrigan held another conversation with Izzy about who to hire as the next boys coach when Izzy resigned after that third season. Miles Minturn was a no-brainer. Avery saw it coming, the baby bump. "Yes," Izzy told her principal, "but I want to eventually get back to my girls. I'm a hugger, not a high-fiver, and Tanya's our girls coach!" Izzy sat out a year and then took a teaching and coaching position at Ft. Meade where her mother-in-law could watch her granddaughter during the day while Jorge and Izzy taught. As of the time of this story being put to paper, Ft. Meade had not won a State Championship yet, but Izzy's girls were challenging Tanya's teams for Corridor League supremacy.

Isabella Soto was back to hugging.

The End